Kelly Creighton facilitates cre[...] groups and schools. In 2014, [...] journal, showcasing the con[...] published books include: *Three Primes* (2013, poetry); *The Bones of It* (San Diego Book Review's 2015 Novel of the Year); and *Bank Holiday Hurricane* (shortlisted in the Saboteur Award's Best Short Story Collection category and longlisted for the 2017 Edge Hill Prize). Her work is featured in Salt Publishing's *Best British Short Stories 2018* and has been noted in the following prizes: Michael McLaverty Short Story Award, the inaugural Seamus Heaney Award for New Writing, Cúirt New Writing Prize for Fiction, Fish Short Story Prize, Abroad Writers' Conference Short-Short Story Award and the Gregory O'Donoghue Poetry Prize. She was the recipient of a 2017/18 ACES Award from the Arts Council of Northern Ireland. Kelly lives with her family in Newtownards, County Down.

kellycreighton.com
@KellyCreighto16

'Creighton has a poet's eye for imagery and a novelist's understanding of the value of a good plot.'
The Irish Times

'Creighton [is] a writer to reckon with.'
The Irish Examiner

Praise for *The Bones of It*

'A brilliant crime debut, chilling, compulsive and beautifully written.'

Brian McGilloway

'Blackly comic in tone, *The Bones of It* is a Bildungsroman that evolves into a slow-burning psychological exploration of the mind … an engrossing tale of the consequences of living a life steeped in a culture of violence.'

The Irish Times

'… true discovered masterpiece of fiction. If she keeps this up, Kelly Creighton can be that Next Great Writer. *The Bones of It* is not just a novel to read, it is a novel to experience.'

San Diego Book Review

'Compelling, compulsive, compassionate.'

Books Ireland

'Scott's is an authentic voice, and Creighton a writer to reckon with.'

The Irish Examiner

Praise for *Bank Holiday Hurricane*

'The 16 stories are by turns gritty and moving.'
The Irish Times

'Kelly Creighton's collection floored me. Distinctive, powerful and filled, at times, with an electric high-wire tension, they contain a lyricism that comes at you sideways and will knock the wind right out of you.'
Bernie McGill

'Often dark and unsettling, excavating relationships that are in tatters, looking at patterns of behaviour that make for dysfunction and unhappiness … a wonderfully written collection about love, loss and cruelty.'
The Irish Examiner

'It's a compelling collection that you will read quickly – and then want to immediately read again, to savour the language and to reconsider the lives laid bare before you.'
Claire Savage

ALSO BY KELLY CREIGHTON

POETRY

Three Primes (2013)

FICTION

The Bones of It (2015)
Bank Holiday Hurricane (2017)

THE SLEEPING SEASON

DI Harriet Sloane Book 1

Kelly Creighton

FRIDAY PRESS

First published in 2020
by Friday Press
Belfast

Copyright © 2020 Kelly Creighton

The moral right of the author has been asserted.

All characters and events in this publication, other than those clearly in the public domain, are fictitious and any resemblance to real persons, living or dead, is purely coincidental.

All rights reserved.

No part of this publication may be reproduced, stored in a retrieval system, or transmitted in any form or by any means, without the prior permission in writing of the publisher, nor be otherwise circulated in any form of binding or cover other than that in which it is published and without a similar condition including this condition being imposed on the subsequent purchaser.

ISBN: 9781708710927

www.fridaypressbooks.com
@friday_press

For Jude and Jonah

Prologue

Bad dreams eat me up. This one came first:

I am fetching firewood with my father. I can smell the woodsmoked scent on my jumper, taste the wax from his Barbour coat. My three eldest siblings are teenagers again. Like spiders they drop from the dark well of that winter and crawl back into my memory. Tall, lanky and dressed in black, both boys have their backs to me as they sow stones into Lough Erne, while Coral shudders on a frost-stiffened margin of grass nearby.

Then we turn away and walk toward our holiday chalet until Coral screams. It is a needle piercing the air.

'Someone's in there,' she shouts. 'I can see them! Look!'

'Stay where you are,' says Father, letting the logs drop onto the grass.

'I'm going in,' says Brooks. He thunders into the lake.

'Get out of there! Get out now,' shouts Father.

Brooks is moving but only just. His feet are heavy as stone slabs, the water up to his knees, then further, to his shoulders; next, his head is gone. Brooks turns into a fly in a cup of tea. He is unable to hear how our father damns him up and down. He comes up for air, then he is trawling a man out from the iced mere, pointlessly trying to turn the body face up.

Addam takes a whiplash glance at Father, then wades in. But Brooks, instead of relinquishing a portion of this tragic find, shrugs him off, shouts, 'I've got him, dicksplash, get out of the road!'

Father is angry at them both. I think he is angry at me too. He orders me to leave, then goes to meet Brooks who lowers the man to the ground with a thud. His blanched, giant water-swollen hands roll away from his lifeless person; his head turns away so I can't see his face. Coral crouches beside him like she might go in for a pulse. It is now I notice his fingernails are missing.

'Coral, come away,' Father orders. He takes off his Barbour coat and throws it over the dead man's head. 'Get you all inside,' he says, putting his hand squarely on Addam's chest. 'I'll head next door and call local branch.'

'What about an ambulance too, Daddy?' I say.

'Yes, a private ambulance too,' he mutters, crouching beside me. He takes my hands inside one of his and rubs them tenderly like I've never seen him before or since. 'Do you understand, Harry?' he says. 'It's too late to help him now.'

Without understanding I nod.

'He's dead, H,' Coral says.

'Get inside. Now!' Father shouts as if afraid to leave his children with this decaying, waterlogged stranger.

Charlotte is indoors. As is Mother, and Grandmother, who lives nearby and who we always gather like a stray sock, on our way through to the chalet. Before we had gone out, Charlotte, in her sultry possessiveness of Mother, had the old mortar and pestle out of the scullery and was grinding winterberries and leaves into a perfume as a gift for her; she is in the same position when we return. Grandmother is still dealing herself a game of solitaire in the kitchen; the string of Christmas lights Mother has threaded around the curtain rail throbs its rhythm of colours onto the plastic tablecloth as Grandmother snaps her cards face up.

'What on God's earth has happened to you?' she asks Addam. Then she sees Brooks soaked entirely.

The smell of him is foul. Charlotte wrinkles her nose,

then pinches it.

'We found a body,' says Coral. 'It was floating in the lake – a man – and he's dead.'

Charlotte jumps up and goes to Mother, burrowing her head into her armpit like a tick. Grandmother hands the boys fresh towels to dry off, but they are in no hurry to change. Brooks's hair is plastered to his face and blacker than ever. With every jumpy movement his shoes squelch on the floor; the tiles pool with his brown water.

'Could hardly get at him,' Brooks says. He is shivering with shock and cold.

'Weighed a tonne,' says Addam.

Charlotte grasps at Mother until Mother dislodges her, tells her to take a seat.

'Right,' she says. Calmly she goes to stoke the fire, glad to be busy with her hands. 'Girls, out you all go.'

'But it's nice and warm in here,' I say, edging towards the hearth.

Flames are taking tiny jumps, like someone spitting into the air. I hear Father's boots loosen the gravel outside.

'Girls, out and let your brothers get changed,' Mother says.

'Could hardly get him,' says Brooks. His eyes are intense, sparkling with worry.

The door opens and Father appears, carrying the logs we collected. He sets them beside the fire and updates us – there is no one at home next door and he will have to walk further. We know the score. Get out of the way.

Eventually the RUC officers come to the chalet where they fawn over my parents, delighted, it seems, to have Charles Sloane, the Chief Constable himself, order them about.

'The body's been in there ten to fourteen days,' Father says to them in the kitchen. I watch from the living room. He knows how to talk to his inferiors and establish his authority. Then he asks a question which surprises me. Perhaps it is to demonstrate that he can be humble too. 'Wouldn't you say the same?' he asks.

'I don't know, Chief. He's in good nick.'

'The water's cold enough though,' Father says. He spots me looking at him and edges the kitchen door closed with his foot.

Stridently I walk off, but I can't resist returning to eavesdrop.

'But the stones in Jamesy Lunney's pockets, Chief?' an officer asks.

'They just delay the find. Enough time and they resurface.'

Another voice comes through the door, another male. He sounds happily out of puff.

'We've found Jamesy's belongings, for all there was of them – that oul' tatty sleeping bag, a bag of jumpers, jeans, all piled up. About a hundred yards from the house in that direction.'

'They come back up where they go in.'

'That's right, Sir.'

*

Since I was a girl I've had this dream. Sometimes I still brood over it, over how many bodies there are lying on the floor of the lough, waiting.

But there are other bad dreams too. Dreams that come with knowledge and age. Dreams that come with the job.

Dreams of people I have tried to save but couldn't. Dreams of trying to save myself. Dreams of the things that are broken in people, things that you just can't see for looking. Dreams of Jason Lucie. Our old bedroom. And a gun.

That one eats me up the most.

Chapter 1

I wasn't supposed to be on shift that Monday in October. I was supposed to be off, and free to wake on my sofa at some senseless hour as usual, then potter about my third-floor two-bedroom apartment in St. George's Harbour overlooking the Lagan and the towering yellow profiles of Samson and Goliath beyond it.

My living room was a rectangle partitioned off by the dining table where I completed my casework. The window had no blind, letting the sun stream in when it was ready to.

I never knew my neighbours: the young English couple renting the top floor apartment above and the older local couple living below, nor the ones below them. But I knew their sounds. The people above liked to listen to The Strokes. *Last Nite* was a favourite; they always played it before going out. Their footsteps were noticeable but soft and beating. I knew that the woman had the manners to take her high heels off when she entered the apartment. I learned this when the woman from the floor below commented on my mine the morning after I staggered home from a night out. Did I know the clacking stilettos made on my wooden floor? After that I avoided her.

Family never visited the apartment. Father would have called, only I put him off in case Greg was there. Charlotte didn't call because the place was unreasonably small if she had her kids with her – five, like we'd grown up with. And Brooks would have dropped in any time, but he'd disappeared off the face of the earth. Greg was the only person who came by invitation.

Jason Lucie, on the other hand, liked to surprise me. He

was the most charming man I had ever known, with his pale skin, eyes the colour of sandy silt, red hair and a wide smile that put people at ease. When he stood on the bridge looking up at my window he would be wearing a hoodie, the hood pulled up, his smile imperfectly still, sending a message to me. He wore that hoodie because I bought it for him, and because sometimes I slept in it at our house in Osborne Gardens when I was cold in bed.

Jason knew my routine, so when I jogged along the Lagan, he would be standing on East Bridge Street, doing nothing but staring. For over a year – once he found out where I'd gone – he was there almost every night. That's why I liked to shake up my work shifts and my runs. I wasn't giving anything up; I was just timing it differently.

At other times the thought of going anywhere outside of work terrified me and I would sit at home and wait for Greg to call. My life became like that – a waiting game. Waiting for people to give up on me, you could say.

Anyway, I was supposed to be off that day. I was eating breakfast when Detective Inspector Diane Linskey, my partner, phoned with the news.

'I said we'd take it. Is that alright, Harry?' Linskey paused hopefully.

'Yep. Of course,' I said.

'It'll get us both out from behind the desk.'

'Oh yeah, we've been getting much too cosy behind our desks.'

Linskey laughed.

An hour later I pulled into Strandtown PSNI station, then went inside and put my handbag in my locker. Outside Linskey was waiting by our navy-blue Skoda hatchback.

'Hello, stranger,' she said with cheery routineness. She

put on her sunglasses and attempted to stare through the low, strong October sun.

'Tell me more about this boy,' I said as we drove down the Holywood Road.

'A missing four-year-old – River, you call him. He's gone missing from his home in Witham Street. His mother called it in.'

'Anything strange or startling?'

'The mother was hard for the operator to get much more from. An officer has been out, but I thought this was one for us.'

'Great.' I yawned.

'You need an early night, Harry.'

'Chance would be a fine thing.' I yawned again. I hadn't slept for a couple of weeks.

'You can drive on the way back to the station,' she said. 'It'll stop you falling asleep on me.'

'Aren't you funny!' I said.

We stopped at the lights at Holywood Arches from where there was a glimpse of CS Lewis Square, a small community garden with murals of long-haired hippy women dancing through fields, a welcome replacement for ones of men nursing rifles and resentment.

Fronting the Newtownards Road, a fair old smattering of shutters were permanently down, only unlocked for potential buyers. Or there were fake shop fronts that were trying to dupe those not paying full attention. The road was a graveyard for businesses in their infancy; the only shops awake were those that had always been there. But this didn't stop the constant pulse of traffic. It was a go-through, get-past place as much as anything, reminding us Belfast people that there's life beyond our floating city.

In between the Gold Buying Centre and the Charter for Northern Ireland office, turning right into Witham Street, we toured a lane of small red-brick terraces, ending with five relatively new three-bed homes that sat proudly facing the hunched shoulder of the old graffiti-scarred transport museum. Four of the newish-builds were semi-detached, but the address we were going to was a detached property with a tasteful dim pink door and a topiary plant either side of it and without the small audiences of weathered garden gnomes that adorned most of the houses in the street.

'This is surprisingly cute,' Linskey said.

We got out of the car. A woman with short red hair came out hurriedly to greet us. She was still in her pyjamas.

'Mrs Reede?' Linskey asked.

'Yes.'

'We're here now and we'll help you find your boy.' She shook the woman's hand and placed a reassuring hand on her shoulder. This kind of case got Linskey going; the stakes were high – a child was involved. She loved cases where she could help a family.

We followed Zara Reede into her home where she clawed the cream-coloured throw off the sofa and placed it around her shoulders like a shock-absorber. She raked her fingers through the tormented locks of her hair and told us what happened. After she woke that morning she went downstairs, made a cup of tea, had a smoke at the back door and got back into bed, thinking that her son River – the missing child in question – was being unusually quiet.

'I called out to my partner Raymond,' said Zara, 'asked if he would check in on Riv. I thought Raymond was shaving in the en suite bathroom. But he didn't reply when I called him, so I called Riv. But he didn't reply either. Then I knew something was wrong. I got up, looked out, saw Raymond in the garden. When I went into River's room he wasn't there. So I went downstairs again … usually River puts the TV on soon as he gets up. I don't like him to, but you know how wee boys are.'

At this Linskey nodded, being the mother of two boys now aged eighteen and twenty. 'Yes, I remember,' she said.

We watched Zara pace. Linskey grew her eyes at me and gave a slight tip of her head at the banging coming from the back garden.

'May I take a look around?' I asked.

'Yes, Detective.' Zara pressed her lips inside her mouth, a dimple forming in each tear-stippled cheek. 'But you'll not find River here. We've looked everywhere. You know, in cupboards and places like that.'

Up I stood anyway, glancing at the wall to the right of the fireplace which was a shrine to the boy: six photos of River in various toothless stages. I took a moment to take them in, to learn his face.

'He's changed loads since those were taken,' said Zara.

On the Mexican pine mantel was a small gold carriage clock and an overloaded pot of amaryllis trumpets. The photo Zara had set out for us rested against the plant pot. I lifted it up.

'We'll get this image of River circulated as soon as possible, Mrs Reede,' I told her.

I knew there was a lesson to be learned from the pied cheeks of mothers of missing children. It was on their top lips, shiny with the glassy liquid that streams from their nostrils and spreads all over their faces like a rash of fire.

'And he was wearing his pyjamas?' Linskey asked. 'Isn't that what you said on the phone?'

At this point Raymond came in: a stout man with a head of thick, black, curly hair. He wore a pair of grey cords and a bland pullover, and walked as though he was soaking wet. He wiped his hands on a rag, reached out and shook mine.

'Thanks for coming,' he said.

'Detective Inspector Harriet Sloane,' I said, then gestured in Linskey's direction. 'This is Detective Inspector Diane Linskey. We're going to get this photo and the description of River straight into circulation. It's best to act fast, Mr Reede.'

'Marsh. My surname's Marsh,' he said. 'We're not married.'

Zara turned to look at him, cloaked in the plush throw. It fell in pleats around her like a baptismal cloak. She gave us a feeble smile, showing her teeth, straight and white if not a bit big for her small face. She was attractive. Would be any normal day. Beautiful and repulsive.

'I'll have that look around now,' I said.

'Knock yourself out,' said Raymond.

In the kitchen, dinner dishes from the night before were jammed in the sink and there was a strong scent of sesame oil, soy sauce and stale beer. Linskey was asking the same questions of Raymond we'd already put to Zara. He wasn't answering but using all his concentration to lower himself onto the sofa with the rigidity of a person who had just undergone an operation. Eventually he sat, his left leg out straight. He took a deep breath from down in his belly.

'Mr Marsh, would you say that River is wearing his pyjamas?' Linskey tried the question again.

Raymond straightened himself up, then slouched backwards, his fleshy hand still pressing the rag on the arm of the chair.

'Pyjamas,' he finally said. 'Yes, stripy pyjamas. Blue and

green.'

The far end of the kitchen dissolved into something of a dining area containing all the paraphernalia typical of a couple for whom this home was not their first. The rooms were small but cushy, and the house seemed to fold in at the corners to better support all the furniture inside. A square table was pushed flush to the wall and there was an imposing book case shored up against the opposite side. In it was an array of cookbooks with names such as *Healthy Eating for Children*, and *Eat Yourself Happy, Eat Yourself Smart – for Children*, umpteen books about Omega oils, and organic, sugar-free, gluten-free and GM-free eating, and parenting self-helpers – *Raising Boys*, *Breastfeeding Now and In the Future*, *The Good Mother's Handbook* and *How to be a Good Mum*.

Another thing I noticed about the house was a distinct lack of toys: not one truck or dinosaur, no puzzle pieces anywhere among the rubble of Raymond and Zara's lives. I asked if there was a sibling we could speak to; I'd noticed that on the cream leather sofa was a cross-stitched cushion bearing the legend, *Excuse the mess, my children are making happy memories*. Children. Yet the house wasn't messy, not with child-mess anyway.

'No, no other children,' said Zara. 'Just Riv.'

She looked affronted and I found myself apologising for what, I wasn't quite sure.

There were some things, however: a packet of extra-large nappies on the counter, and on the side of the bookcase, three charts pasted onto primary-coloured sheets of paper. The soothing cornflower blue chart was for sleep; the traffic-light red one was labelled 'good/bad boy', and a suitably urinal yellow chart was apparently for the potty. Each sheet was ruled out into lines, with red crayon Xs and little sticky gold stars summing up the success/fail rating of each day.

Zara's pacing grew impatient in the living room. She asked Linskey when we would be going, and when we would be coming back, and when she should expect to hear from us again. Raymond told her these things take time.

'Yes,' Linskey murmured. 'The moment we have any information.'

In the sink, among the plates and glasses, were numerous plastic spoons. Little Calpol measures. And on the mini island, its body constructed from wooden pallets, a steel toolbox was opened out, a hammer lying beside it, nose angled against the cold Formica surface. Zara came in, crouched to the bottom shelf of the bookcase, pulled out a huge hardback catalogue, eased it open with both hands onto the island: *Next Catalogue, Autumn/Winter 2015* – last year's.

'I've no photo,' she told me, 'but what I noticed …'

She paused, flicked through silky photographs of pleasant-looking children posing in starchy school uniforms.

'His coat.'

She pressed her fingernail into a photo of a blond boy with a broad white smile, then tore the photo from the catalogue and handed it to me.

'River has taken his coat?' I asked, somewhat surprised.

Zara nodded. Her shoulders shuddered, then shrugged. 'It wasn't on his hook in the hall,' she said.

'So, you think …'

'Yes, he must have. I can't find it anywhere.'

'We'll ask all the neighbours to look for River too,' I told her.

'Raymond did that already … I've stayed here, in case.'

'Children usually come back pretty quickly.'

'When they get hungry?'

'Zara,' I said gently, 'do you have any enemies?'

'Do you?' she replied.

When the floorboards chirred above us her eyes darted to the ceiling. She frowned, dashed into the living room, calling Raymond. He sat in stillness. Linskey, however, was gone. Zara strode to the hall, bare feet slapping the tiled floor.

'Hello? Detective?' she called. 'Can I help you?'

'She's just checking the lad's bedroom,' Raymond told her, his hand reaching out for the TV remote control.

Zara's feet banged their way up the stairs.

'Doing some work?' I asked Raymond. He gave me a distrustful look. 'The toolbox ...' I added with a smile.

'Yeah.' He set the remote control down and levered himself up. 'Come here till I show you, Harriet.'

He walked to the back door; bin lorries beeped in the distance. He pointed. 'See the fence?'

My eyes landed on the house behind, hidden behind the fence he was talking about. The slats of the fence were diagonal, all butted together, but there was a patch where a mismatching piece of darker wood overlapped.

'The builders never gave us a fence,' Raymond said. 'That belongs to the woman out the back. It's rightly rotted through. That'll have to do until we get the money to put up our own. She has these dogs, you see. And there was this gap ... River can get through. Has no fear, like.' He blew out, his tumbling fringe breezing about his eyes.

He had bad skin, his nose misshapen by crystallised acne. I held the photo of River and the picture of the coat he may have had on when he left. I tried to envisage the boy at the fence. Willed him to appear over it.

'He's not over there, if that's what you're thinking,' Raymond said. 'First place I looked. Anyway, River left through the front door.'

'Any signs of forced entry?'

'None.'

In the hall was a photo of Zara and River on the wall, and the coatrack, just like Zara said there was. I was aware I was being watched from the landing as I looked at Zara's and Raymond's winter coats, and the hook that held a little navy-blue gym bag that said *strandtown preschool* on it in white lettering.

'Just his little gym gutties in there,' Zara shouted, helium-lunged, pre-empting my question.

'So, River would've come down here?' Linskey asked, walking down the stairs marginally in front of Zara who no longer had her throw; it swathed the bannister instead. A pair of baggy grey pyjama bottoms were wearing her.

'River would've taken his coat from this rack,' Linskey went on. 'And … where would he have gotten the door key from, Mr Marsh?'

'The keys are in here, Diane,' Raymond answered. He stooped to open the drawer in a pine telephone table.

Zara pursed her lips, but Linskey couldn't see it.

'There's a little canvas pouch,' Zara announced. She edged past Linskey and lifted it into her palm – tilted it so we could see into it, as if she was offering us a boiled sweet each from a bag. Only, nothing.

She tossed the weightless pouch in her hand. 'The key's in the door,' she said, 'but it's usually kept in here.'

Raymond gestured at the top of the door. 'Got a bolt put up there too,' he explained.

'And did either of you put the latch on last night?' Linskey asked.

Raymond's jaw hung open slightly, his eyes flickering

softly to the side giving the impression he was trying to remember. He leaned against the door jamb in the axis of the hall and the living room, his face grey apart from the white spikes of October morning light that flickered over him through the trees out front, like he was being seen through fluttering eyelashes. He scratched his head.

'I can't be certain,' Zara interjected. 'Maybe … But was it last night that I double-locked? Frig it, the days are rolling into one!'

'River would've let himself out easy enough anyway, Zee,' said Raymond. 'He was a wee climber, sure.'

Was? My interest piqued at his use of the past tense.

Zara explained. 'River used to climb something dreadful, especially when he was two and three. Desperate for it!' She looked out their front door at the woman standing at the end of the gate that twinned theirs. 'Raymond, she's still out there,' she said. 'Flip sake, get a life, love!'

'Who is that woman?' I asked.

'Ness.' Raymond smiled. 'She's a neighbour. Ness'd be able to tell you about River's climbing. He climbed into her tree before – remember, Zee? Couldn't get him down, wee monkey man.'

Linskey told them that boys were more likely to hide outside while girls were more likely to stay indoors. Zara ran her hands through her hair; she reached for her throw and slung it over her shoulders.

'I don't need to hear about what girls do,' she snapped. 'It's not a girl I have.'

*

The neighbour backed off as Diane and I proceeded down the

short path. Vanessa 'Ness' Bermingham, a woman in her sixties, petite with a titanium globe of hair like she was growing out a shorter style, went into her house, easing the front door of her end terrace shut.

'Well done, Harry,' said Linskey, 'you didn't yawn once.'

I started up the Skoda and looked side-on at the house. Through the window I could make out Raymond who had nestled himself back into the sofa, finally able to turn on the TV to wash away the awful silence. And there were two women, Zara and Ness, who stood looking out of their own living room windows, neither of them pulling away.

Chapter 2

When Chief Superintendent Dunne entered the room, I celebrated his presence by getting out of my seat. He perched on the table just to the side of my desk, so I sat down again. Linskey was at the table behind. The Chief took his tie from his suit pocket, lifted the collar of his shirt and snaked the strip of black material around it.

'I've sent Simon and Higgins to the Marshes' street,' he said, teasing a knot and straightening it.

'Yes, Chief,' I said. 'That was the mother on the phone.'

Zara had phoned the station to let us know that the coat had a hood, in case it hadn't been obvious from the photo. She'd thought about it and panicked, got on her laptop and checked the website. She thought the photo didn't look as though there was a hood. She asked if it was too late for me to tell everyone that the coat – already shown on both the BBC and UTV news bulletins – did indeed have a hood. Her voice crept small and meek down the telephone line.

I tried to reassure her that we would keep updating their information bit by bit, but only until River was found. I had to stay positive that a fruitful find would be the only outcome. I added that we would be back soon to the street he had gone missing from, that officers would work their way along more houses, quiz more people on the street and in local shops. That we'd do everything in our power.

It was then Zara reported back to me that there was a police car pulling up outside, sounding calmer for seeing it, and she ended the call.

Chief Dunne recreased his collar. 'Okay, Sloane,' he said, 'you'll have to update the press office about the hood. But tell them *they* forgot to mention it. Don't admit that you forgot to mention it. Doesn't bode well.'

I said nothing, wanting to add that I hadn't forgotten a thing. Zara had forgotten.

'I'm about to do it now, Chief,' said Linskey. She lifted the phone handset from its cradle.

The Chief pressed his earpiece tight against his ear and stared through me as he listened. I looked back over my notes.

'You need to go to Shaw's Bridge right away,' he said. 'To the playground. A child's green coat has been found.'

'Chief?' I said.

He turned toward me. 'Yes, Sloane?'

One point of his collar was tucked underneath his tie. I tapped my collarbone with my pen but he didn't take the hint. Instead, I proceeded to tell him what Raymond had said about the fence.

'If River could get through the fence, I think we need to check the house behind theirs, Chief.'

He frowned deeply. 'You insisted that our young man left through the front, Sloane.'

'I did. That's right. Still, I think we need to check it out.'

'You need to get to Shaw's Bridge is what you need to do, Sloane. And Linskey, with this new information I suggest you hold off contacting the press office just now.' The Chief did not look at Linskey as he spoke to her; he peered past, out of the window at the brick wall.

'Constable Higgins and Sergeant Simon are the first attending officers. They're there already. They're talking to a man walking his dog near the park. It's a lead. Go with it.'

He walked away.

Linskey set the phone down. 'Let's get going then, Sloane,' she said.

'How Jocelyn sticks him is beyond me,' I said once we were outside.

Jocelyn Dunne was the Chief's wife. She and Diane had been friends for years; since school, even. They'd even been on double-familied holidays to the Dunnes' villa in the Algarve back when Linskey was part of a couple and did that kind of thing.

'You'd know,' Linskey said, 'with your dad. They have to be a certain way. We all do, but more so for them. More so for your dad. I'm sure people used to ask how your poor mother stuck Charles. It's intense at times.'

Poor Mother indeed. 'You don't need to tell me!' I said.

Linskey had been RUC for a time. Father was only ever RUC; he'd retired when the constabulary became the PSNI (or when he was sacrificed for the PSNI, as he put it). Linskey knew him as her ex-Chief Constable; she also remembered my mother when she fully functioning: the renowned judge, Adelinde Brooks, Justice of the Peace, then Judge Sloane, serene and strong. But I could barely recall Mother before she became a vegetable.

'What was he like – Dunne – when you were in Portugal?' I asked Linskey. 'Go on, spill!'

She looked at me over the roof of the car. 'Well, he's kept himself in shape,' she said. 'I like a good pair of legs on a man. My dad ran too. The smell of sweat always gets me going.'

'You're gross,' I said. 'So that's why Jocelyn puts up, you reckon? The calves?'

'You'd need to ask her. I've given up trying to work out relationships.'

'You and me both,' I said, starting the engine.

The car heater came on, blowing out what smelled like

Irish Cream on a drunk's breath. While Linskey contacted Simon and Higgins, my thoughts turned again to young River.

'Are you still with your fella?' Linskey asked them.

Chapter 3

The coat was the thing that struck a chord: River's little green puffa jacket. It was padded, snug for the October weather. It gave the appearance that the boy model was much larger than he could possibly have been; it gave him a bulky outline, plump with muscles. River, by Zara's account, was slight, like her. Light brown hair, like neither her nor Raymond.

I turned the car into the car park at Shaw's Bridge and came back on myself where I could already see the coat. A man was there with his dog, a mink-coloured Weimaraner, beautiful and aloof. They were standing before the short black iron gate. A marked Mitsubishi Shogun was beside the hedge; Higgins and Simon were nodding as the man spoke. When we reached them on foot, Linskey greeted the dog with a stroke.

'It was me that phoned into the station,' the man said. He was in his late fifties, owner of an aquiline nose and bright auburn hair pulled low in a ponytail at the nape of his neck.

'It does look like the photo,' Simon told me in an aside.

The man said, 'Couldn't believe it … well, I walk her away from home when she's in season. And I'd just heard on the car radio about the missing boy, about this green coat they're looking for … I mean, *you're* looking for. Then look …' He marched over to the entrance of the playground, the dog trotting alongside.

'Please, sir, we need you to stay out here so there's no contamination of evidence,' said Linskey.

'Oh, I haven't touched the coat at all. I've learnt not to disrupt evidence, you know, from watching a glut of crime movies.'

'Of course,' I said. 'You did the right thing, sir.'

The coat hugged the top floor of a climbing frame with yellow and green plastic compartments between the rope ladder and the slide. Its arms were tied around the bars, hood upright. If glanced at from a distance, it looked like a child playing hide and seek, huddled in against the frame as though counting, anticipating turning around and giving chase. I took the photocopy from my pocket. The levitating coat certainly looked a lot like it.

I crossed the playground, the surface giving under my boots. Under the dripping trees, roots knitted out of the ground. Dry leaves were lifting and falling onto beds of rotted ones. Some had crumbled like stale bread; like old bone. But the coat itself had the look of being carefully positioned by an adult, considerate of the child without it.

River might have been there – at Shaw's Bridge, in the park – and left it. Alternatively, it might have been taken from a bench or from the woods and set in the playground by someone thinking the child was more likely to go there next, rather than return to the place where he or she had lost their coat.

Traffic made its deafening lap of the road; birds glugged in the trees. I couldn't hear what the man was telling Linskey; Linskey took her pad from her inside jacket pocket and made some notes. They remained at the gate.

The swings swung, though they were empty, their chains soundless, without the screech I remembered them giving under me. It had been years since I had been there.

I was about to glove up, mask up, when a gust of wind lifted the coat's hem away from the frame, giving me a peek of the personalised, iron-on nametag. 'River', it read, tailed by an inky frogspawn of a football. I used my personal radio to contact the station to let them know we needed forensics on the scene right away. Simon and Higgins stayed where they were so as not to leave their footwear impressions.

'We need perimeter control,' I shouted over to them.

'How much?' asked Simon, a tall, long-boned man with thinning hair under his hat.

There were two entrances to the park and to the right of the play area was an open space for picnics.

'Cordon off access to the car park,' I told them. 'Don't let anyone in.'

I tried to picture my twin sister Charlotte in Zara's position; she'd be taking it out on everyone in sight if one of her kids were missing, especially Timothy, her youngest. Timothy was four years old, the same age as River, only Timothy had cerebral palsy and complex medical needs while River was the picture of health. I looked again at River's smiling little face in my copy of the photo Zara had given me. Then I thought of him not coming home, and I had to shake the thought from my mind.

Linskey was thanking the man for phoning the information through when I reached them.

'DI Linskey, can I show you something?' I called out. At the climbing frame, I told her to look at the small rectangle in the hem that showed itself briefly in the breeze.

'Looks like it's our boy's,' Linskey said. She kept her voice low.

The man lingered.

Linskey turned back toward him. 'Thanks again for the description of the woman, Mr Hammitt,' she shouted and watched as he waited, smiled and felt her meaning tighten. I know that cold side of her.

'Any time,' he replied. He fixed a chunky brown scarf around his neck and headed back toward his car with a lead wrapped around his hand and his dog trotting off.

'It's our boy's then. What's it doing all this distance from home?' Linskey asked. 'They never mentioned being over here yesterday.'

I remembered Zara being certain that River was wearing his coat. Not that it mattered that much, but it was a good coat to get lost in: bright and attention-grabbing. It wasn't such a good coat if you went on to lose it too.

'So, Mr Hammitt saw someone?' I asked.

'Yes, I have her description here – a woman in her fifties, blonde bob, about five two. Black or dark grey coat. She was walking two dogs.'

While Simon was at the car getting the tape, Linskey spoke to Constable Higgins: 'I want you both to get back to River's street. Keep asking questions … especially the street out back that runs parallel – Ribble Street. Start with the house directly behind.'

Higgins goggled at her, his deep brown eyes narrowing until they were nearly all lash. Those eyes really would have been quite beautiful on a girl. At twenty-six, Constable Carl Higgins was a law unto himself; he was waiting for the results of his sergeant exams. He had thick hair he was clearly enjoying, and kept it in a long Liam Gallagher style with mutton-chop sideburns. He played drums in an Oasis tribute band – I'd seen him play at a couple of our Christmas parties. Outside of his greens he wore only two outfits – a cashmere jumper and creased black trousers, or a white shirt buttoned up to the neck and creased navy-blue ones. He had no doubt spent a clean fortune on both ensembles. Even his socks were Louis Vuitton. It was integral to the style that you should be able to notice this.

'D'you not think we'd be better here?' he asked.

'Absolutely not,' Linskey said.

'Alright,' he said and walked off to help Simon.

As the rain arrived so did forensics. They erected their portable tent over the frame, bagged the coat and dusted the wood for prints.

So close to my own childhood home, I couldn't stop thinking about my family in a way that had become unusual for me. I remembered one evening, when everyone else had gone into the drawing room after supper, Father and I sat on around the elongated oak table and he began, in a way that was unusual for him, to tell me about a case he was working: a teenage boy who had vanished into thin air. I recalled it feeling abnormal that Father should talk about this in such depth and with such frankness when one of his own son's was unravelling, flitting in and out of the family, and his original mind, because of drugs. Brooks used to go missing for days at a time, and Mother would cover it up, saying he was staying at a friend's. I had asked Father why he thought the boy had gone missing, perhaps wanting to understand Brooks on some level too and why he had become the reason for my parents' late-night arguments. I'd forgotten Father's reply to my question until that Monday we found River's coat.

'Someone going missing is not an event in their life but the indicator of a problem.'

'Is he coming back?' I had asked Father, my voice full of hope. I was eleven and had recently started Victoria College, the local girls' grammar school. I wanted to be taken seriously and Father granted that wish.

'Probably not, Harry,' he said.

'How do you know?' Had Father heard something? Had there been a new development he hadn't updated me with, something that had escaped his mind as we ate supper?

'It doesn't matter how I know.'

In the kitchen, Father dried the dishes faster than I could wash them. Mother popped her head around the door.

'Do you want some coffee?' she asked.

'I'll bring you one in,' said Father.

'No, it's alright.'

My parents were not compliant but they did comply. Mother's heels bit the tiled floor. She fetched herself a mug. Father stood silent. Coffee and silence and a sink of cold sediment-filled water. What sort of couple had they become? Charlotte came in and pulled herself up onto the counter. Mother smiled at her, tapping Charly's knee so she would move her legs out of the way of the cutlery drawer. She took a spoon, made her coffee and gave the spoon straight to me to wash.

Father went into the drawing room where he opened a broadsheet across his lap. Coral was sixteen and lived in her room; she was a real bedroom girl. She attributed it to her studies, but I knew she spent hours making mixtapes from the radio.

Father ran his hand over his brow and shook out his paper.

'How do you know the boy isn't coming home?' I asked.

'Who?' asked Charly, only to be ignored.

'He's eighteen,' Father said.

'Same age as Addam,' I said.

'He's more man now than boy.'

I wasn't sure. To me Addam still seemed like a boy. There was something babyish about him. He still played computers and went to Scouts. Brooks mocked him for it, when he was about. They could barely be in each other's company a minute.

'Adults make their own decisions in what they do,' Father said. 'That's the point of growing up.'

'What is?'

'Time to go out on your own.'

Mother joined us and the silence came pinballing back.

But that night Father came into my room and shook me awake. Charly, in her bed, turned toward the wall, her eyes budded shut, her lips smacking gently.

'He's home,' Father whispered.

'Brooks?' I asked.

'No.' Father's enthusiastic gaze dropped, excited more by the prospect of sharing his work with me. 'The boy who had gone missing.'

'That's good.' I yawned.

'Just wanted to tell you.'

'I'm pleased.'

'Right.' Father stood up.

'Why did he leave?' I asked louder than I meant to.

'Plenty of reasons. He might not stay, but at least we all know now.'

'What?'

'That's he's alright.'

'That's good.'

'Right, back to sleep, you.'

Chapter 4

'The Chief has been in touch,' Linskey said. She stood against the gate. Her face was whiter than usual, her grey eyes cooler.

'What did he say?' I asked.

'He wants someone to check in on your friend Donald.'

'He's not my friend.'

'You know what I mean.'

'And you volunteered us?'

'Do we really have any choice?'

'Let's pretend we do,' I said. 'Any particular reason we need to see Donald Guy?'

'Just to touch base.'

'Touch base,' I repeated.

'Chief says it's precautionary. Probably nothing.'

I nodded, hoping this was true. 'Want to go check in now then?'

'Yes, let's head over that direction,' said Linskey, looking at the playground again.

It was procedure to call on Guy in cases like this; it would be terribly negligent not to. Not that that knowledge made it any more pleasant.

I couldn't help but yawn again as I acclimatised to the warmth in the car. Linskey swiftly turned the heating off. We went right round the Malone roundabout and back along the Outer Ring, down Cregagh, Orangefield and on. Guy's address was on the pad on the dash though I knew it by heart. Two minutes later we were in Ballyhackamore, at a second-floor flat buried behind a row of busy shops and restaurants. He was hidden away where, it seemed to me, he would be hard to keep an eye on. Which was worse? Seeing his ilk or not? Visits to his place were never a joy; this was a necessity.

Linskey felt the same, as evidenced by the groan she emitted as we approached the entry to his place, a marked car already beating us there.

Donald Guy: fifty-two years old, lived alone, visited by probation officers weekly. He had served three of his six years in Maghaberry for ten counts of child abuse, for hundreds of indecent images of children, for making and distributing all scales, thirty of those images in the most abhorrent category. He'd been out of jail for eighteen months. Since his release had been working in Albertbridge Home Supplies, a local hardware shop on the edge of Connswater Retail Park.

In my experience paedophiles are one of two types. One is the type that grooms a community – the church leaders, school teachers – the types who are trusted, so that when they're eventually complained about – after roughly two hundred offences – they can stand there, maintain eye contact, use fluid hand movements, their clothes unimpeachable, their name revered, and make the complainant look like a liar.

My colleague Detective Amy Campbell worked on these cases exclusively. It was she who told me about the other type, the type that didn't enter the community, the outsider who looked like your stereotypical creep, the kind of person you would never see near a school. That type worked in a different, underground way, lived an unexamined life. Campbell explained that the second type could sometimes be a later version of the first – what happened to a type one paedo once they had been forced to become covert. As much as I respected her – someone had to do the job – I hated to hear Campbell talk about it.

Donald Guy was now a type two. I didn't know if he had ever been the first type, the charmer; it was hard to picture him charming anyone. He stood in his hallway saying he had been expecting us; Campbell had phoned his landline to say she was on her way – he was banned from owning a smartphone or computer. His skin was tinged yellow, like he was vitamin D deficient, the whites of his eyes were pink.

The search team set about his rooms while Linskey and I stayed with him. I didn't fancy going through those rooms again, seeing where he gratified himself to thoughts of those images. He'd once looked at me with some indication of shame.

Linskey cut to the chase. 'Donald, have you seen the boy?'

'No, I haven't,' he said, walking into his living room. He looked into the gas fireplace, embers brightening the shins of his trousers.

'You know who I'm talking about?' Linskey asked.

'Yes, I do,' he said. He sighed and looked from Linskey to me. 'I can't help you.'

We were bookending him, brushing his knuckles. He didn't look bothered that people were plundering through his home. We could hear them, the emptying, the removals. Donald knew he hadn't a leg to stand on, not with his past crimes. Whether he had hurt River or not, whether he knew where the boy was or not, he couldn't complain about any bombardment of his home and his life because this was the way it would always be for him.

It was six o'clock in the evening. The plastic tray of a microwave meal sat on the arm of his chair, a fork resting on it. The room was sparse: TV, a clock, a rug on the floor. This was how he lived now, the opposite of Zara and Raymond. It was closer to how I lived, though I didn't like to acknowledge the thought.

'I told Detective Campbell,' Donald said. 'I was just home when my parole officer called. I told him too – I was working in Albertbridge today. Working from eight this morning till four this afternoon.'

'That wouldn't cover last night,' I said. We had no time frame for River leaving the house or being taken.

'There's nothing I can do about that,' he said. 'I was here. Sunday's my day off.'

Donald took care of himself with the minimum amount of effort and expense – just enough to get by. He was thinly occupied. I could tell he had given up on life. In the past, he would have had this questioning look; he would have asked, 'What do you think of people who download those photos?'

I would have told him – because I had to – that I made no judgements.

'You must have some thoughts,' he'd have said. 'Do you think this makes me a bad person?'

'I think you need help,' I'd told him at the time. This was before he had served time, back before the PSNI knew about the boy he had been abusing.

Acting on intel from the National Crime Agency, which had traced his access of illegal sites, Linskey and I had initially arrested Donald for possession of indecent images. Then he was out on bail. Linskey went off work on sick leave – she was going through her divorce at the time – and I had my own shit to deal with. But when I, along with Campbell, went to his house to follow up ten months later, it turned out he had managed to befriend Sorcha Seton in that time. A local alcoholic, Sorcha worked in Neptune Bingo on the Newtownards Road and rented an apartment in Edenvale that always smelled of Malibu and leather. She had a strong jutting chin that sprung coarse white hairs and eyebrows that stayed high up on her forehead as if to keep her permanently heavy eyes open. Sorcha had raised a family who had abandoned her – or she had abandoned them, I'm not sure which. Then she had had Rhys, her little 'late one', her little strawberry-blond surprise. Rhys was four and Sorcha fifty-four, and Donald, fatter then, lived in the flat next to Sorcha's.

Back then, Donald had led us to his bedroom where three PCs were running simultaneously.

'What will we find on those?' Campbell had asked him.

'More,' he'd said, looking into her eyes for some kind of response.

He wasn't like some, craving a reaction he could feed off. It wasn't like that. And because I wasn't the one to look through the images – to tally up the stages, to look at those little violated bodies, distressed faces – I was able to see him as human. Unlike Amy Campbell.

Campbell was disgusted, but that was what she'd signed up for. There was no achievement like seeing a predator go down, she told me. But then she changed too; in later years, Detective Campbell became all 'hate the sin, not the sinner'.

Back then, I'd had some empathy for Donald. He was ill; that's how I saw it. I didn't judge him too harshly, and had to distance myself for my own sake. Undeniably, if it had been one of my nephews he'd hurt, it would have been different. But it wasn't. At that stage, it was images and images only. I told myself, to get through it, that it was indirect abuse.

Then Sorcha found out about Donald's arrest, and gradually there was a drip feed of disclosures from Rhys, telling his mother that on the nights she was out – partying, working at the bingo hall – encouraged and cajoled by Donald, her new friend, to do so, reassured that she could leave the boy in his care – Donald had been inappropriately touching the four-year-old.

With Donald's impending court case coming up, the PSNI had a visit from Sorcha, and from then on, things were very different. I couldn't think of Donald asking me if he was a bad person without wanting to go back in time and scratch the eyeballs out of his head. Of course he was an abuser.

During the time he was on bail he had committed a contact crime. I was revolted both by how slow the legal process was and by how he couldn't help himself, obviously, didn't even want to try. Yes, he was ill all right; yes, he was a bad person for not getting help, for not going to his doctor's and saying, I am having these urges and I need them stopped. That's what Donald should have done, to my mind.

Now he was a different person; now he was disillusioned. I was disillusioned too, but paid not to show it.

'Donald, what are you doing about your urges?' I asked.

'Don't have them any more,' he said. 'I'm on tablets. Leuprorelin. Chemical castration. I'm as dangerous as a prepubescent boy.'

We stood looking at each other.

The search team shambled into the room. 'All clear,' said the officer before they left.

'Thanks,' said Donald, 'that's all I need – the neighbours seeing this!'

'You hardly have any.'

'It only takes one.'

I coughed away an unprofessional response while Linskey went to the door to speak to the team. Then it was just Donald and I in the room.

'I don't want to be that other person,' he told me. 'If I have to be that person, I'm not saying I'd kill myself, but it would make everything different.' He looked as animated as

I'd ever seen him. He was at once the predator and the prey.

But this victim act I didn't buy. You only value other people's lives when you treasure your own. That's what worried me about the likes of him. And Donald Guy looked like a man with nothing left to lose.

Chapter 5

I went home for a cup of soup that I ended up pouring down the sink, eating a dry slice of bread instead and drinking a coffee. Feeling the silence. Even rush hour was silent in the apartment. I took my coffee out to the balcony to watch the darkening sky. The Lagan was stirring; people were coming and going along East Bridge Street, heading in and out of the city, some rushing for a train that would take them out of this place.

I lifted my mobile phone from the patio table. I'd been ignoring it. There were three missed calls from Charlotte when I only wanted to hear from Greg. I wiped the calls from my phone and looked in the window at the TV. I had a habit of keeping it permanently on, with the volume low or off and the subtitles displayed. I'd gotten like that – aware of the silence of my own life; not wanting to disturb the peace.

Chief Dunne was on the news, talking about River. There he was, collar all straight and correct as he solemnly told reporters there was now a hunt for a missing child. There had been a Child Rescue Alert out since early that afternoon. The forensic teams were concentrating all their efforts on Shaw's Bridge, combing and sweeping the playground and car park, but the ground was too cold for imprints.

After I ate, I drove back to the station through Short Strand, stopping at the lights near the yellow painted wall with the word HOPE spelled out in clays dots with faces pinched into them.

'Yeah, hope,' I muttered.

At the station I picked up Linskey and we drove on to Witham Street. Outside Zara's, a blue sign glared from the stone-clad hut of Tamar Street Baptist Mission Hall: *Believe in the Lord Jesus Christ and thou shalt be saved. Acts 16:31*

New faces peered into the back of the car, people who were now part of the party, searching for River on our backseat. We passed a wheelie bin, a stack of red, black and green recycling containers on the road from every door in the street except Zara's. Some neighbours had dumped the contents of their bins onto the pavement, while others were giving their bins a rattle and a meaningful peak inside.

By this time Zara's house was boiling with people, busy with inactivity. Initially she didn't notice us enter, what with all the commotion. She had changed into a purple mohair cardigan and white leggings, brushed her hair into smooth red curtains. She looked completely different; now she was bright, stylish, spirited.

'He's not with you then?' she asked.

'I'm sorry,' I said. 'Not just yet. But we have some news. There is something.'

She didn't look ecstatic. If it wasn't River, River in person, then it wasn't enough.

'There's Harriet and Diane back,' said Raymond, tucked into the corner of the room in a twittering huddle of people tied like a knot around him. In stark contrast to Zara, he looked to me like a bit of a layabout – unkempt and unshakeable.

He was speaking to a lady who stood holding a sandwich platter in front of him while he scoured it thoughtfully. He took a sandwich and smiled at her with the kind of thankful smile you would give a caterer at a party.

East Belfast has the type of neighbours you would want in a crisis, the type that gravitate towards you and bring egg and onion sandwiches. The room smelled positively sulphuric.

'The neighbours have been brilliant,' Raymond said, aimed more at Diane.

'It's great to see you have lots of support,' Linskey replied.

The woman with the platter smiled sympathetically, her eyes dipping, her chin becoming lumpy.

'Zara, Raymond, can we speak to you in another room?' I said.

'Well, yes,' Zara answered.

She viewed her mobile phone and then the kitchen where people were smoking, drinking a flood of tea, scoffing yet more sandwiches and buns, turning to look at Linskey and I before going back to their conversations. Unlike Raymond, Zara seemed imposed upon by all the people.

'Upstairs,' she said. 'That's off limits to everyone.' She walked ahead of us.

'I'll be up in a minute,' Raymond said as I looked back for him. He was chewing his crust, caught up in conversation that sounded like it was nothing – certainly not about River. More like avoidance speak. Wake speak.

Upstairs, a dressing-gown belt was draped over the bannister. Brian Quinn, a member of forensics, was in River's room. Quinn held an evidence bag with River's toothbrush inside and another with his hairbrush. He nodded at me and got back to finding DNA samples.

There was a wooden rocking horse on the landing, the scent of aftershave wafting from the bathroom. Zara went into her room, the walls white enough to nip your eyes, especially since it was after nine and she had turned on the bright ceiling light. She sat on the bed, creasing the taut crisp lines of her white linens. Linskey sat beside her, starch-spined, the end of the bed dinting.

'We've found River's coat,' I said.

Zara covered her face with her hands. Aren't you going to ask where we found it? I felt like asking her. She took a deep breath, then stood to throw the window open, her hand upsetting the venetian blind that had sliced the sky into strips; it tinkled and shook. A lone cacti on the sill shielded itself against the bumps with a terracotta pot.

'I feel a bit sick,' she said. 'It's coming.'

She balled her fist and covered her mouth again; she breathed in through her nose, out through her mouth. She threw her mobile phone down and jumped up off the bed, leaving her wrinkles in the sheets, and shot along the landing to the bathroom. We could hear her dry wretches.

'Are you okay?' Linskey called out once Zara had stopped spitting.

'Yes,' she called back.

When she returned her eyes were watering, both hands clutching her right side. She sat on the bed again, further back than before, and pulled her legs to her chest. Her expression showed a degree of self-awareness.

'Do you need anything?' I asked.

'I'm fine,' she said. She lifted her phone again and looked at a spot on the wall in front of her.

To the side was a chair with a pile of clean laundry on it. I lifted it carefully onto the bed and sat down.

'The neighbours have been good,' she said. 'But it's weird hearing a local MP saying River's name. Though he goes by Reede. Anyway, they are talking about our River. That's the main thing.'

Zara had not corrected us when we gave out 'Marsh' as his surname. A boy lost was a boy lost. Still, we needed to work together. This was important.

'We'll update the press,' said Linskey.

'You said that River had his coat, Zara,' I said, 'that the night before it had been on the coatrack. But it was found in a park.'

Zara's eyes drank me in. She looked hopeful – or was trying to look hopeful.

'A park a good distance from here,' I added.

'Did you take River there? Maybe he left his coat there yesterday perhaps,' Linskey said.

'No,' said Zara. 'River had his coat when his dad brought him back yesterday at tea time.'

The landline rumbled. Zara ran downstairs to the hall table and snatched the mouthpiece from the cradle.

'Hello?' she said, then again, more frantically. 'Will you speak!' She hung up. 'No one there,' she said, hesitant to rejoin us, but she did, carrying the phone with her. Back in her room she set it beside her mobile.

'River's dad, you were saying …'

'Yes.' Zara tapped her fingertips to her forehead.

'I'm sorry, I must have misunderstood,' I said. 'I thought that Raymond was …'

'No. No.' Zara shook her head. 'Raymond's my partner. Sure I told you that.'

I felt like saying that just because she had called him her partner didn't mean the man wasn't River's father.

'Would River have gone to the park with his dad?' Linskey stepped in to ask while I rearranged my thoughts.

'His dad wouldn't have brought him to a park,' Zara answered.

'Where did they go?'

'You'd have to ask him that.'

'How do you know they didn't go to the park?'

'I don't see the importance of this line of questioning,' Zara said. She sighed and looked at the phones by her side.

'It's important,' I said, 'because lots of officers are going to start combing the woodlands there in the next while looking for River. But if he was in the park, then they may be wasting— '

Finally, Zara interrupted me to ask which park.

'Shaw's Bridge,' I said.

'But that's miles away! He couldn't walk there,' Zara stated as she realised the seriousness of this new find.

'Exactly,' I said. 'So if he was there and his coat was just left, then we'd be better changing the search area.'

Zara shuddered. 'Search area?' she asked. 'Like on the news? When you hear that phrase your heart nosedives. The next thing you hear is the word *body*, isn't it?'

She fell against Linskey and started to cry, pressing her face into Linskey's shoulder.

Linskey wrapped her arms around her. 'It's just procedure, Zara. It's best to be safe,' she said.

I tried to get more out of Zara: could she be certain the coat came back from River's dad's house? Who was his dad? What time had he brought River home on Sunday? How long had he had him, and so on. But Zara was inconsolable. She had to go and be sick again, this time sounding more convincing.

Raymond came up the stairs. He got near the top and stopped, putting his cheek against the mahogany bollard carved into an acorn. He knelt slightly on the top stair, studying the boot tips under his corduroys that were never zipped up.

'Is Zara unwell?' I asked.

He was sipping glances of her around the wall as she

threw up. He tapped his rounded stomach.

Linskey slipped into the bathroom. 'Any chance you're in the early stages of pregnancy?' she asked Zara in a gentle voice.

Zara insisted she wasn't, then she got up, washed her hands and came back into the bedroom. She glared at Raymond.

Brian Quinn popped his head around the door to let us know he was getting back to the station. I went out of the room to speak privately to him. He held his kit in one hand.

'I powdered both doors,' he said, 'seeing there was no obvious break-in, but they are covered with prints, which could be family. There have been all sorts coming and going.'

'I noticed.'

'What can you do?' Quinn asked. 'I'll see myself out.'

I glanced into River's bedroom. His sheets were tangled; there were a few teddy bears and a blue circular plush rug in the centre of everything, parted in the middle like a sea from a fairy tale. There were no books on his bedside table. No lamp. There wasn't even a lightbulb in the ceiling. A stuffed Thomas the Tank Engine lay on his pillow.

'I want you both to come to the station with us,' I said to Raymond and Zara.

'Why?' Zara asked.

'It might be easier to talk there.'

'I don't want to go anywhere in case River comes back.'

Linskey explained that someone would come to the house and wait for him.

'It is procedure,' Raymond said.

I followed him downstairs while Linskey helped Zara get herself together. People were still there, chatting in low, doughy voices.

'I am going to need the contact details of River's father,' I told Raymond in the kitchen.

He fetched his phone and gave me a mobile number. He told me that River's father was called Shane Reede, that he had no landline and that he had recently moved into Brandon Terrace.

'Very close to here,' I said, glancing at Raymond's mobile screen, picking up certain wounding words in a stream of texts.

'That's right,' Raymond said, turning off his phone. He had a stain that looked like gravy down the centre of his pullover. He pushed the platter of sandwiches across the kitchen island to me.

'No thanks,' I said.

He took another egg sandwich himself. I got the details of Shane's car: he drove a black Ford Focus. 'But he drives all sorts with his job – sometimes a van, sometimes a jeep,' said Raymond, crumbs falling on his belly. 'Sorry I can't be any more help. I'm not a car man. Shane chops and changes vehicles all the time.'

'Do you drive, Raymond?'

'I have a car on the DLA, a Renault Megane, but I don't drive it. Zara does, as my carer.'

He went to a cupboard full of bottles and blister packs, and popped two pills into his hand and shook out three or four of something else from a bottle.

'But Zara and you are … together?'

'You tell me what *together* means and I'll tell you if that's what we are.' Raymond smiled and put the tablets into his mouth. He cupped his hand under a running tap, drank the water and, with a backward flick of his head, swallowed the lot.

'We're a family. That's what counts, isn't it?'
'Do you mind me asking what your disability is?' I said.
'Meet Peg.' Raymond knocked his knee.
'And do you mind me asking …?'
'Not at all. I had an infection. There was no accident, no diabetes, no long-term anything. It was over quick. Can't work now, though.'

'You've a lot of tablets.'
'Get me through. A to B.'

Zara was standing behind Raymond with her bag; behind her the house was emptying out.

'I don't want people here, milling about when we're not here to see them. I don't want people upsetting things any more than they have already,' she said.

'Good thinking, Zee,' Raymond said, wiping his mouth on his sleeve.

*

Much was made of them getting into the Skoda, a bit of a show in front of the house for the burgeoning crowd. They were going to give details; they were helping the PSNI find young River. There had been the hand-holding with locals and a multitude of kisses on cheeks, pats on the backs, backs of their hands.

'He's probably out wandering, Zara,' someone said.
'River'll turn up the minute he's hungry,' said another.

I suddenly understood Zara's earlier quip; she must have been sick of hearing those positive remarks. It wasn't other people's sons who were missing. The crowd spluttered their reassuring, almost dismissive comments. Zara explained that she was too upset to drive and the detectives were kindly giving them a lift.

She sat in the backseat, her thumb in her mouth. It was quiet on the way to the station.

*

The news is usually dank and damp; rarely does a glimmer of hope come through. But news of River's disappearance was both, both a nightmare *and* something that could be rectified, something that *might* come good. It put that old 'no news' axiom to the test.

River Marsh, the four-year-old from East Belfast is still missing. He was not in his bed this morning.

The photo beside the story let everyone know who to look out for, what made him different. What also made him different was that he was missing when it was time for other little boys his age to be at home.

River Marsh. I admit that Linskey and I had scoffed at his name a bit. But we were wrong about it. River Reede wasn't much better, but now we didn't scoff at all.

Belfast, this city that had been destroyed and rebuilt, was shocked by the news; it was a city easily outraged but not easily shocked. This news felt wrong, this headline. It was a front page from another country. There were plenty of men in vans, attempted abductions, kids approached, kids asked to get into strangers' cars. These things were rife in other places. But in Belfast it was never this – a boy missing and not found within an hour or two, part of a custodial battle perhaps. Kids did not just disappear here.

River was different all right. That's what I realised as I watched the Chief's speech on the telly for the third time. Locals were being urged to check their sheds, garages and –

because of River's history of climbing – their trees. It had been repeated so often it was old news now. People had already done these things, repeatedly. Hope disappeared fast. You could feel it slipping away through the airwaves.

That night the search team went through the boat house on the upstream side of Shaw's Bridge and the periphery of the woods. There was talk that the next morning, as soon as it was light again, the search would move into the water.

Chapter 6

Zara waited for Raymond to be done. Across the room the fingerprint expert, Stuart Thomas, a Welsh man in his late forties with generous eyes and broad shoulders, lined Raymond up in front of the LiveScan machine. He told him to put one hand in, then the other, finger after finger. He watched Raymond as he swayed slightly and put a hand behind him as if, even if Raymond were to fall, he was catchable. I offered Raymond a seat but he refused.

Zara kept a close watch on the process too. I told her it would help us eliminate people. Anything I did or proposed doing she asked if it was necessary, even down to taking a statement from her. Raymond didn't question a thing; he cordially obliged when I mentioned the scans. He seemed almost excited to stand in front of the machine.

'We're all reduced to numbers,' he said over his shoulder, pressing his index finger against the screen, Stuart holding it in place.

I stepped forward to watch Raymond – his face, his tongue, how it folded on his lower teeth and protruded out of his mouth giving him the profile of a bullfrog. Really, there was nothing remotely handsome you could find in that face. What in the world had Zara seen in him?

Chief Dunne walked through the room holding a cup of coffee, doing that thing where he seems like he is not paying attention. But believe me, nothing escapes that man. Simon was sitting at a desk flicking through the pages of a document, his pink skull shining through his hair; beside him Higgins was bent over, one hand on the desk, the other thrumming his pen on a pile of paper, his face up close to the computer monitor.

I noted his 'hat hair', a little tuft sticking up.

Dunne stopped to talk quietly to them, standing at such an angle that Zara, Raymond, Stuart and I were just to one side of him. He was in to see what the parents of our young man looked like, no doubt, and get a read on them. It was what he did, not that you'd necessarily notice. Everything about the Chief was alert and not about to switch off anytime soon.

When Raymond's scans were done he stepped back and sat down. Then it was Zara's turn. She forgot about the cluster of keys she had set on her lap and they dropped to the floor as she got up. Raymond stooped to get them, but I got in there first, dropped them into his hand.

'Thanks, Harriet,' he said.

I noticed the questioning look Stuart gave Raymond for his over-familiarity. It probably seemed weird to Stuart, being male and all. The Chief, drinking coffee, allowed his eyes to take Raymond in, then Zara, who walked to the scanner smoothing her clothes down. Stuart guided her, speaking as pleasantly and distractingly as a Family Liaison Officer speaks to a child. She looked back at him with doe eyes. She looked really pretty, for a second I felt a pang of jealousy. I know! Me? Jealous of her? Here in the Venn diagram of the scan room pity and envy overlapped in me. It was madness, I know that now.

'That's some piece of gear there,' Raymond said.

'Yes,' I replied, 'it's all different nowadays, with technological advances.'

'We'll have our answers wild and fast then.'

Then there was a racket, Higgins saying, 'How did that get in here?'

Circling the room above us was a parakeet, yellow and

green, a red hat of feathers topping its head. Dunne soon left the room, like it wasn't his problem, and closed the door behind him. Raymond was mesmerised. A smile brought his tongue to the edge of his mouth. I couldn't see anything but that; I couldn't see past that expression on his face. Raymond was happy. It would be good to be that happy. He was not taking his situation seriously.

'Well,' said Linskey as she entered the room, 'we all done here?'

'Close the door behind you,' Higgins shouted.

She paused, saw the bird and then obliged.

'Nearly done,' said Stuart, trying to ignore the bird. 'I just need your autograph please, Zara.'

She signed the form dutifully.

'Done,' Stuart said.

'What's going on here?' asked Linskey.

Higgins put his hand out, the back of it steady. There the parakeet settled.

'First time you get the bird,' said Simon.

'I wouldn't say that,' said Higgins.

We all gathered round, Raymond and Zara included. Stuart was saying, 'This is someone's pet. Obviously used to being handled.'

'Okay,' I said, trying to get everyone away.

'Get a cage,' said Linskey. 'If no one comes for it later, I'll take it home.'

'We'll go get one now,' said Higgins, looking at Sarge Simon.

'I doubt it takes two of you,' I remarked.

'Okay, *I'll* get a cage,' Higgins said.

Zara's face tightened; she was growing impatient. I thanked Stuart. Linskey led the couple to the interview suite, and I followed along the dark corridor behind them. She turned and gave Raymond and Zara that mumsy little smile of hers, her snub nose creasing up, and opened the door to the waiting room.

'Take a seat, Raymond, and we'll be right with you,' she said. 'We're just going to speak with Zara first, okay?'

'That's fine,' said Raymond as he hobbled in. 'Zee,' he said as an afterthought, 'you'll do fine.'

*

Although we'd told Zara she could have a solicitor and that we could sort that out for her, she waived her right to one.

'There's no call for all that palaver,' she said. She was sure River would come home, then she looked unsure.

I couldn't help but think about Donald Guy when I was with Zara. I remembered the look in Sorcha Seton's heavy eyes, the fear, the weight of her own guilt.

Linskey pressed record: 'Monday 17th October 2016, just about. It's 11:24 p.m., and we have Zara Reede in the interview suite.'

'Procedure?' Zara asked with a little smile.

Zara picked at her nails, the cuffs of her oversized cardigan covering almost the length of her fingers. The prettiness that had been on her in the scanning room had gone. Now she seemed small and frail, quite ill looking. Her elfin features gave her a girlish look, as did her impish haircut, and when she opened her mouth her front teeth, big, straight and white, perpetuated the youthful myth. But when we took her date of birth, it turned out she was the same age as me – thirty-seven. Only a few days between our birthdays.

'When was the last time you saw River?' I started off

asking.

'Sunday night, at bedtime,' said Zara.
'What was he doing?'
'The bedtime routine.'
'What time did River go to bed?'
'Eight or so.'
'What was he doing on Sunday during the day?'
'I don't know – he was at his dad's.'
'How long was River at his father's for?'
'Since Friday at dinner.'
'What time is dinner in your house?'
'I don't … six o'clock?'
'What did River do with his father over the weekend?'
To this Zara, stated again that she didn't know.

There was no energy from her when she spoke, like she was pinned right in the middle of some storm or other, like she was no longer a person but a space where a person once was.

'How can you be certain they didn't go to the playground?' I tried again.

'Because they don't do that. Not playgrounds.'
'Is there any particular reason why not?'

There felt like there should be a reason. I thought about when Mother was working at court and my siblings and I would go over to the very park at Shaw's Bridge where River's coat had been found. We loved it there. Then Charlotte's five loved it too, but she would never let them go alone, as we had done; besides, there was no disabled swing for Timothy. Instead, his sisters would take a break from playing themselves on the seesaw and spin his chair about until he laughed, until his little body went rigid, his breathing quenched.

'Does River not like parks?'

'I suppose he does,' Zara muttered.

'Can you just speak up for the tape recorder?' Linskey directed.

Zara didn't appreciate the change in Linskey's tone. She was no longer Zara's shoulder to cry on; she'd become systemic and practical. I could see Zara drawing herself in, pushing her back against the chair, slumped over.

'I suppose he does,' Zara repeated in a tight, loud voice.

Linskey, fearing she'd lost her, changed tack. 'River spent Sunday at his dad's home, is that right?'

'Yes.' Zara sighed.

'Shane Reede is River's father. Is that correct?'

'That's right ...' Zara's eyes flitted to me; she was primed to give me the 'so what' response.

'We have an address for Shane. Could you confirm it for us please?' I asked.

Zara confirmed it. There were officers already headed there with Reede's details.

'So, how long does River see his father for?'

'As long as he wants,' Zara answered.

'As long as who wants? Could you just clarify?'

'As long as Shane wants.'

'And how often and how long would that be?' Linskey was poised with her pen again, ready for Zara's answer.

'At the moment Shane sees River one weekend in a month. Has done for the last four months.' Her words came fresh and fast now, in a tone like they had almost been learned by rote and she had no interest in going into detail. She was bored and would rather be anywhere else, do anything else, than talk about this.

Her cardigan was gathered around her belly and it fell

open. There was a dark patch on her blouse around her breast. Why would she keep a pregnancy from us? I supposed there could have been a stack of reasons.

'Shane stopped seeing Riv when he was living over the border,' she added.

'Where?' I asked. 'Where over the border?'

'County … Monaghan?'

'You don't know where he was living?'

'We split on bad terms. Shane was off with someone else. I let him get on with it. Things ended with them, then he came up here to be near River. So, I thought …'

'And yet a weekend in the month is all he sees him after coming all this way to be near his son?'

'It's all he's asked to see him,' Zara said abruptly. 'Well, he hasn't asked to see River at all. He came to the door one night four months ago and said "I'm back".'

'Out of the blue?'

'Yeah!' Zara frowned, clearly pissed off at having to back up her claims.

'We just need to be sure,' said Linskey.

'I know, I know. It's just there are far more important things … like where is my child? Have you spoken to the officers waiting at the house?'

'They'll get in touch as soon as they hear anything.'

I don't know what possessed me: I reached over the table and squeezed Zara's hand. She pulled her hand away and onto her lap, her cardigan falling open further. Linskey sat up, flicked through her notes.

'Zara, are you pregnant?' she asked.

'No, I already told you in the house.'

'You haven't just had a baby, have you?'

Zara glared at us, eyes watering, nostrils flared, stifling a yawn. She set me off with one of my own. 'No! Of course not,' she said.

'It's okay. Okay,' Linskey paused. 'Zara, can we get back to Shane? Is there a custody agreement in place?'

'No. Well ... Shane left, he came back. I was phasing them in with each other. River couldn't remember Shane initially, so it was an hour here or there, then a day, then an overnight. So this is where we've got to. In time, yes, if he wants more time, if either of them want more time, I'll help them do that.' Her elbows hit the table. She steepled her hands and let her face fall against them. 'I'm sorry, I'm so tired. I think I've got a virus of some sort. Or maybe it's everything else. Stress.'

'We'll take a break here,' said Linskey. She glanced at the clock, wrapped the interview up. 'You're doing brilliantly,' she told Zara, beaming at her.

Zara gave a wary smile in return. 'When will we hear something?' she asked as if there was a schedule.

'Most kids come back within forty-eight hours, nearly all within seventy-two,' I told her.

'And what if he doesn't?'

I said we'd cross that bridge if we came to it.

Chapter 7

'Shane Reede,' Raymond was saying, 'works in a mechanics garage in Orangefield – RAD Car Parts off Ladas Drive.'

I slipped out of the interview suite and handed over the details to Sarge Simon. When I returned Raymond confirmed that Shane brought River home at dinnertime and his times corresponded with Zara's.

'We ate dinner – pizza from Dominos for us lads, Chinese for Zara. But it didn't agree with her – too spicy. River was overtired. He hardly ate anything. He was bouncing off the walls.'

'How do you mean, *bouncing*?' I asked.

'E numbers, most likely. Zara doesn't like him having orange juice or sweets, and when he goes to Shane's we've no idea what he's eating. It's hard for Zara because she's quare and regimented with him.'

'Regimented?'

'No, not regimented, just in a routine.' Raymond interlocked his fingers; his breath fell into a wheeze. There was a crackle of silence.

Linskey tilted her chair forward, wrapped her ankles around the chair legs. 'Raymond, is there anything you think we should know?' she asked. 'We just want to see little River safe. The child's welfare is always paramount to us, as I'm sure it is to you.'

'Yes. Definitely,' he said.

His stubby, underdeveloped-looking hands scratched his belly in small urgent movements.

Rolling over me was this feeling. I felt sorry for Zara now; that's what it was. Not just sorry for what she was going through, but sorry for how she had ended up living with Raymond. I could picture Zara when she was younger. She would have been brimming with potential. To have ended up where she was, with a man like Raymond ... I felt certain she must have been lacking in self-worth.

'He's a hyperactive child. River can be hard work,' Raymond said.

'What are you saying about River, Raymond?' Linskey pushed.

'He was hard to handle, until Zara changed his grub, you see. But still, he doesn't sleep.'

'How so?' I asked.

Sometimes it sounded daft to me, asking these questions, but they were necessary when we had someone like Raymond in for questioning – or 'assisting the PSNI with enquiries', as we put it at that stage. He was on the verge of telling us something useful and all he needed was a nudge here and there. Zara was the opposite – a hard nut to crack – and I wasn't sure that we did. How much could we lean on her? How far could we push her without sounding like we were accusing her of something? And what was there to accuse her of at that point? There was no crime scene, no corpse; it was purely a missing person's case. Still, the questions had to open themselves out for the answers to pass through.

'River would go to sleep at eight o'clock,' said Raymond, 'then waken at one a.m. and stay awake until four.'

Raymond told us that River had been hard to shift in the morning, especially on days when he had preschool, which he started only a month earlier – Strandtown Preschool, a church nursery on the Belmont Road. I took the details in the hope that we wouldn't have to go there, that River would show up before the next school day, that he'd appear back in his own bed in his blue and green pyjamas.

Zara had said at the end of her interview that she just wanted to wake up the next morning and realise it had all been a dream. Everyone wanted that. Except Raymond, it seemed. He didn't seem concerned that a four-year-old child was out in the big world – in the streets of East Belfast, or further away – without an adult to accompany him. Or maybe there was an adult. That was the subtext of everyone's thoughts, the thing the neighbours dismissed but the fear in their eyes seemed to say.

Raymond implied a few times that River could handle himself, and maybe he could in nursery, at home or wherever, but there's a difference between a boisterous child who is confident and savvy in familiar surroundings and one who is streetwise. I couldn't even imagine Gus, my fourteen-year-old nephew, being talked about in terms like these. I had to make Raymond see sense, to flit from the reassuring copper I was with Zara and remind him that the boy was at risk. Apart from anything, they lived beside a busy road. Wasn't that enough?

'Is there anyone you could imagine would have taken River?' I asked.

'Nah,' Raymond said. 'They'd bring him back as soon as they realised what he was like.' He laughed; his joke struck me as ignorant, not malicious.

'What is River like?' I asked.

'Well, he'd be hyper,' Raymond said.

'Is he hyper the way all four-year-old boys are?' asked Linskey.

'Couldn't tell you. He's the only one I know.'

'It must be hard, the lack of sleep.'

'The sleep terrorist, I call him. It's torture, absolute

torture.' Raymond scratched his head.

'Why do you think he doesn't sleep?'

'That's the million-dollar question there!' he said. 'I'm sure he could have a wee bit of a sleeping pill – you know, the way people give their dogs a painkiller. They can't have the whole thing, but if you work out the weight of an adult and the weight of the animal, then you can give them a quarter, say, of an aspirin. It's not recommended but everyone does it. There's no harm.'

Linskey was writing furiously.

'Years ago, there was this old woman lived beside us,' Raymond went on. 'I grew up on a farm near Limavady, see. This farm was overrun with cats. There was this one cat who, well, that old woman used to go around saying this cat was a raper – she meant rapist. This cat, a big black one, well, he kept getting all the cats in the area pregnant. It's not like it's a consensual thing. Have you ever seen cats in mating season? Anyway ... the girl cats would be hissing, and when they were in season they would disappear. They'd eventually come back and you knew where they'd been and what they'd been up to. And the cats we had, two ginger females, which is very rare – ask anyone who knows anything about cats and they'll tell you – they'd disappear and then come back. So, did they enjoy it or not? I was always confused about that. It's in their make-up to mate, but were they being raped? I don't know. The animal kingdom is a cruel place.'

Raymond stopped for breath, wheezing in that slow way we'd come to know over the course of the day.

'But this old woman,' he added, 'she was way past what my mother would have called *the change*, and she was a spinster – never had a man as far as anybody knew. But she got the doctor to give her the pill because she was sick of all these kittens. She never drowned them nor nothing, never gave any away. People didn't neuter their animals then. My father told her that the vet was just away and that one of our cats was expecting again. And she told him that when the cats were coming up to being in season, she cut the contraceptive pill into tiny pieces and put it into the females' food. So it wasn't foolproof, but the cats didn't fall pregnant as often. It was a good idea when you think about it. I've never forgotten it.' Raymond reached for his plastic cup of water and took a sip.

I had that feeling I had when I looked at Donald Guy … or when I thought of Jason. Linskey looked up from her notepad, a smile mixed in a frown.

'And you've asked his doctor for something to help River sleep?' she asked trying to unzip the loose covers of Raymond's meaning.

'Oh, aye,' said Raymond. 'The doctor won't give River anything for it. She can't, you see.'

'Why not?'

'It's the meds he's on already.'

'What medication is River taking?'

'It's for his fits – just wee ones where he stares into space. You call them petit mal seizures. It's like epilepsy but not as bad. The wain'll be eating his breakfast and you'll see him stop. He comes out of it quickly. People think he's just daydreaming. But the meds control it. The worry is that he'll have a big seizure, but he never has. A tonic-clonic. They're the boys, alright. I knew nothing about any of this until recently and now I'm an expert!'

Linskey and I looked at each other briefly in a way I liked to think others couldn't see, but Raymond suddenly looked concerned.

'What is it?' he asked.

*

We brought Zara back in on her own to ask her about the epilepsy.

'That's right,' she said, folding her arms.

'And River needs medication for this condition, is that right?' Linskey asked.

'River was due his half spoonful of Epilim at a quarter to eight, just before bed.'

'This is important. Why didn't you mention it earlier?' I asked.

'I hoped he'd be home long ago.'

'But if we'd known this …'

'Does that mean you aren't already doing everything you could be doing?' Zara asked. 'Are you suddenly interested now you know about the seizures?'

I tapped my pen on the desk.

'Listen,' said Zara, 'you know those baby-on-board stickers people put on their car windows?'

'Yes.'

'I used to have one. It was one of the first things Shane bought when we found out we were having River – him being into cars. Shane, I mean. River couldn't care less. Trains … now, yes. Well, River arrived. Shane collected me from the hospital in this Jaguar. He'd borrowed it from someone for the day just so I could write a flash answer in the baby book under *First car I drove in*. "Someday we'll have our own," Shane would say.' Zara bit her lip and inspected her nails. 'We never got a Jaguar. I had a little runaround, like a shoebox. I wasn't bothered, but I took the baby-on-board sticker and put it in the back window. I was proud. Stuff the car – it was what was inside that counted, you know. My wee man.' Now she became tearful. 'I was driving along the Bangor to Newtownards carriageway one morning. River was nine months at the time, all strung up in his car seat. These two young guys in sporty cars started chasing each other along the carriageway. I ended up between them somehow. They didn't overtake and just go do their own thing. The one behind me – well, he wasn't for stopping, so I just … I had no choice, I had to go off the road. It happened in a split second. I just hit this fence – went straight through it. Ended up in some field upside down. I don't know how I moved, because I was sore after for ages.' She sighed. 'Maybe adrenalin took over. But first thing I did was looked around and there was River, still in his car seat, upside down. He'd slept through everything. For a second I thought he was … you know. I got out. This man who had stopped by the side of the road came and helped me get him out and he drove us to hospital. I was a bit battered but there wasn't a scratch on that boy. With something like epilepsy you blame everything. Was it that crash? Was River injured in his head and it just wasn't visible?'

Linskey gave her a little knowing nod.

'Anyway, the car was a write-off. Shane brought us home in another new motor. He hardly visited River in hospital. He was more concerned with the wheels, as usual. He'd went and got a baby-on-board sticker for the back. You know, the first thing I did was pull that sticker off that window and rip it up.'

'Why, Zara?'

'Does anybody look at those things? Those boy racers didn't look and go "oh no, better be careful here." They didn't give a shit. People either care or they don't. Before that man stopped to help, others drove on past. People will either help you or they won't. I never thought to play the epilepsy card. It didn't even occur to me,' Zara said.

Chapter 8

Did Zara live on another planet? Why did she think we wouldn't be interested? That people weren't doing all they could? That the neighbours wouldn't be out all night searching for her child?

I offered to work all night too, but the Chief told Linskey and I to go home, that we would need to be fresh for the following day, because if River wasn't found within the first twenty-four hours, then something was seriously wrong and we would need to step up the search.

Before I left the station, Sarge Simon informed us that he had run Shane's car details and been out to his house at Brandon Terrace, and found nothing, although he did comment on the décor. Having been a painter/decorator in a past life, Simon never quite got away from flock wallpaper and feature walls; he would sit in a victim's home and tell them that whoever did their edging had done a good job. He and Constable Higgins would head to RAD Car Parts the next morning and let us know as soon as they had brought Shane in for questioning.

But Raymond was a funny one to pinpoint. Granted, the boy was not his, but he had shared a roof – shared Zara – with him for the past year and a half, was something of a father figure to him. And Zara, it seemed to me, had acted as mother to them both.

Raymond was forty-five, though he looked older. Even Linskey commented on his looks after we let him go home, how he was so clunky compared to Zara's petiteness, gross to her prettiness. An oil and water mix.

'I don't believe it. Do you?' Linskey asked me before we

went off shift.

'Which part?' For me the list was growing.

'I don't see the two of them as a couple.'

'He said she's his carer.'

'Doesn't sit with me.' Linskey folded her notes, ready to hand over to Inspector Seymour who was on nights. She looked in at the parakeet and tapped the cage; it was chirruping sweetly. 'You should get yourself a pet, Harry,' she said.

'The management company doesn't allow us to have them. Besides, you're my pet.'

She laughed as she creased the page on which she had written out a schedule of feeding instructions for the bird and set it in front of the cage.

*

I arrived home at one a.m. The heat had knocked itself off long before and the apartment was cold again. I liked to be shrewd, taking advantage of the heat that rose from the floors below. I only heated the place if Greg was calling.

I texted him to see if he had finished work, knowing I wouldn't sleep anyway and he may as well be here with me. He didn't respond, so I expelled any nervous energy by pacing, shoeless. I reminded myself of Zara, so I sat on the sofa with a glass of Merlot, waiting for Greg to text back. But he didn't. I knew he would tell me he was still at work. I suspected it was also the perfect defence for being late home too. Rarely does anyone question you when you say you have to work.

But eventually sleep came to me. I had that dream again about Christmas at Lough Erne and Jamesy Lunney, who we found dead in the lough. When I was younger the dream was a recurrent thing that eventually petered out. But in the last four years, it had come back again all too vividly, especially while working certain cases.

The chalet at the lough had always been cold. It lay neglected during term-time and was always full of cool air no matter what time of year it was. The walls seemed to pull themselves together, release loose plaster as if the bricks rubbed together for warmth. The air tasted like a candle put out on your tongue. In the dream it was always the same: the candlewick taste faded away, the walls crumbled completely, and I would be by the water, warding off a cold-edged wind pushing up the lough. I never seemed to have the presence of mind to lift a coat. In the dream I never learned to remember. Where were the coats kept anyway? And which one was mine?

The coats I wore weren't memorable – not enough to have permeated my subconscious. Not like River's coat, that soft, corrugated blob of green. All night, that was the scene my mind kept bringing me to, interspersed with all the unrelated mumbo jumbo of my emotional to-do list: try to be a friend to Linskey; try to be a better sister and daughter; decide what the fuck to do about Greg.

I used to always dream about Jamesy Lunney. But I'd dream about different people on different days. I watched Brooks tussling with another version of himself in the lough, as if he'd been duplicated the way Charlotte and I were, and I would wake asking myself which half of Brooks was left, if any of him was. I would wake up wondering if he was even still alive. And how would I know if he wasn't?

Some nights Jamesy Lunney was not dead. Some nights it was little Timothy, who could have passed for a fish in Brooks's arms. I would be haunted by that in a way I hadn't been when I was eight years old and my brother had pulled that dead man from the water and threw him down at my feet.

That day had been too bright, too chilled for us to be afraid; we were too together for Jamesy to haunt us then. It wasn't until Brooks kicked a hole in the door of his own bedroom in the middle of the night that I felt scared. That's when I saw my brother inside the storm for the first time.

Inside the chalet I sat in the soft centre of the matt-rimmed sheepskin looking around at the rest of the family as they talked and waited for the RUC to arrive. And that's the part, right there, where I snuck out, when it becomes all dream instead of memory. In reality, I stayed put, trying to summon up the courage to go and look. It was the lead up to the dream being over, the big reveal of the face that had remained hidden since that December day in the late 1980s.

What usually happened was that I would go down to the scene of the find, hands and shoulders shaking like I was carrying two overfilled bags. The dream went like stepping stones: I was on this one, then I was on that one, then I knew I was on the final stone where there was nowhere else to go but wake up.

I woke on the sofa, disorientated and with a crick in my neck, Merlot zingy on my teeth, sour on my tongue. Moonlight made knives on the walls through the open blinds. Of course I had a bed. I had bought a new one when I moved in; I couldn't bear to bring the bed from the old house.

It was four a.m. I turned the volume up on the telly and sat with my arms circled around my knees. Stayed like that for a while. But I must have drifted off because it was after eight when I woke again. I could feel the cold unclenching like two fists in my stomach. And when I was no longer submerged in sleepiness I thought about River.

Then I had a call from the station. Ronnie Dorrian, Shane Reede's boss at RAD Car Parts, was claiming that Shane had not weighed into work the day before.

Chapter 9

An end terrace house in Grays Park Gardens in the Belvoir Estate was where we would find the Hammitts that Tuesday morning. Under the flat run-off porchway stood a woman who looked like she was expecting visitors. Jan Hammitt, waiting at her bottle-green door, wore a pink top with a black collar, little swallows on the print. She was smiling like Linskey and I were the visitors she had been expecting.

I opened the short cast-iron gate and saw the chicken-wire partition at the end of the drive that was no doubt for the dog. Behind it came the cooing of pigeons.

Jan shook my hand. She had exceedingly long fingernails, as if to elongate her fingers the way high-heeled shoes work on short legs. The tips of her nails were as white as if they'd been dipped in melted candle wax.

Inside the house she dived straight in. 'That wee coat,' she said, 'Sandy told me about it. Is it the boy's? Is that right?'

'The coat is River's,' Linskey said as she sat on the fabric sofa: it was brown on the seats, bottle green at the back. The house smelled of cooked breakfast and hearth fires.

After a moment the back door opened. We could hear footsteps, and claws clopping on kitchen tiles.

'The police ladies are here, Sandy,' Jan shouted.

'Yes, so I see,' Sandy called back. His voice was like gravel. He came into the lounge. 'Hello, again. How are you doing?' He touched Linskey on the shoulder. I saw her flinch.

Sandy removed his chunky scarf, his weathered leather coat, fixed them over his armchair and sat down. His hair, in the muted light of the lounge, was not as bright as it had looked outdoors. You could tell he dyed it. His face was brown, a tan that only made his skin appear more wrinkled than it was.

'Dusky's just having a drink, then she'll be in to greet you,' Sandy said.

The Weimaraner remembered us. She entered the room and nuzzled her head under the crook of my knee, her mouth dripping water onto my trousers; then she did the same to Linskey. The smell of eggs and bacon was replaced by that of wet dog.

'Are you walking her close to home because she's off season now?' Linskey asked.

'No,' Jan told her. 'It's put Sandy off going to Shaw's Bridge after what he found. Hasn't it, Sandy?'

Sandy ignored the question, not wanting to look weak. He stared at the dog, then sat back, his spine to the back of his chair, his watery blue eyes looking bloodless against the reds and browns of his hair and skin.

'There's a new photo of the boy, I see,' he said.

'That's right, Mr Hammitt.' I nodded. 'But we're here because of the coat you found, and to see if there's anything else you remember seeing yesterday.'

'Have you traced that woman yet, the one out walking her dogs?' asked Jan, twiddling a silver locket on her necklace, pressing it against the underside of her chin.

'We haven't heard from the woman yet, no. There's a public appeal for any witnesses to get in touch.'

'You really need her before you can move along,' Sandy said.

Jan studied a bunch of flowers on the mantel. A petal drooped; she pulled it off and threw it into the fire. A feather of smoke escaped. The cabinet she was standing beside held DVDs – crime movies mostly.

'I'd love to have been more help but that's all I have to say,' Sandy told us. 'There was mention of the coat on the radio. I got out of the car, walked with Dusky along the water towards the park, then down to the boat house and back.'

'Is this the walk you always do?' Linskey interjected.

'At certain times. But not usually. Usually I just walk her around the estate here. I got to the gate of the playground and saw the fluttering of something bright green out of the corner of my eye. I couldn't believe it when it was a coat. I took out my phone straight away and called it in. Then I waited until you got there to make sure no one touched it. Think I already said all that yesterday, though.'

'You must think me terrible,' said Jan. 'Would either of you ladies like a cup of tea or something cold? How about a wee bacon soda for breakfast?'

We refused but thanked her. She sat on the arm of Sandy's chair and listened, self-conscious and distracting, picking imaginary fluff off her skirt and blouse.

'When was the last time you were at Shaw's Bridge, Mr Hammitt?' Linskey asked. 'Before yesterday, I mean. Were you there on Sunday?'

'No, no,' he said. 'She just came into heat yesterday morning. It must have been months ago.'

'You saw that woman with her two dogs.'

He nodded.

'Would you remember what she looked like if you saw her again?'

'Umm. I can't ... she was leaving.'

'Her car – can you remember what it was?'

'A hatchback, maybe a Volvo. She was able to open the back up and the dogs jumped in.'

'What breed were they?'

'Well ... I wasn't taking it in but something tells me that they were spaniels. I did look, with Dusky being on heat. They seemed female, just in the way they went by us, or maybe neutered males. One was smaller than the other. Maybe a Springer Spaniel and a Cavalier. Two small dogs, anyway.'

'Hopefully the woman will get in touch,' I said.

'Yes.' He stroked his chin and with a deep breath sucked in the gloom. 'It will come out in the long grass.'

'Poor little boy,' said Jan. 'Beautiful child. What his parents must be going through.'

'Mr Hammitt,' Linskey started, 'where were you between the hours of midnight on Sunday and nine a.m. yesterday?'

'At home.'

'He was here,' said Jan. 'Our daughter Meggi stayed on Sunday night. She had a few days off work so she stayed over. Yesterday we all had coffee together and a fry-up. Then Sandy took Dusky for her walk.'

'Can you vouch for Sandy? Can your daughter?'

'Yes. She was house-sitting for us last week, minding Dusky. We were in Marbella, you see. Meggi's been going through a divorce, so we thought it would kill two birds. Give her space. But you can call her if you want. She's back to work today, but you can get her.'

Mrs Hammitt wrote her daughter's name and phone number on a piece of paper and I put it into the depths of my pocket.

'I suppose there'll be loads that people don't tell,' said Sandy. 'Like when that boy went missing ten years ago, that little Brody Pottinger. They never let on but his mother – that Verda headcase – already had a conviction for child abuse. None of that came out in the papers though.'

'That boy showed up safe, Mr Hammitt,' Linskey said.

'He did indeed,' said Sandy. 'But I always found it strange that they kept that private. I knew there was something dubious the minute I saw Verda give that press conference. Then the next thing, he shows up. Was hiding in the bloody roofspace under his own steam they said. She bloody put him up to it!'

Linskey narrowed her eyes at him. I looked out the back window at the pigeon carrier.

'What's the collective noun for pigeons?' I asked Sandy.

'A bloody nuisance,' said Jan.

'A flock? A loft?' Sandy shrugged. 'It's only a hobby.'

'You aren't missing a parakeet?' asked Linskey.

'I don't have parakeets.'

'No? That's fine.'

'If you think of anything else, Mr Hammitt, please give us a call,' I said.

We all moved to the front door.

'I'll call.' Sandy looked at Linskey.

Jan stood there shivering while her husband came all the way outside and stood at the gate, reminding me of how we found him at Shaw's Bridge. The couple stayed in position until we left.

'Jesus, that was odd,' Linskey said on our way out of the estate.

'Which part?' I asked.

'I worked on the Pottinger case and no one knew about Verda's conviction. Chief Dunne said it would colour the case. He was right too. There was no crime in the end. Just a naughty boy, hiding out.'

'It's a wonder Sandy remembers it,' I said. 'Maybe because of the name – Pottinger, like the Pottinger's Entry.'

'Certain cases stick in people's minds,' said Linskey. 'You

know, I still get people mention Brody to me. But we did a good job to keep Verda Dolan's problems out of it. I always had a soft spot for Brody – with all them brothers and sisters sure he hardly got a look-in. Could you blame Verda for giving them the odd smack or two?'

'Hmm,' I said. 'I remember her now. She should have spent ten minutes getting an IUD and less time on her back.'

'Jesus, Harry!'

'How many kids did she have?'

'Six.'

'How many men?'

'Fair play to her.'

'Where did she find them? Specsavers?'

'That's awful,' said Linskey.

Verda Dolan – her face came back to me all right. Hammitt had a point. She *had* looked like she was acting at that press conference. She was as false and insecure a person as I'd ever seen, and believe me, I knew what to look for. I sometimes wished I'd been assigned that case instead of Linskey. I remembered that long face of Verda's, her pea-green eyes and her furry voice. She'd worn the same maroon jumper day in, day out, carelessly rolled up at the elbows. Her family tree was more like a map of the London Underground.

'Fancies himself as a bit of a detective – Sandy Hammitt,' I said.

'Did you see the books?' asked Linskey. 'The crime books?'

'No. Did you see the DVDs? All crime too,' I said. 'Was he in the constabulary? Is that how he knew about Verda's conviction? Surely he would have said.'

As we pulled into Shane's street Linskey took a card from her pocket, handed it to me.

Alexander Hammitt, Senior Engineer. Shorts Bombardier.

'He gave me this at the park yesterday,' said Linskey. 'They let him go a few years back – Sandy and ninety-nine others. Now his job is sunning himself in Marbella, by all accounts.'

'Jammy git,' I said.

Brandon Terrace was a short street, one side of it terraces, the other side the backs of apartment blocks, and bookended by two busier streets. Shane's house was dilapidated, a fact the landlord had tried to conceal with white paint that had turned pinkish and was flaking off the pebble-dash finish like dried camomile lotion on an angry dose of the pox. There was a wall around the yard, the top bricks missing alternately as if purposefully arranged like that.

I knocked on Shane's door, looked in his windows at the browning, wrecked louvres. We walked down the grassy entry behind his house, through his yard and peeked in the back window. Planes were returning to City Airport, humming overhead. His house was deserted, and his car nowhere to be seen.

I contacted the station, asking someone to get in touch with the DVLA and check what car Shane was driving at the moment and run the plates. The Chief informed us of a new development: a dead dog had been found in the water at Shaw's Bridge.

'A fresh death,' he said. 'With weights tied around its paws.'

'A spaniel?' I asked him.

'No. Think the opposite of spaniel and you're in the right ballpark.'

'What in the world does that mean?' Linskey asked me as we drove to River's preschool.

'Not cute and cuddly?' I guessed.

'Glad someone speaks his language! I suppose we'll have to get onto Sandy again and ask him if he remembers seeing a stray going about.'

'Any excuse to get talking to your number one fan,' I teased her.

Chapter 10

Strandtown Preschool was in an old church on the Belmont Road with an ornamental bell-tower and a car park housed behind verdigris spiked railings. Three huge trees dripped leaves onto the road.

The playgroup leader was Miss Olivia Sands. When Linskey called her that morning, Miss Sands had asked that we wait until noon before coming over. The children would have left by then; she didn't want them getting more worried about River than they already were.

When we arrived Olivia was standing huddled by the palm tree at the door, a modern double-glazed version of the traditional windows, right down to the arched shape and the leaded panes. With her long, straight, black hair swishing against her back, Olivia took us through the main hall with its freshly painted magnolia walls and scuffed wooden floorboards where two childcare assistants were finishing up for the day, one stacking chairs, the other tossing toys into plastic boxes, the sounds echoing in the high-ceilinged room.

In the kitchen, we would have refused Olivia's teas and coffees had we been offered but we weren't. We sat facing her, but Olivia Sands didn't sit down. She bounced about, boiled the kettle, saying she was gasping, that she needed caffeine, after the morning she'd had and all the questions she'd had to answer.

'I'm happy to help you, of course,' she said, 'but what do you tell kids? Plus I don't think it's my place.'

She bent down to a low shelf in the cupboard, chimed the cups until she found one she was pleased with. She leaned back against the counter, her hands by her hips, flexing her fingers. She stood still for a second to answer a question I asked: 'Do you have any concerns about River?'

'Plenty,' Olivia announced, then started to busy herself with milk and sugar and boiling water. She threw a teaspoon into the sink and finally sat down. At last we were able to get her full attention.

'I never slept all night,' she said, closing her eyes like she was miming part of a children's story. She had thick eyeliner on her top lids, licked up towards her brows.

'I don't think many people slept last night,' Linskey replied.

'Like I said on the phone,' Olivia resumed, 'River's a lovely wee boy and I just hope he gets home soon. I'm not religious' – she lowered her voice – 'I shouldn't say this here, really, but I prayed last night, really prayed that I would … I don't know, be a better person, nicer to people I can't stand – not that I'm *not* nice – if he would just come home safe. I should shut up. It just sounds daft now.' She took a sip from her cup of thick rusty-looking coffee.

'So what *are* your concerns about River? What stands out?'

'It's his mum,' she said. 'He's only been here a few weeks, but sometimes I think it would be easier if she'd just take him out of the nursery and go somewhere else.'

I sat forward and squinted at her.

'It's not River,' Olivia continued. 'Not his fault. It's his mum, as I say. She makes things difficult. River's a lovely child.'

'In what way is River's mother difficult?' I asked.

'She's never happy with his care provision. I've worked in lots of different nurseries and I know what I'm doing, but she questions everything.'

Olivia looked like a child herself. I understood Zara's

logic instantly.

'Is this your first management job, Miss Sands?' I asked her.

'Yes, but I know what I'm doing. Most parents love it that I'm young and have new ideas and the kids, they say, can relate to me. That's not Mrs Reede's issue.'

'What do you think her issue is?' asked Linskey.

'It's a personality clash. It's that she knows she can say anything and I have to be professional – that's all it is.' Olivia pulled her hair into two tails over her shoulders, then carried out a concise scan for split ends.

'Are you aware of any health problems River might have?' Linskey asked.

'Oh, his ADHD – is that what you mean?'

'ADHD?' I repeated. 'No. It was more along the lines of epilepsy my colleague was asking about.'

'Epilepsy? I haven't heard anything about epilepsy. Not at all.'

'What is this you were saying about ADHD?'

Olivia looked as though she had been lured back to some memory or other. She took another sip of coffee. 'River has trouble standing still,' she said.

'Does he have a diagnosis?' I asked.

'I don't know how much you know about ADHD.' Olivia examined our blank faces. 'It's almost impossible to diagnose before the age of four.'

'But River *is* four.'

'Yes, he is – a July birthday. One of the oldest here, so he should be more competent at certain things. River has the signs of it, from my experience. He's a good boy, just has a short attention span.'

'Is that all ADHD is? So, he's like any other four-year-old

boy?'

Olivia laughed. 'I had all this with Mrs Reede. She's in denial about him.'

'What makes you say that?'

'Well, I said to her that I recommended testing and she went ape. Absolutely crazy. It wasn't just me – it was the other staff in the nursery too. We've been doing this for years. River fidgets. He has no patience. You can't read him a story, he has no interest – I mean none at all. He's very talkative and a real climber.'

Linskey looked at me. 'Does he climb here?' she asked Olivia.

'Yes, he does,' she replied, smiling a slow sad smile, fluffing her hair at the roots. 'Bless him, I feel bad talking about him like this. He's a little devil with the face of an angel. Really, he can't help it. We have another boy with ADHD here and one with an ASD – autism, like. We had behaviour specialists out for them and both specialists picked up on River. It's just that the earlier the intervention, the better the help. It's for him. I'm not trying to make life easier for me, but for his mum – for Zara. She thought I was trying to point the finger at her. She was livid. Obviously I couldn't say he had already been observed. He has little spells when he stares at the wall and it's like he can't see you. He doesn't respond to his name.'

'Those spells are his epilepsy, apparently,' said Linskey.

'I said to Zara that he seemed absent and she told me he was a daydreamer.'

'River is receiving medication for his epilepsy,' I said. 'The doctor has already diagnosed him.'

'I should've been made aware of that.'

'Is it possible that you wouldn't have accepted River to

the nursery if Zara had told you about the epilepsy?' asked Linskey.

'We haven't had a child with epilepsy yet, but … maybe we could have had training. I'm not sure.' Olivia frowned.

Zara knew fine rightly, I thought. She wanted River in mainstream education, even if it meant sending him to school without the right provisions and awareness. I had a feeling that the same thought was dawning on us all.

'The climbing frame outside,' Linskey said, pointing out of the window. 'I'm sure River must love that.'

'He did,' said Olivia. 'Zara doesn't want him on it any more. I may as well tell you this, in case she does first and it looks as though I'm hiding something. We were playing capture the flag with little pirate flags on the frame outside when River climbed up and tried to take it down. I believe in letting children explore, letting them climb. They need to burn themselves out. It's gone now, but there used to be a flag with a little skull and crossbones on it. We took it down after he fell and broke his front teeth.' Olivia sucked in her lips as if she was expecting judgement.

'How did Zara take that?'

'Obviously she wasn't happy. She talked about changing nurseries, so if you're telling her that you came here, I'm sure she'll mention that we had words. *She* had words. She said she was going to home-school him if she couldn't find somewhere that wasn't going to *victimise* him.' Olivia's chin tremored with emotion.

'What about River's dad? Shane Reede?' Linskey asked.

'Zara does all the paperwork – the lifting and laying. Sometimes the big man's in the car waiting.'

'Have you noticed if he walks with a limp?' I asked.

Olivia was looking at a point just past me. I turned to see

what it was. There was a quote from the Bible inscribed on a framed mirror; she was trying to check herself out in the margin.

'I never noticed that,' she said. 'He's older than Zara. He's a bit ... of a funny one.'

'How so?'

'I don't know. No reason, really. I thought he was the grandad.'

'That's Raymond,' I said. 'Is there another man that comes – maybe on a Friday, Miss Sands? River's biological father?'

'I thought he *was* the dad,' she said. 'He was with River and Zara at the open day.'

I got a call then through my earpiece to say that Zara's hospital records had been checked.

'I have to nip out for a minute,' I said.

I got into the car and spoke to Sarge Simon on the radio.

'The doctors have no record that Zara Reede has had any pregnancy other than when she was pregnant with River,' he said.

'Thanks for that,' I said, feeling somehow like I was betraying Zara by checking up on her. People knew that their medical records could be used against them. It often stopped them seeking help when they most needed it.

I looked at the climbing frame; it wasn't tall at all. There was a flag holder at the top; the children could easily have been reached by an adult. Suddenly the game didn't seem like the bad idea it had when Olivia told us about it.

Linskey came to join me in the car.

'It was all about her, wasn't it?' I said.

'Ah c'mon, she's Miss Honey from that kids' book *Matilda* – too sweet for her own good.'

'Bet Zara had a field day with her.'

A rap landed on the window. Olivia was peering in, winding her hand, miming at us to roll down the window.

'I started to tell you,' she said, crouching down, holding onto the slim spine of glass. 'It's the climbing frame. The park, I mean. I heard on the news that the police are checking the park at Shaw's Bridge, but he wouldn't have been there.'

'Why do you say that?'

'After River broke his teeth, Mrs Reede said: "Any wonder I don't take him to the playground. He hasn't been since he was two".' Linskey and I must have been looking at her without conviction, because she added, 'River took a little boy's glasses off him and snapped them in half. Mrs Reede said there were loads of people in the playground and all the parents turned on her, so she never took him anywhere for ages after that because people were so cruel. She said they were bullies.'

'Thanks for telling us,' Linskey said.

Olivia gave us a blazing smile.

'Do you use behaviour charts?' I felt compelled to ask before we left.

'We don't, but a lot of the parents do. I suggested it for home, but that was another thing that riled Mrs Reede.'

'Okay, that's great. Thanks,' I said.

Olivia stood up and headed back towards the church.

I thought about charts and meds, how Zara seemed to be like a sponge who took advice but never gave credit. She was stubborn and pig-headed, but she did what was best for her boy, at least that's how I felt right at that moment. But my mind, it changed with every word and in every breath.

*

Another photo was released to the public, the one Sandy Hammitt had been talking about. In this one River was smiling. He was at the seaside at Portrush, hunching down to look at a sandcastle. There were sandworms noodling beside his bare toes. He looked proud.

It sparked renewed interest, this photo, and the phone lines began to purr, one on top of the other.

Chapter 11

In the lab, River's green coat was suspended inside a glass cabinet like an exhibit at the Ulster Museum. Forensic scientist Kate Stile, a tall, young woman with a doughy face, explained her findings to Linskey and me.

'First let me tell you both about the DNA we found on the coat. Someone has coughed on the fabric and the DNA is unknown.'

Linskey walked around the cabinet to see the back of the coat where I met her coming from the other direction. Three dark fingermarks scarred the fabric.

'That fingermark.' Kate pointed at one on the far left.

'Whose is it?' I asked.

'It's small. A bloody smear. More than likely it will be a match for River himself,' she said. 'Boys cut their knees, hands, elbows all the time.'

'I know,' I said. 'Check everything, accept nothing.'

'And there are two more fingermarks here and here,' said Kate, pointing. 'Bigger ones, caused by adults this time. They also look like blood. The fingermarks have been run through the Ident1 database and come back as belonging to two separate individuals. One, in fact, matches a set of prints collected after a house break-in Donegal at the start of this year' – she looked at her notes – 'on 6 January 2016. I had a colleague look at the results to corroborate, and she confirmed what I thought. Based on the minutiae it's likely – same pattern of pores and whorls, double loops, same friction ridges.'

'And they were never caught, the person who committed the break-in?' asked Linskey.

'No, they weren't. A car was also stolen from the garage of the house, the keys taken from the hooks in the kitchen. The car was found burnt out three miles away. So whoever did that is one of our guys.'

'He's been keeping his nose reasonably clean, then, if he isn't on the system,' I said.

'Stealing a car doesn't come out of the blue. There'll have been a build-up of petty crimes,' said Linskey.

'Nothing serious enough to make its way into the system though,' I said.

'Or he just hasn't been caught yet,' said Kate.

'Then another unknown who's not in the system?' Linskey asked for clarification.

'Yes,' said Kate. She pointed at the third fingermark at the base of the coat. 'This one hasn't got a match.'

'Could any of it be old blood?' I asked her.

'No. I'd say more recent.'

'We have to eliminate everyone who'd help River with his coat,' said Linskey.

'We'll get the nursery teachers to give their prints too,' I said, 'though I think a certain person might be mortally offended.'

Linskey nodded. 'Miss Honey.'

'We have his parents' prints, don't we?' asked Kate.

'Yes, his mother's and stepfather's prints we do have,' I said. 'Though the boy's bio-dad hasn't weighed in yet. We'll get his prints as soon as and see how they compare.'

'And the dog that was found in the water?' asked Linskey. 'Have we had any word on it?'

'I believe it was unchipped when tested,' Kate said. 'Unlicensed too. Some people shouldn't own animals, don't you think?'

'Some people *are* animals,' I said.

Chapter 12

'It sounds like Zara has a victim complex,' I said to Linskey as we drove through mid-afternoon traffic on our way to Zara's doctor's surgery.

'That's the worst thing a parent can teach a child – that they're a victim,' said Linskey. 'All we need in life is resilience.'

I agreed. Thing was, the good, the bad – you started to think you deserved it. Resilience was the thing I'd learned from my parents. It's why they still went on despite everything.

'Ever see Jason?' Linskey asked.

People didn't mention him much – I certainly didn't – and her question caught me off guard.

'Yes,' I said, 'sometimes.'

But I hadn't, not in a while, not standing outside the apartment peering up at my window, like he had done relentlessly for so long. I wanted to brush over it, sweep it into a groove, but Linskey wouldn't allow it. It was how she got info out of people.

'Where do you see him, Harry?'

'At the gym.'

'Didn't you get custody of the gym?'

'I thought I did,' I said, staring out of the passenger window. 'Anyway, I'm running now.'

'Running away?'

'Am I? From what?'

'Processing things.'

'It'll be two years come January,' I said. 'I've had plenty of time to process. That'd be like me asking you if you see Geordie.'

'But Jason only filed for divorce recently, didn't he? That opens up the scar again.'

When I'd been considering joining the PSNI, almost the first thing everyone told me was how impossible it would be to hold down any semblance of a love life. They didn't say it outright. I'd been invited to a talk facilitated by women from different ranks on the service. They each gave their insight into life on the job. The further up the ladder the women had climbed, the more likely they were to be single. But not through choice. They tried to have it all, but something had given way – their marriages, in most cases.

Maybe it wasn't an accurate sample group, considering there must have been those who'd given up the job instead. Then I wouldn't have got to hear their story. But I was also acutely aware that each woman who stood in front of the room, these PSNI women I'd patterned myself on who gave out their name, age, rank and marital status, like Miss Northern Ireland hopefuls, couldn't have it all.

I remembered Linskey saying, 'I'm thirty-five. I'm a constable and I'm married.' She had gone on to tell us about the path, how she couldn't see herself doing anything but police work. It was Diane Linskey who convinced me I was doing the right thing. 'No two days are the same,' she had said.

It sounded like everything Father had told me. Exciting and challenging. When I whinged about being on the beat for two years – I wanted to get stuck straight in – he told me how the years were short because the days were long, and he was right.

Linskey lived for policing ever since her teenaged brother was killed and no one was convicted. She didn't mind saying this to a full room, but she never mentioned it again after. She had been the only speaker that day who wasn't separated or divorced. Now we both were. But it wasn't my career that broke my marriage.

'How was Jason?' Linskey asked. 'Do you talk? Does he act civil ... at the gym?'

'At the gym, he does. Yes,' I replied. 'Whatever civil is!' I only said it because I couldn't bear to get into it.

'Start using the gym in work,' Linskey told me. 'He'll think you're trying to bump into him.'

'Told you, I'm starting to run again. Out in the open.'

'I think you need to talk it out with him.'

'I don't want him back, Diane. I never want him back.'

'I know ...' she started.

'Then what's the point?' I snapped, angry at Linskey for pushing it.

I'd never understood the violence of some people's love. A kid born as the result of a one-night stand is a Love Child; a strangulation victim is usually caught up in what we call a Crime of Passion. I'd always hated those juxtapositions. Love, to me, was always about acceptance. But habits are made, and broken, in ninety days.

Three months into my relationship with Jason, I saw that he was a man with strong values. I saw that love doesn't always turn a blind eye or plod happily along. I saw that he loved with vehement conviction.

Jason was charming. Everybody loved him. He had red hair, pale milky skin, hazel eyes and a wide mouth that was always smiling. Jason was giddy in my presence for the first while. It was all-consuming. But for quite some time, since we'd started trying, the sex hadn't been considerate. Three years of trying for a child. Yes, I could have just said no. I did, in a way. He could smile all he wanted, he could charm people as much as he liked, but he couldn't have everything his own way. And I just wished Linskey would drop it.

At the doctor's surgery, we got out of the car and went inside, overtaking a man and woman on mobility scooters with rain covers. With a look on her face that angered me even more, the receptionist told us that Dr Lancaster had patients to see.

'What do you want to see her about anyway?' she asked, a line of patients looking us up and down for jumping the queue.

'Dr Lancaster told me on the phone that she could see us now for a few minutes,' said Linskey. 'I believe it won't eat into anyone's time but hers.'

I heard a tut in the queue that seemed to come from a brash blonde woman who wore her handbag across her chest, like milkmen once wore their money bags. She was wearing three quarter length trousers and a powder-blue 'Help for Heroes' hoodie. I gave her the look that made me the Bad Cop out of Linskey and me.

'Well,' said the receptionist, 'she didn't tell *me* about it.'

'Rita,' said Linskey, looking at her name badge. 'Would you give her a wee call and tell her we're here?'

I knew how this would go, that Rita would pout and do it. But I was angry.

'Rita,' I said, 'you look really familiar. Have I ever arrested you?'

'No, you have not,' she said, her skin reddening in a scarf around her neck. She lifted the phone and told us to go to Room 4, round to the right. Dr Lancaster was free. I bit my smile down as we walked off.

'Naughty, naughty,' Linskey whispered.

Dr Lancaster had the notes ready: the Epilim, the request for sleeping medication, which she had advised Zara to hold off on until they could get to the root of the problem.

'So River *has* got epilepsy?' I asked straight up; I'd no intention of keeping her back from her patients.

'River spent a few nights in the sleep clinic and sure enough, he displayed abnormal brain patterns on his EEG,' the doctor told us.

'What about ADHD?'

Dr Lancaster hesitated.

'Do you think it's a proper disorder?' I asked. I remembered Charlotte saying it should be called D.A.D. instead because kids with the disorder were usually lacking a father figure in their lives.

'Yes, it's real,' the doctor said, 'but there are a lot of misdiagnoses about. There's this fashion – has been for a while – to label and not try to find the root cause. I was happy to send River to get a proper examination from a team of multi-disciplinary professionals.'

'Did they detect ADHD?'

'He was identified as having the symptoms, yes. They're planning a review in a couple of months' time, and there's the possibility he may start some sort of behaviour-modifying medication.'

'And would that be okay to take with Epilim?' I asked.

I could feel Linskey looking at me. Other than methods of contraception, I used to know nothing about medication. Then Mother's condition surfaced. I learned even more when Charlotte's youngest son Timothy was born. I thought about Raymond calling himself an expert in epilepsy. I felt like an expert in disability – in long, lingering, in-your-face disability –

and I was going to advocate on River's behalf, for River and his hidden disorders.

'We were cutting his dosage – five millilitres to two millilitres,' said Dr Lancaster. 'Which could definitely explain the hyperactivity. A lot of change – an adjustment stage.'

'What if he stopped taking it altogether?'

'I wouldn't recommend it.'

'And Zara isn't pregnant, is that right?'

Dr Lancaster brought up her notes. 'Not that I know of. Zara hasn't been to us for a test, that's all I can say.'

Linskey gave her the smile that usually wrapped up our meetings.

'There was an incident,' said the doctor.

Linskey sat forward and her smile slipped away.

'Two years ago was the last time I saw Zara for herself. I prescribed Diazepam for her nerves. It was a temporary measure.'

'Can we ask why?'

'A neighbour brought River home once from pulling the flowers out of their flowerbed, Mrs Reede explained to me. The neighbour, a man I think it was, dragged River by the scruff of his neck the whole way home to tell her what had happened. She hadn't even realised River was out of the house. Mrs Reede was terribly upset. She was crying, said she got into an altercation with him.'

'So she got put on medication for this, for her nerves,' I said.

'There was a house move, a split from her partner and it was the pre-diagnosis time of her boy,' Dr Lancaster said impatiently.

'I think she's only lived in the house eighteen months,' I said.

'There were two moves,' the doctor corrected me. 'One after her separation and another when she moved in with Mr Marsh.'

'You know Raymond?'

'I'm his GP too.'

'And Zara is his partner?'

'She's his carer.'

'What does this mean?'

'What I will say is that Raymond has been a calming influence on River, to my mind. Although ... there is something.' Dr Lancaster read from her computer screen. 'While in Raymond's care – Zara was out at a meeting – Raymond took River to the hospital with burns on his torso and legs from pouring a scalding cup of tea over himself. The boy spent two days in hospital. A skin graft wasn't deemed necessary in the end.' The doctor looked at us before turning back to the screen, the cursor flashing to one side.

'Age stood him in good stead. The surgeon at the Royal decided that River's skin would repair itself fully. There's just the trace of a scar now on his outer thigh.' With one finger, she traced a small semi-circle on her own leg. 'River came to me for aftercare.'

I thought about the meeting Zara had been at. I'd gathered she was a homemaker, an at-home mum. Zara wasn't a 'meeting' type of woman.

'So what we have is an incident and that Zara has been struggling,' I said.

'An accident, I'd guess,' said Dr Lancaster. 'I will say this for Zara, she never asked for any more Diazepam after that batch. She said it spaced her out and she couldn't take it. A lot of breastfeeding mums don't like to take medication.'

'Was she still nursing? River would have been – what – two?'

'Absolutely. Yes.' Dr Lancaster smiled, showing a dead tooth. 'Zara has never requested antidepressants, which is unusual in the mothers of children like River. The statistics aren't good for the parents of children with special educational needs either. And the divorce rate is high. Eighty per cent.'

'But Zara's still married to Shane Reede, isn't she?' I asked.

'Separated.'

'But we were under the impression that the separation happened pre-ADHD, or at least before anyone had suspicions that the condition might be present.'

'Some relationships fold without extra pressure,' Dr Lancaster said. 'With special needs children, it's even harder. Now, I need to get back to my patients.' She rose from her chair. 'I hope that was a help to you.'

Chapter 13

Most theories on crime are devised by people who are not criminals. Hence, more than one hundred calls were made to the case's designated number to advise us to check this and that. Just theories. There wasn't one sighting.

Afternoon and evening linked their shadows together on Tuesday, the day after River disappeared. Chief Dunne gave another statement to the press office in which he stated we were now exploring the possibility that the disappearance was the result of a criminal act. Yet more photos of the child were released and the public thanked for all their efforts to find him.

Linskey sat across the desk, her hand over the mouthpiece of the phone, relaying information from Brian Quinn in forensics.

'No signs of a break-in on the windows and doors. No prints other than the family's upstairs. No footwear impressions.' Then her eyes blazed. She nodded, put down the receiver. She asked if I remembered the dressing-gown belt. Vaguely I did.

'It was over the bannister,' I said.

'That's right. There were the fibres from it at the end of the bannister, on the wood and on the handle of River's door, but nowhere else that was checked.'

'They were using it to lock him in his room?'

'Exactly.' Linskey wet her lips a little. 'Do you think they were doping him to make him sleep?' she asked. Taking the lid off her pen she began to write notes as they occurred to her.

I yawned, massaging my shoulder with one hand. I let my head roll left to right and back, heard the cracking of my neck.

'Could be, and the sink was full of little medicine spoons,' I said.

'It's one theory,' said Linskey.

I had dismissed the spoons, just like the belt, because in Charlotte's house the teaspoons always seemed to go missing, *like socks*, she would say, hovering over the kettle, doing her caffeine dance. I would find these little plastic spoons in the drawer for her instead of silver ones. I would see the older kids with them wedged in their yoghurts. It was like they preferred using them for their novelty.

'Isn't it weird that Zara isn't on meds?'

'I don't know. You're damned if you do, damned if you don't. A mother's place is in the wrong,' said Linskey, wrapping clear tape around her fingertip, peeling it off.

'But could Zara have been getting Raymond to get medication for her?' I said. 'Could she have been taking his?'

Linskey didn't reply; she started writing again. All I could hear was the swish her pen made on the page and the faint beeping of the green man outside, guiding everyone safely across Holywood Road.

While Linskey was busy with her own thoughts I took a spin to the old petrol forecourt off Ladas Drive. This was RAD Carpets, the sign told me, but the '*pets*' in 'Carpets' had been struck through and '*parts*' written above it. Blame the illiterate signwriter for that oversight, I thought, or the boss's thick Belfast accent while giving the order.

'You the woman looking for Shane?' a man said. I recognised his voice from the phone.

I asked him his name.

'Depends who's looking me.' He winked.

'Detective Inspector Harriet Sloane. Are you Ronnie Dorrian?'

'That's the one,' Ronnie said. He was in his sixties, shorter than me, and had sleek strands of hair covering his bald head and a long face with two waxy red cheeks.

He invited me into the office where a pin-up was tacked to the wall. I had the feeling she was the only person with a vagina who ever graced the room. And what a vagina! It was on full display, the camera looking up at her mortified expression from crotch level. She was in the most uncomfortable position imaginable, her inflated breasts squeezed together by two rake-slim arms, her perfectly manicured hands holding her legs apart so you could see her perfectly manicured bush. Her make-up was garish, her brown hair big and backcombed. The fading colours told me the poster was as old as I was.

'He's not here,' Ronnie said, wiping his black oily hands. 'Shane's back in Monaghan. He had some emergency to deal with back there yesterday.'

'An emergency bigger than this one?'

'That's everything he told me,' Ronnie said. 'Said he'd tell me everything when he gets back, and he'll be back first thing this morning. I'm expecting him in anytime now, love. He's supposed to be working late on that motor over there.'

'Do you know if he's heard about his son?'

'No. What about him?' said Ronnie.

'His son River. He's been missing since yesterday morning. It's all over the media. A little four-year-old.'

'I don't pay attention to the news.' Maybe Ronnie was telling the truth. There was no radio playing, no newspaper lying about. Just CD cases of Neil Diamond. 'And we're more colleagues than mates. Maybe he wouldn't tell me anyway. That's really personal business.'

'When you're talking to him next, tell Shane that my colleagues and I would like to speak to him at Strandtown PSNI station.'

'I will do, aye.' He made to leave the office.

'Did Shane say anything else that you can think of?'

'Oh, I thought you were done, love. Let me think … He did … thinking about the wee boy now … Shane said something about that clampet his ex lives with now.'

'Raymond Marsh? He was talking about Raymond?'

'Aye, that's him. Marsh.'

'What did he say about Raymond?'

'He's a shifty one. He thinks he's the boy's dad, according to Shane. He hurt the boy before, this Raymond.'

'Shane said this, and he said it *today*?'

'No, no, another time, love.'

'Just to clarify, he wasn't talking about Raymond today when you spoke?'

'No, not today, another time. That clampet, he was supposed to be minding the child when he got scalded.'

'That was a long time ago now.'

'You know about that?'

'I do. Do you think Mr Marsh did it on purpose?'

'Sounded like it,' Ronnie said.

'Would you be prepared to make a statement to that effect?'

'Nah,' he muttered. 'What do I really know anyway? Sure, if you've already heard, then you know and it's up to you now. At least I feel better for having said. You know, a clear conscience. If it turns out that Raymond has hurt the child I'll be able to sleep at night.'

Ronnie looked chuffed with himself. It was best I said nothing, so I didn't.

'Shane's very private,' he continued. 'He tells me very little, love.'

'Enough of the "love", alright?'

Ronnie looked taken aback.

'It's Detective Sloane. Now, when you gave him the job here, did you get any references?'

'I did, but we have this helper – he fucken shreds everything. Thinks he's being helpful. Sorry about that.'

'Sorry about what?'

'For swearing. My da always told me to never curse in front of ladies, especially ones who talk posh.'

I rolled my eyes. 'Who is this helper?'

'Wee Syrian kid – Kage. I took him in and gave him a job. You have to help people like that. I went to Uganda for a fortnight a few years ago. You have to help people who need your help or you'd feel like a rotten bastard, isn't that true? People like me and you are the same, and when I say that, what I mean is that we're blessed, like, aren't we?'

'Kage, you say? What age is he?'

'Definitely over eighteen.'

'And you have kids yourself, Mr Dorrian?'

'The potential's there, love, plenty of it' – he winked – 'but none that I know of.'

'There's the blessing right there,' I said, taking the smile off his face.

Chapter 14

When we went to Witham Street later that evening, Raymond was sitting with Ness, the next door neighbour, a cheerful fire plumping in the grate. They were watching the news, Raymond with an inane grin on his face and Ness's delight palpable that their houses were on the TV. She was bubbling with laughter and picking at her eyelashes. She was wearing a white coat, even though she was indoors, and kept her small square handbag on her knee.

I asked if she would give us a moment to talk to Raymond and she said it was no problem, but she sat on until Raymond told her he'd be straight round to debrief her when we left. At this she scoffed, got up and walked to the front door; the snib clicked shut.

'Where's Zara?' Linskey asked Raymond.

'Upstairs.' He rubbed his nose and sniffed. 'You looking her?'

'Please.'

He plodded out to the hall, held the balustrade and called her.

Zara shouted, 'Be down in a mo.'

We avoided each other's eyes, the three of us. Raymond sighed. He asked if we had found Shane.

'He's on his way home,' Linskey said.

Raymond nodded. 'Has he been in Monaghan?'

'Do you know the address in Monaghan, Raymond?'

'Yeah, it's in the address book ... I think. I could be wrong.' Raymond tried to dismiss the thought with a wave of his hand. 'Zara never spoke to him when he lived over the border,' he said.

'We couldn't find a place in his name,' I said.

We all sat down in the living room.

'No, you wouldn't. It was his grandmother's old farm he lived in. Wouldn't be in his name, see?'

'Could you get me the address please, Raymond?'

He got up and walked towards the kitchen, paused, then turned back. To make sure he didn't renege on the offer of the address, I followed him in. Linskey edged up on her side of the sofa and watched around the door frame.

I put my hand out for the address book. It was covered in circles, the rings of coffee cups over the years denoting its age, like a tree. I flicked through it. Most of the pages were blank; the few names there were there had been scored out altogether, or one person removed – possible divorces. I didn't see a single entry that hadn't been altered in some way.

Raymond jammed a finger at the page. 'There's the boyo there,' he said.

I examined it. By now Linskey was at my side, trusty notebook out to write it down. I gave the address book to her and she leaned on the island. Raymond said he wouldn't have the first idea how to get to Shane's grandmother's old house.

'We need to get Zara down for a chat,' I said.

Raymond paid no attention, so I went upstairs to fetch her.

The top stair creaked; drawers in Zara's bedroom clattered like dropped crockery.

'Hello?' she said nervously.

The door was open just a crack. She was sitting on the bed, something whirring nearby, and a mink throw fussed over her shoulders, falling to a fold in her lap, her mobile phone on top of it.

She opened her teeth like gates. 'Get out! I'm not decent!' she shouted.

'It's Harriet Sloane,' I said. 'I've news about Shane.'

Zara looked from left to right and back at the door; the action was scented with panic. I let myself in.

'It's okay,' I said. 'Just thought you might like to know about River's father.'

There was a bottle on her bedside table, a plastic tube going into it; the bottle was being filled with milk from her mink covered nipple.

Zara tutted. 'Is nothing sacred?' she mumbled.

'Unless … unless you have something you want to tell me about Shane,' I said, pretending I didn't care that Zara was expressing milk, that I wasn't taken aback by it. What in the world? River was a preschooler.

Zara looked at the open door, now behind me, and then the bottle and the white pithy sides of her book stack, spines hidden, sitting there like a nameless still-life. I chanced sitting on the edge of her bed. I tried to be kind to her, now I could see how she wore her motherhood so closely it looked like she might unskin without her boy.

'We'll find River,' I promised her, knowing that I shouldn't.

'If he's not back by the morning it'll have been forty-eight hours,' Zara said, 'depending on what time he left, which we don't even know. I could've been sleeping soundly in my bed all night and him away. Where's the invisible string that joins a mother to their child? Where was my motherly fucken instinct?' She swept the books beside her bed onto the carpet, knocking the bottle over, her milk spilling and gulped up by the chocolate brown carpet. Her breast was exposed, the nipple dripping liquid into a crinkle of stomach skin.

'There's every chance he'll walk in the door,' I said. 'No news is often good news.'

'Often is not good enough,' she replied, looking at her mobile phone.

I lifted the books – text books, mostly about mothering – and arranged them back into their pile. Raymond was calling up to see if everything was okay.

'Fine, dear,' said Zara, sounding as though she was rehearsing an answer, or it was an answer too well rehearsed.

'Alrighty then,' he called back.

'I'm sorry, Detective,' Zara said. 'What were you going to say about Shane?'

'He's on his way back. He contacted his boss, Ronnie Dorrian.'

'You haven't heard from Shane himself?'

'Not directly, no. Zara, after sleeping on it, do you think Shane might have a reason to take River?'

'After sleeping on it?' She curled her top lip. 'Do you think I can sleep with my baby missing?'

I apologised, knowing I shouldn't. 'If Shane doesn't come back and we have to go to Monaghan to get him, where would we find him?' I asked. 'Are you sure you don't have an address?'

'Yep,' said Zara. 'It was a different life he had down there. I've no idea where he was, who he was with or what he did. *Sorry.*' The last word came out almost sarcastically, like a childish song. 'He told me lie after lie, that man. I stopped asking him questions.'

Cars went down in the street, the headlights running along the walls, and for a moment a necklace of lights fell across Zara's collarbone. She saw me glance at her. She pulled the throw up and tucked it under her arms. Linskey came upstairs to ask if I was ready to go, and when she smiled kindly at Zara and didn't seem taken aback by what she saw, it alarmed me how differently two people could view the exact same scene.

Chapter 15

At nine thirty a.m. on Wednesday 19 October, it looked like business as usual at Albertbridge Home Supplies. The car park was full of traders' vans as their owners stocked up on panels, paints and screws. From the doorway, I spotted a large window looming over the cashier desks. From behind it and down a few steps, came the area manager, Alice Groves, shaking her blonde bobbed head like there was water in her ears, ruffled to see Linskey and me.

'Come through,' she said, waving us up into her office.

She was a woman in her fifties, and wore a trouser suit and a black velvet choker that looked like it was garrotting her. She turned to ask a young man working at a cash desk to bring us another seat. He glanced at his approaching customer and disappeared while we tailed Alice into the office.

The cashier returned with a swivel chair. 'That's from the lunch room,' he said, then hung back. Alice looked out at the shop floor at the queue of two workmen.

'Alright, thanks, Gary,' she said. She waited until Gary was back down the last step and behind the till before she resumed. 'I hadn't a clue that Donald Guy was a paedophile,' she whispered. 'Not until this all happened.'

'As I explained on the phone, we had a tip-off that Donald wasn't in work for all of his shift on Monday,' Linskey said. 'Obviously that concerns us.'

'Without a doubt,' Alice said. 'It concerns me too. Like, I knew he did time – that's not unusual, the way we work – but it's being honest that stands by you. We aren't the type of place to need criminal checks. If someone's a thief, then we don't really want to be employing that type. Goes without saying. But Donald has courses. His CV, here it is.'

She set the pages on the desk on top of a lattice of order forms and invoices. There was a passport photo paper-clipped to the corner of the printouts. Even Donald's passport photo looked like a mugshot.

'Since this wee boy disappeared you get people saying things …' Alice twiddled the back of her earring with her thumb. 'Some fella refused to work with Donald a few months ago in the warehouse, but I'm glad now that he was working out there. We don't just get tradespeople. People come in here to do DIY. At the weekend, a lot of kids come through these doors.'

'Alice, in the tip-off we received during the night, someone gave information that Mr Guy was in work for only half of his shift and that he took off at lunchtime,' I said. 'A colleague of ours, Detective Amy Campbell, showed me Mr Guy's roster. Isn't he supposed to be working from eight to four on Mondays?'

'That's what he was supposed to do,' Alice said, looking unglued. 'He clocked in.'

'How does one clock in here?' Linskey asked.

'You come here, to the office, at the start of the shift and sign in. Look, there's his signature.' Alice pressed her finger against Monday's form that was stuck to the window.

'Do you have a similar system for clocking out at the end of a shift?'

'No, but you have to walk through and past there.' Alice pointed out at the shop floor from our raised vantage point. 'You couldn't just leave. You'd be seen. Detectives, can I ask what Donald actually did in the past? You know the way people talk. Did he abduct a kid? That's what Gary's saying. Gary's our assistant manager.'

'Mr Guy has a conviction for making and possessing indecent images and sexually assaulting a child over a period of months,' I said.

Alice's expression didn't alter. She rubbed her forehead. 'No abduction?' she asked.

'No abduction,' I said.

'I'd hate to think that he'd take that wee boy River and do anything to him.'

'We have to investigate every avenue. With Mr Guy's crimes being known to us, we have already visited him. He is under surveillance all the time.'

'He's okay, you know,' Alice said. 'Out of all of them, he's the only one who doesn't give me any earache. Just keeps his head down and gets on with it. Goes to show!'

I was glad she was so pleased. 'But you believe he was here? At work?' I said.

'I do, Detective.'

'Do you have any proof, Alice?'

'I was off at the start of the week. The manager of the shop was here – Crispin. He claims Donald was too. He called me yesterday to tell me all of this. Wish he'd told me sooner.'

'Do you have those CCTV tapes of the warehouse?'

'Yes. Here, they are.' Alice pushed two tapes towards me. 'I'm waiting for a delivery,' she said. 'I don't have time to go through these myself. That okay?'

'Perfect,' I said.

We took the tapes with us.

Chapter 16

The staff at Strandtown Preschool had all been eliminated as the sources of the fingermarks on River's coat. With this news, I sat in the meeting room where Higgins was throwing ideas around. He was convinced he had it.

'A man and a woman,' he said. 'Maybe they've taken River to play the part of their son? You know, a couple who can't have kids of their own.'

Linskey stared at the ceiling. 'God give me strength,' she said. 'Let me guess – you're a flat-earther too, Carl.'

'Why not?' Higgins said, but no one responded. 'It's not *un*likely.'

'It's very *un*likely,' said Linskey.

'We're looking for a jeep, is that right?' asked Simon.

'That's right,' I said.

Ronnie Dorrian had confirmed it when we spoke, and Raymond had told Linskey the same thing the night before when I had been upstairs with Zara. Shane drove a different car every time he dropped River home. On one occasion, according to Raymond, someone on the street had done a double-take when they saw Shane coming to the house – had they just seen their own car drive past when it was supposed to be in RAD getting work done? Shane had wriggled his way out of it by claiming that he'd been taking the car for a test drive to check the repairs.

Raymond was no petrolhead, which I imagined was a pleasant change for Zara and far removed from bad associations with car-loving men, but it meant that Raymond couldn't tell Linskey the make or model. Zara just palmed me off with 'a jeepy thing' when I asked her.

But what Raymond could tell us, which was even better, was that the spare wheel cover had a cartoon of a jeep on the back and the words 'I like it dirty' in white writing above it.

'That spare wheel is bound to stand out,' I said to the team. 'Or the testicles Raymond told us about.'

'The testicles?' asked Simon.

'Yes, Raymond said Shane had something akin to a pair of tights with two egg-shaped objects weighing each side down and this was tied around the tow bar.'

Higgins laughed. 'A pair of bollocks? What a legend!'

'Is he for real?' Linskey said, hiking her thumb at Higgins.

'So, Shane Reede can sexually harass motorists while simply overtaking them, is that his game?' asked Simon.

'Right charmer, isn't he,' Linskey said.

I thought of the pin-up on Ronnie Dorrian's office wall. Those accessories on the tow bar of the jeep said Ronnie to me through and through. He had eventually stopped playing the dumb chauvinist long enough to confirm that the vehicle was a black Suzuki Vitara. I think it was to take the heat off the Syrian family – a father, two sons and a daughter – who were washing and valeting cars in front of the garage.

'A black Suzuki Vitara with a couple of swingers hanging from the tow bar,' said Higgins. 'That should be easy to find.'

'Good,' I said. 'It sounds like a job for the boys.'

*

We waited at Shane's house in Brandon Terrace for this jeep to pull up. The road was landmined with cracks and weeds. It was here, looking at that sorry state of a house and feeling glad it was only a weekend home to River, that I admitted to

Linskey I found Zara to be a hard-boned soul, despite her nice house and her nice face.

'I can't make out if she's a saint or a bitch,' is what I actually said.

'You have to admire her though,' said Linskey. 'Four years old and she still has River on the boob. Even with a mouthful of teeth … or not. Expressing milk for when he returns. She's formidable in some ways.'

The most recent photos of River showed his front teeth missing and the bottom two as well, though they fell out on their own. Just as I was thinking about the photo a white transit van rocked our Skoda as it passed. I had to wonder if it was Shane. We sat on and after five minutes the transit came back the way it went without stopping.

So we tried to follow it. We circled the area but kept coming back to Brandon Terrace. With no sign of the van, we got out of the Skoda and went around the back of the house where the blinds in the kitchen were still shut fast, the third slat up buckled on the right-hand side. Through the gap you could just about peer in. It was completely dark.

At the front of the house two boys were playing in the street, hitting a football off the kerb, every time getting nearer and nearer to our car and to us as we stood trying to agree what to do next. We couldn't waste any more time waiting for Shane to return. We should have had him the day before.

'He's not been home in days,' said one child as he dinked the ball. He was in a school uniform that had that end-of-day tattiness. He looked to be about nine.

'Hey youse, what are you looking for?' asked the other, possibly a younger brother – seven, perhaps. He wore wet-look gel and a thin red tracksuit. 'What do you want that man for? We'll let him know you're lookin' him, missus.'

We ignored the kids. I didn't tell them to go on about their business, though I was sorely tempted.

Shane had taken a year's lease eight months before and his agreement was ending, from what we could gather. That was what worried me. His landlord told me that he had never been called out to fix a thing, and the neighbours had never complained to him about Shane, which was a miracle in itself.

'And Ivan isn't DHSS, so that's great too,' the landlord said.

It turned out that the house in Brandon Terrace was leased under Shane's middle name: Ivan Reede. Yet he *was* DHSS and he had been flying under the radar, working cash in hand at RAD. Doing the double with deft precision.

Shane had given the landlord a reference from a Mr Cleary in Monaghan. The address was the same as the one we had got from Raymond. Cleary, we deduced, was living in the house Shane used to live in in Monaghan, a house that was registered to Isobel Reede.

Linskey and I decided to visit Shane's neighbours in Brandon Terrace.

In the second terraced house a woman opened the door and welcomed us in. Laura was a big, convivial woman who sported darkened glasses that sat on the end of her nose and purple lipstick that had left Crayola-like marks on her teeth. She said she had last seen Shane on the Saturday morning. She worked in the newsagents and had served him there, where he bought some milk and a comic for River.

'The wee lad told me I needed to lose weight. I had to laugh,' Laura said with a smile. 'He has no filter – always says something funny. It's never cheek, to my mind, like with some kids.' She nodded at the pair outside who had progressed to kicking the ball at her kerb. 'Nobody could be bad to wee

River. River!' She rolled her eyes. 'What's wrong Jack or William? I told him, "I'm trying my best to drop a few pounds." I didn't notice, in all honesty, if Shane was about. Besides police cars, there's been no one at that door during the evenings. But then I'm not here most evenings – most nights I go and sit with my mother who's in a home now – and of course I'm working during the day. Maybe you'd be better asking the girl next door to me.'

The third terraced house was occupied by a young African woman: Rashida, mother to six-month-old twin girls. One slept on the sofa with pillows at the edge to stop her falling off, the other one, a black-eyed beauty, Rashida held outward. The child's spine fitted the length of the mother from hip to rib. She curled in on herself, holding toes in fingers, drool splattering on her vest and her mother's forearm, and on the floor.

Linskey just about melted. 'Don't you just love them at that age,' she said.

Rashida smiled and, with one finger, gathered the drool from her daughter's chin and wiped it off on her jeans.

'Oh yeah, him two doors down has a wee fella, doesn't he?' she asked. 'Haven't seen him though.'

I told her that Shane's son was the boy on the TV, the missing one.

'I don't get a chance to watch much TV at the minute,' she said, nodding at the baby. 'But I did hear, the way you hear things, in the shops. I hope he's okay, the man two doors down. His son is a little loud, but I think they're okay.'

Outside Shane's house I could feel my guts churn. My head pounded as huge dark clouds whipped above us and the rectangle of sky we were depending on suddenly shut off like someone had turned all the lights out.

Chapter 17

By five p.m., when the Chief got off his call with the gardaí, he called a meet. He wanted to get a couple of our officers to Monaghan. Linskey offered us up, seeing it was our case. He told us to go on ahead and keep him posted.

Before we set off, Linskey phoned her son, Luke, the only one who still lived at home, to tell him she would be working away from home for the next while and that he would need to look after himself.

Luke was on speakerphone. He said he'd be fine and told his mother to be careful.

'You too,' Linskey replied. 'And feed the parakeet, please.'

Luke groaned.

'I can't believe you took that thing home,' I said when they finished the call.

'They were feeding it left and right at the station. The thing was about to explode.'

'You're just a softie.'

'And you're cold-hearted.'

'No,' I said, offended. 'I just wouldn't want that responsibility.'

'Yeah, yeah, yeah,' said Linskey.

We soared down the motorway in silence, but eventually spoke about River. Even though he was nothing more than a case and a few photos to either of us, he had suction, that boy. He drew people to him. The confidential phoneline had now received hundreds of calls, most from well-wishers hogging the line, but also from people who thought they could find out what stage the investigation was at, as if the helpline was to help the public, not River and his family.

Rain began to pelt down. I set the wipers to full whack. I hadn't had the chance to get out running since the previous Saturday morning; now it was Wednesday teatime and my legs were cramped from sitting at the wheel. Just before Craigavon, Linskey got me to pull over to a service station for something to eat.

'My blood sugar's getting low,' she said.

She always had this excuse; she couldn't just say she was hungry, as if hunger was an abnormal desire to have. So I stood outside to stretch my legs too, grains of icy rain sliding down the back of my collar. Then came a call in my earpiece: the woman from the park, Ms Smith, the one Sandy Hammitt claimed to have walked past, had come into the station to say she had been at Shaw's Bridge on Monday morning and hadn't seen anyone – not Sandy, not Dusky, not River or his coat.

'She spoke out of the side of her mouth, like she's had a stroke,' Higgins said. 'She wasn't the full shilling, if you know what I mean.'

'Okay, copy that,' I said and got back into the car.

Linskey bought me a bottle of Lucozade and a sub filled with tuna and onion. 'Get that into you, skinny,' she said. 'All the carbs you eat too – it's not fair.'

We sat mulling over this latest development.

'Maybe we should go and see Ms Smith when we get back to Belfast,' I said, never completely happy when something was left in Higgins' hands.

As we ate we watched people filling their tanks, running from their cars to the garage, running back out, dodging the rain as best they could.

'I had a feeling about Alice, the manager of Albertbridge Home Supplies,' Linskey said, wiping her mouth with a napkin.

'Why is that?' I asked her.

'When I thought about the description of the woman in the park Sandy gave us, I started to think about Alice.'

'I suppose … same height, same age bracket.'

'I was tempted to ask her if she had dogs and ever went walking them around Shaw's Bridge.'

'Why didn't you? And she did seem fond of Donald, in a sick kind of way.'

'Well, it wasn't Alice anyway. It was just a fleeting thought.'

The rain had become torrential; I could hardly hear Linskey when she asked, 'How's your mum doing, Harry?'

It was always Mother; no one mentioned Brooks any more.

'No change.'

'Your dad must be having an awful time. I saw him recently, and I hope you don't mind me saying, but he looked frail. Maybe it's the care of your mum.'

I was chewing the sub, careful to leave the filling. 'I don't know,' I said. 'He's old now.'

There were other things to worry about other than Mother and bedsores. Brooks had made himself disappear; he'd told us so he wouldn't be a worry any more. Not that it worked like that. Father acted like he couldn't care less, but I knew he cared more than he'd admit. Maybe that was the father's burden.

I couldn't picture Jason Lucie as a father. If I had have been able to picture that, to picture both of us as parents, then maybe I would have gone there. Thank God I didn't. The way it worked out had shown me his ugliest side. Imagine being stuck to that because we shared a kid. It would have been the most hellish of hells. By the time our relationship ended, I couldn't pick love out of any corner of our marriage.

'Any news on the love life?' Linskey asked, as if she was reading my mind.

With her marriage wrecked by Geordie, who worked in Fraud and had left her for a young barrister, I kept my love life to myself. I had a feeling she knew that my man was married. She always scratched the surface but never asked anything more. For her benefit, I had changed Greg's name to Paul.

'He hasn't called round in a week,' I said. 'He texted me last night – had to work late.'

'Well, you've been busy yourself,' she stated.

I rolled the tuna up in the wrapper and Linskey put her hand out for it, gathering all the rubbish in a brown paper bag. She got out of the car to put it in the bin now the rain had eased off. A man with pruney eyes walked in front of the car, seemingly unaware of the rain. He had a carton of milk swinging in his left hand, and under his right arm a newspaper was folded, River's photo showing, a boy adoring his sandcastle.

'Feeling better?' I asked Linskey.

She said she was. 'You haven't asked me about my love life,' she added.

'Oh, what's this?'

'Nothing to tell, really. I got talking to this fella online. Well, we met at the city hall, but didn't he turn up with a mate in tow.'

'For moral support?'

'Don't be so naïve, Harry.'

'What!'

'Even men in their forties chance their arm for a three-way.'

'Listen to you – a three-way. You watch too much MTV. And another man? It's usually— '

'I know.' Linskey started to laugh.

'Bisexual?'

'Oh, don't! He could be bi and I could be asexual at this point.'

'And? Would you, do you think?'

'Away and fuck,' Linskey said. 'Absolutely not! Just … no!'

'What did you do, then?'

'Went to the loo, via my car, and got out of there.'

'Don't worry, Sandy Hammitt fancies you.'

'Oh great! That's what I mean, Harry – I get all the weirdos of the day. Jesus, are there any normal ones left?'

'Yes. Charlotte has one. David's not perfect but he's not deviant. He's loyal.'

'That sounds perfect to me,' Linskey said. 'Your Coral has it right – maybe women would be easier.'

'Even more drama, if you ask me. Though not with Coral's Rose. Love her to pieces. But generally, most women. How do men stick us, I wonder sometimes.'

Linskey beheld me with disappointment. 'Fair game, I'd say,' she replied.

Chapter 18

Father and I went fishing for my twenty-second birthday. It was the weekend before my main plan, which was to go to Dublin with my sisters, though Coral was in full baby-making mode with her (now ex) husband and refused to drink, and Charlotte got engaged the day before and decided she wanted to be at home with David instead.

As for the rest of them: Addam was playing missionary in Africa and Brooks was living in England and having a stab at being sober and a husband to Lydia, their marriage more of a short forgiving phase than a commitment; I think it was lost in a sneeze.

And Mother. I don't know, she probably would have enjoyed Dublin but I didn't think to invite her. Fifteen years ago, they still used the holiday home; Mother was still healthy and being in Father's presence wasn't such a chore for her.

The fishing trip ended up being the only thing worth remembering about that birthday. And out of that trip the only conversation I recall was about Hans Clarke, who had a restaurant in Belfast. Clarke was being threatened, embezzled by so-called decommissioned individuals who still enjoyed the flavour of the few extra pounds they gathered from protection money. Father told me that Clarke had suddenly shut up shop and fled, and was initially accused of doing a bunk – tax evasion – which turned out to be hearsay. Clarke had been asked for protection money when he set up his restaurant and had refused at first, being from England and not accustomed to city centre politics in the smouldering afterglow of the Troubles. So they had put his windows in and fucked about with his suppliers. Eventually he had given them something.

Clarke also had a wife – no one ever mentioned her name let alone remembered it, but I did: it was Meredith – with whom he lived out Hillsborough direction. He gave his family a beautiful home and a prep school education for Hanna-Caitlin, their only daughter, who had horses and did dressage.

'You can see how people can get used to a way of life,' Father had said.

We Sloanes had always been comfortable, and while Father came from quite humble beginnings near Lough Erne, Mother came from a family in Bangor who weren't hurting for money – lord mayors and solicitors a long way back. She was the first woman in the family to be a success in her own right, and one of the only female judges in the province. Us kids went to prep school; we didn't have horses, but we had a chalet to run to and skiing holidays every other year.

Anyway, the restaurateur went bankrupt and the extortionists burnt out his car for touting on them. In the end, this was when Linskey came into her own, on the job and in Father's – and subsequently my – books. Hans Clarke smothered Meredith in bed, then went into Hanna-Caitlin's room with the intention of doing the same, but she was awake, using the toilet. So when he went in he was startled, and so was she. He put his hands around her throat and squeezed until he had taken the life from his own daughter, a fifteen-year-old girl who, to add to the tragedy and the questions that arose, was two months pregnant.

When Clarke was found to have drunk a concoction of white spirits, alcohol, rat poison and every tablet in the medicine cabinet, gossip began to percolate that the motive was that the father had impregnated his own daughter. Eventually a sixteen-year-old boy came forward to say that he had been seeing the girl, which at the time both surprised and pleased me. Hanna-Caitlin's boyfriend knew about the pregnancy and they hadn't told anybody else.

Hans Clarke left a note to say he couldn't let his family live without the things they loved, that he couldn't take everything away from them. Forensics were able to tell that he wrote the note after he had killed Meredith and her daughter. (I refused to refer to them as *his*, correcting Father when he called them Clarke's wife, Clarke's daughter.) Hans thought it better to take their lives than their wealth.

Father had sat reeling in a fish, grappling with it at the same time as telling me that it was Linskey who found the bodies and insisted on being the one to tell Meredith's family, who lived around Warrenpoint, and that she had dealt with the family really well. Now I wonder if he was telling me: Look, here's a woman who can do this job and do it well.

Linskey was a constable then. Father spoke about her with respect, which was more than most got. She shared his work ethic too. She offered to go to Hanna-Caitlin's school to answer any questions the pupils might have. Father was impressed with how Linskey broomed their worries away. People, especially young people, always think these things are catching, and they looked at their own dads differently after what happened to Hanna-Caitlin.

It was Diane Park's shining moment – Park until she divorced Geordie and reverted to Linskey. She had the makings of a fantastic detective, according to Father. She never jumped to conclusions, even when everyone was gossiping about Hans tampering with his own daughter. She didn't let things slip past her either.

But now Linskey seemed off her game. There was something I couldn't put my finger on, but she had changed.

Why didn't she ask Alice if she had been at Shaw's Bridge if she had thought it?

'People hear the word *case*,' Father said. 'They say they are working on a *case*. They picture a suitcase and imagine they can unpack the evidence, then repack it – try to make it fit. Park was scared, but she did it without getting overwhelmed.'

He thought that being emotionless, or at least having the ability to conceal those emotions, was a virtue. I could do it too. I also knew fear, the flavour of it, how it tasted like gunmetal.

I thought of Linskey finding Hanna-Caitlin strangled on her bathroom floor. That must have been a worse sight than the car accidents we'd been called out to, teens mangled, their faces smashed from the impact of the dashboard, blood everywhere.

But a child who still looked perfect and had been purposefully taken – that was the worst of the worst, if you could rate it. And for what? A motive I found brittle, superficial.

What would we Sloanes have been like if we had suddenly moved into a local primary school, lived in a terrace in East Belfast? Maybe wealth had more importance than I realised when I was an idealistic, somewhat emotional twenty-year-old. Everything fluctuates.

Chapter 19

In Monaghan the night sky looked unfazed by the day just gone. There was this agitated churn of landscape, the land sectioned off with toothpick fences. After the rain, the air felt weightless, as if the night could just evaporate. It didn't feel like autumn.

I unstitched my legs from the car seat and got out, our boots clacking on the stones of the drive. I shone a torch around the building. There was on old derelict barn where the lane elbowed off to the left and vanished. Moonlight dusted the bricks and the air tasted like silica. Through the trees we caught the hollow rush of breath.

Before us was a dark beefy presence. I shone the flashlight at his feet and he shone his at mine, like we were actors holding spotlights, facing off.

'Can I help you folk?' the man called out.

We walked towards each other.

'Police from the North,' he said. 'This to do with the young lad's father?'

'Shane Reede?'

'Yes, Shane.'

'Is Mr Reede about?'

'He isn't. Saw him just earlier. Said he was heading home.'

'Can we take your name, sir?' Linskey asked.

'Cahal Cleary.'

I shone my torch to the side of him to see his face better. It was heavily pockmarked at each temple and ribbed his cheekbones.

'Mr Cleary, do you mind if we ask you a few questions?' Linskey asked.

'Haven't you seen Shane yet?' he said.

'That's what we'd like to talk about,' I said.

Cahal Cleary was a man about sixty. He wore dark jeans and a plaid shirt, like Greg in his down time. Bald on top like him too.

'Come hither,' he said and took the lead. 'I was expecting you might call here, but then you didn't.'

'News has reached over the border?'

'Naturally, with this child alert thing.' He tucked his torch under his elbow, the light off, took a bundle of keys out of his pocket and rifled through them, directing me to shine my light on them with a nod of his head. He found the key he had been looking for and shook it into the lock.

'This can be a bastard at times,' he said, the metal grating as he turned the key.

He let us in and led us into the kitchen, where he turned on a light. There were dried boot prints across the floor and the fresh prints from Cahal's own mud-encrusted shoes. I scanned the room for a smaller set of feet.

'I'm the landlord,' he explained. 'But before I bought the house from Issy Reede – Shane's grandmother, God rest her soul – I'd have always had a key, me living next door and all.'

'Which direction do you live?'

He pointed downhill to the house we had passed with the visitors' light glaring outside.

'Mr Cleary, you said you saw Shane. How long has he been staying here?'

'I saw him earlier. I've been up here a couple of times since I saw the boy on the news.'

'Do you know him – River?'

'No, I've never seen the young'un so. But it said youse were looking for him and that his dad's name was Reede, that youse were trying to get in touch with him. I said to my missus, Bernadene, that's our old lodgers – Shane Reede and Bronagh Shaw. The house was actually in her name, Bronagh Shaw. They must have split up after a year or so. I offered Shane to buy the house from me, to keep it in the family. He said that he had a young'un in Belfast. I knew that's where he moved to a few years back, but I'd never seen a young'un here. Don't like to ask questions.'

Cahal took a cigarette from the packet in his back pocket, flipped open a zippo and lit up.

'Why don't you ladies go and have a look about?' he offered. 'There's the barn too. It might interest you. I'll go back down to the house and put a pot on the stove. You're welcome to get a cuppa to warm you back up.'

Cahal walked out, a bloom of smoke trailing him. 'Mind bringing my keys back down?'

'We will, Mr Cleary,' Linskey said.

We gloved up, then walked through the house. It smelled of mouldy cheese and mouse shit and was plainly not lived in. All the bedding was starchy and primped; the rooms had an undaunted thirst for daylight, their heavy curtains trailing the floors. There were cobwebs around the light fittings and in every corner; fluff banked up the sides of the skirting boards. Our presence was stirring the dust only for it to resettle on our clothes and skin and hair.

Linskey gave me a sticky smile. 'It doesn't look as though River has been here,' she said.

After we searched the cupboard spaces and under the beds for a teddy or a child's forgotten toy, or the kind of thing we weren't anticipating, we gave up and turned all the lights out. I wondered why Cleary hadn't had the electricity stopped when the house had been lying vacant.

Outside, the grass had grown in tufts. We entered the broken-beamed barn, heard the flap of bats above and shone our torches at the tidiness of it all. There was nowhere River or Shane could be hiding there, or that Shane could be hiding River.

We took the car back down to Cleary's house, which had a similar layout but was cleaner and warmer, with fresh October air coming in the UPVC windows that had been left on the latch. Bernadene Cleary segmented a tiramisu and set it in front of us. Linskey took a slice with her tea; I took the tea alone. Linskey used low blood sugar as an excuse to eat rubbish. She was getting podgy and resentful of me for not joining her. Everything was happening to Linskey and Linskey only. Even if I were two stone heavier than her, which wouldn't be hard with our height differences, Linskey would have said it was okay for me, that I could carry it. I was getting a bit fed up with her personal observations.

'He dropped in this afternoon, Shane did,' Bernadene said. She was quite a striking looking woman. Her hair was cropped and peppery brown and she was tall and lithe. She would have been called a tomboy in her youth. 'Shane stayed in the house last night. He told me he was down to see a friend he hadn't seen in years.'

'Who was the friend, do you know? Did he say?'

Bernadene considered her husband who was pulling a seat out to sit facing us.

'Shane didn't say,' Cahal replied, as if he could feel her gaze. 'His friend had needed surgery of some sort and he was worried he wouldn't pull through.'

'So it wasn't Bronagh then, but a man?'

'Bronagh lives in England. Yorkshire. I still forward the odd bit of mail. Well … I used to until she put a letter in the post to thank me and let me know that it was all rubbish and that I'm to bin any more that comes.'

'Do you have her address – or the letter?' I asked.

'You think she took the boy?' Bernadene asked.

'They just need to cover everything. Correct?' Cahal said.

'Shane was telling us all about this friend – the man and the surgery,' said Bernadene, 'and Cahal was trying to tell him about the boy, to see if it was the same boy, this River Reede, and if he knew or didn't.' She stole off to the side of the room to write down Bronagh's address for us.

'Did he know, by then, about River's disappearance?' I asked.

'When I was giving him his mail – cos we get the odd letter for him too,' Cahal explained, '"Shane, did you see the news. This young'un called River Reede in Belfast, missing since Monday?" He looked at me strange. I thought he didn't hear me, then he said, "Belfast, you say?" and I said, "Yes." Then he said that he'd left his mobile at home and could he use the house phone. Then he called his ex-wife.'

'We didn't even know there was an ex-wife,' Bernadene said, handing me Bronagh Shaw's address. 'Don't people surprise you?'

'His grandmother never told you?'

'She had dementia.'

Linskey left half of her cake and took out her notepad to write down a few sporadic notes. 'Shane phoned Zara …' she said.

'Dunno the woman's name, but when he got off the phone, he was white as a ghost and a bit unbalanced, for sure.' Cahal nodded at the corner of the kitchen counter. 'He was gripping that. I told him he shouldn't drive.'

'He didn't look right.' Bernadene nodded.

'Did he say he'd spent the weekend with his son at all?'

'No, said nothing about that. Just said the police had been at his work looking for him and he had to let them know he was on his way home.'

'He didn't arrive home,' I said. 'We waited for hours.'

'Oh dear, I hope he's okay. He tore off,' said Bernadene. 'Shane was driving with his emotions. Didn't I say that, Cahal?'

'And he still stays up there, in the other house?' asked Linskey. She got a nod from Bernadene. 'Is Shane paying rent?'

'Well, no, he hasn't since he left in February. The girlfriend left first, in December. Then him, a coupla months later. But he still had a key and said he'd let himself in and knew I wouldn't mind because he was only visiting, seeing how it was an emergency, he said.'

'The property's been vacant for more than six months, is that right?'

Now Cahal did what people do when they are no longer out giving other people's information: he turned defensive. 'Shane shot straight off towards the North,' Cahal said, deftly fielding the question. He stood up, placed his hands in his pockets.

'See,' Bernadene said, shaking her head softly, 'I told him to get everything turned off and shut down until the building works start. It's getting flattened.' She swept her hand across the table. 'It's a wedding present for our son when he gets married in January. We want to give him and his new wife the land.'

'Not the house?' Linskey asked, looking up, squinting while her vision readjusted.

'They want to build their own home. He's an architect, our son, young Cahal. Studied at your Queen's.'

This made me smile, as if Linskey and I, being from the North, which they were practically a stone's throw from living in themselves, had some ownership of the university. Young Cahal an architect. Like Jason. The smile died on my face.

'I've a son studying there myself.' Linskey smiled, and her and Bernadene shared a motherly moment. I imagined Greg's wife with her girlfriends and the women at the golf club doing the same thing.

'You have to respect the property while it's there,' said Cahal, playing with the loose change in his pocket. 'Until it's gone and rebuilt it's a place full of memories. Issy's memories.'

'He's sentimental about that kind of thing, Cahal,' said Bernadene. 'Big Cahal. He likes to go up there and look around, tries to picture where everything is going to be for Cahal and his wife, don't you?'

'Yes,' he said. His face had become as vague as frosted glass.

'And Shane was driving what type of vehicle?' I asked.

'A jeep.'

'Was there anything memorable about it?'

'No.'

'On the back?'

'No, it was a black jeep. Maybe I never saw the back.'

Just then I received a message in my earpiece. I took my personal radio from my coat and spoke into it. Then I turned to the Clearys.

'I need to call the station,' I explained and stepped outside. The sky was like melted tar over the house, a sphere of stars stuck to it. They almost looked bright enough to see by.

'There's been a sighting of a young boy matching River's description, Sloane,' the Chief told me. 'The person he's with is an older man with long brown hair in a ponytail. They're on the Stena Line heading for Birkenhead and are going to be met on the other side.'

Chapter 20

It was bizarre the dream I had when I got home from Monaghan.

I was in Charlotte's house. She was making a tiramisu. She set sparkling sponge fingers into the base of a cake tin, then poured an espresso out of a Starbucks' cup over it. She was in the living room, baking on the top of a chess table like the one we had clubbed together to buy for Father when he retired.

Then the dream flitted to the kids, who were all playing. I was sitting on this beanbag on the floor; I had Timothy in my arms. He was stiffening his body, silently laughing at an episode of *Timmy Time* on the TV; his siblings were getting rowdy. When I looked up to shush them, they stalled their horseplay just long enough to sing 'Twinkle Twinkle, Little Star', spraying the lyrics into the air; then they came to kiss his face – the two bigger boys, the two girls. Timothy's galactic brown eyes were toing and froing on his lax face. His teeth seemed too small for him.

There was a green puffa jacket tied to the curtain pole and a draught blew through the room. Charlotte suddenly said, 'I'm going to put this in the fridge' and she left me.

The big kids were gone and a window was smashed in. The curtains feathered as they lifted and billowed. Then the full moon breathed in on Timothy and he stood up, a moonmark on his forehead like a silver thumbprint.

He spoke, defying the odds of his profound disability. He toddled across the room, then climbed the curtain like a monkey and reached for the green puffa jacket, tugging at its arm. He turned to me and said, 'Harry, tell them I'm cold.'

I put my hand in my pocket and something bit my fingers: teeth; tiny teeth. When I put my hand to my mouth I found all my own were gone.

These words were going through my head when I woke: *sometimes the reeds are ashamed of the river.*

I had fallen asleep on the sofa without a duvet. I hadn't heated my apartment in days and it was freezing. My hands were so cold they were on fire.

I sat in the half-light that spilled through the curtainless window, wanting to talk to Greg.

There were times I could. Like when we went away together to his house on the Algarve and had behaved like a proper couple, though we shopped separately and only ate in restaurants outside of Guia, not unless he wore his baseball cap. It became a running joke: I had packed a fake moustache and glasses and I came down to the pool wearing them.

One night I couldn't sleep. I watched Greg lying in bed under layers of suffocating cotton, half lit, half dark.

'Come back to bed,' he said.

'I wonder what's happening back home,' I said.

I was wondering if Jason had realised that I'd left yet. Not that I'd taken much – only what was mine, what he had no use for. I had told Charlotte I was going away with friends. I had told Father I'd call him in a couple of days. I didn't have to say where I was headed. I had no one to answer to any more.

'Darlin', what did you say?' Greg asked.

He always called me darlin'. I'm sure it kept everything easy. No names to confuse.

He turned on his bedside light, high up on the wall, a determined light crowning the top of his head. There, in that room, I could have loved Greg, or at least pretended for the weekend that I'd taken with him in honour of my pending divorce.

I fetched us breakfast and carried it on a tray like a brimming ash-pan back to the bed, but Greg had insisted that we ate at the table. He opened his box of cereal, a cloud of dust, almost invisible, puffing into the air. Grapefruit squirted in my mouth. That's when we had the conversation, the one and only serious one.

'Do you want kids?' Greg had asked, sweeping his spoon to his mouth.

'No,' I replied. 'Do you want more kids?'

'I'm long done and two is enough,' he said taking a sip of his coffee. I was almost close enough to taste the dark bitterness of the Robusta beans.

'I thought you were offering.'

Greg laughed. 'No, no, no,' he said in his deep Ballymena accent.

I could see the way his face was going, the shape it would be when he was even older, his nose broken from the accident he'd had as a kid that also left a pleasing laddered scar under his chin.

I knew how naff it sounded, but I said it anyway. 'I want to take that love I would have given to a child and give it to myself. I know most people don't understand that, but it's my life.'

Greg lifted my hand and held it. 'Good for you,' he said, his eyes unblinking under thick black brows that needed to be groomed.

Sometimes I had no idea what he was thinking, no idea where he really came from, what type of family. He had an elderly mother; sometimes she was why he couldn't see me. But that could have been a lie. I knew first-hand how good he was at telling them, how he was unemotional and in control and liked things wrapped up neatly so he could understand them before he could move on. When he told me I was beautiful, he may as well have been saying I was reliable. To him they seemed to be the same thing.

I was not an unwise girl to Greg. He cared for me in a way, even if it wasn't something typical in a relationship. But it wasn't a typical relationship. He had no words he used to hurt me. I knew he never would. Most importantly, he wanted my respect. My admiration meant something to him. Greg fully understood the meaning of things. He was able.

'Do you think we'll do this again?' he asked.

'I'd like to,' I said.

I watched him noodle his little sachet of honey onto granary toast, take a bite, seeds caroming off the table. I knew we weren't in a hotel, but I was still tempted to put all the soaps in my bag before we left as if they were complimentary. Of course I didn't. Nor did I leave my bra under a pillow for his wife to find. But I was growing insanely jealous of her, even though everything of hers that I wanted, I had. In doses.

I knew I could never return there. It was hers. But I knew I couldn't go back to my old house either, not even when Jason was at work, even though I was curious to see what I'd been left with.

My phone went off. I slammed my hand on it to silence it. It might wake someone on another floor. Chief Dunne was calling.

'Sloane,' he said, 'two things.'

'Good news and bad news?'

'Not exactly. The man on the ferry was a dead end.'

'Yes, I know,' I said, picturing some poor man being stopped getting off the boat with his son, who turned out not to be River. Naturally, my mind had sprung straight to Sandy Hammitt when I'd heard the description of the man with the ponytail. There had been a light sense of relief between Linskey and me on the way back to Belfast from Monaghan: it was possibly over; River was safe.

'What's the other thing?' I asked the Chief.

'Raymond Marsh has collapsed and died at home.'

Chapter 21

Zara sighed hard. She poured a glass of milk and drank it.

'Do you mind me having a glass of water?' I asked.

'You usually refuse.' Zara opened the fridge where there was no sign of breast milk.

'I haven't restocked on water filters,' she said fetching a clean glass from the rack, still soapy at the rim.

I troubled her for an ice cube, remembering a book about baby food and chapters on breastfeeding I had once read out of boredom when babysitting for Charlotte. I hadn't wanted to turn on the TV in case it drowned out Timothy's breathing on the monitor. And I vaguely remembered Coral saying that she froze her milk when she went back to work, but that could be a cartilage of memory twisting itself the way of my wanting it to.

Zara pulled open the freezer door; as discretely as I could I looked inside. There were four items, one thing per shelf: an ice-cube rack, fish fingers, Goodfellas pizzas and bags of veg and rice. It seemed that the cookbooks taking pride of place on the shelf were purely for show, not that I should judge Zara's eating habits and the low nutritional value in the kitchen on the week her son had disappeared and her partner died. If they were, then maybe the parenting books were as well. There was no breastmilk in this freezer at any rate.

Zara slammed the ice-cube tray against the glass. A couple of blocks clanged on the island. She swept them into the sink.

'You soon get out of your routine if you aren't doing it every day,' she said. 'It was eight o'clock last night and I thought to myself, that's two days I've missed out on saying prayers with River at bedtime. He'd say, "God bless my nanas and grandpas in heaven, God bless Mummy and Raymond, and God bless Daddy".'

The front door opened; then the living room door. A man was walking towards us into the kitchen, his face a mess: a sirloin of a bruise on the left cheek, two old scars shortening the ends of his eyebrows.

'Shane!' Zara screamed.

She ran at him and he caught her in an embrace.

Linskey and I exchanged looks. Her eyes travelled over Shane. I could tell she was thinking the same thing I was: if anyone had a type, Zara did.

Shane was short with dark brown curly hair, younger than Raymond, bulky too, but more muscular. As far as I could tell, he had two good working legs, though he was broken in many other ways. Zara must have had a desire to love unlovable men.

They were still crushed together until Shane pulled away long enough to cough. It sent tremors through him.

'Are you alright?' he asked Zara several times, but she remained in a full-throated fuss in his arms. Shane turned towards us. 'Are you here for the boy?' he asked.

He looked hard at me with what seemed like recognition on his face.

Before I could reply Zara said, 'Raymond died. It was only a few hours ago.' She started to cry. 'He keeled over in the bathroom and hit his head on the sink. They're here to see if I'm okay.'

This wasn't strictly true; it was always about River. He was our first priority. It would have been nice to leave Zara in Shane's arms, but the fact was that we were also there for him, seventy-two hours after his son had vanished. Thursday morning and here he was eventually, and he was on his own.

Zara lifted her head from his chest and looked at him. 'What on earth has happened to you? Where have you been?'

'I was beaten up,' he said. 'Carjacked. Lay unconscious all night.'

'Oh my God,' she said.

'We need to speak to you, Mr Reede,' said Linskey. 'We'd like you to come to the station with us now.'

His eyes bulged like headlights. He asked Zara if she was going to be alright again; she told him she would get her neighbour to sit with her once the officers went.

Then we took Shane out of the house in silence out under that sky, cracked with cinder-blue veins, the traffic chanting on Newtownards Road.

Chapter 22

It took Shane a while to warm up. He sat facing us in the interview suite late on Thursday morning, cold and contracting, his eyes focused behind us at some point on the wall. It was three days since Zara opened River's bedroom door to an empty bed.

Shane claimed to have been carjacked somewhere outside Armagh on his way back from Monaghan. I pushed the unlikely carjacking aside and went straight to his impromptu journey from Belfast to Monaghan.

'Where in Monaghan?' I pressed.

He let his shoulders fall from besides his ears and he sat forward. He made a bowl of his hands and let his words fall into it.

'I was in Carrickmacross, County Monaghan.'

'How long were you there for?' asked Linskey.

'From …' He squinted, clucked his tongue like he was seeing time wind itself backwards. 'From Sunday evening until Wednesday afternoon,' he finally replied.

'You spent three nights there, is that right?'

'I did.' He coughed.

'Where did you stay?' asked Linskey. 'And be specific.'

'My old house,' he said.

'Is there anyone who can vouch for you?'

'Yes, Cahal. Oul' Cahal Cleary. He used to own the house.' The words shot out of Shane's mouth at a faster rate than the chat in the car on the way.

'What do you mean by *used to*,' asked Linskey. 'Shane, what do you mean by *used to own the house*?'

'He's given it over for his son, put it in his name.' Shane eyed me, a look of relief waving over his face.

'When did you see Cahal Cleary?' I asked, lunging at him.

'Yesterday. He told me about River. I still can't believe it.' *Cough*.

'Why were you in Carrickmacross?'

'It was my mother.' He clammed up again.

'What about her?'

'She was unwell.'

'How so?'

'She had a stroke. Well, she said she did …'

'Did you tell Mr Cleary this?'

'No … I said it was a friend.'

'Cahal is a family friend, is he?'

'Not a friend of my mum's, no.'

'Why not?'

'He doesn't know her.' Shane fell into a surly silence. He scratched his ear, the tip of it black to match the black eye, the busted nose.

'But Cahal bought the house from your grandmother, isn't that true?'

'You were talking to Cleary?'

This bothered me. Why was Shane surprised that we'd gone to his home when his son had gone missing? It bothered me too that maybe Zara hadn't been lying, that she really didn't know all the details about his living there, that he'd never explained the housing arrangements in Monaghan to her.

'Yes, we did. We were there yesterday,' Linskey said. 'The house didn't look like anyone had stayed there for three nights. Where did you eat?'

'It was only a place to put my head down. I was at Margaret's.'

'Margaret?'

'McGuire. My mother.'

'And you call your mother by her first name, do you?'

'She was young when she had me. Gran brought me up. Margaret's only fifty-one. I was brought up to think she was my sister and the black sheep of the family. I always knew she did something ... bad. I didn't know until I was sixteen when my gran sat me down to tell me that Margaret was my mother. I always knew it, I think. Deep down.'

'Is she okay? Your mother?'

'Sorta. She was let home from the hospital. It's just when you hear the word *stroke*. I thought, fuck, I better get down there in case something happens, her being my only living relative ... except River,' he quickly interjected, then crossed himself. 'But when I got down there, she wasn't even in hospital – never been, said the doctor came in to see her and said it was probably a minor stroke but left her at home.'

'Do you have an address for your mother?' Linskey asked.

'I wouldn't know what house number, what street. I'm dyslexic that way. I know it to see. It's a bungalow ... with a garage.'

'I find it strange that you didn't mention your mother, and that you told Cahal it was a male friend.'

'Now, I never said male. He must have just assumed, and in a way she *is* a friend. Margaret never raised me. I don't owe Cahal any great explanation. He never had time to chat when I was living with my ex ...' He coughed.

'Zara?' I asked.

'No.'

'Bronagh?'

'Yes, Bronagh.' Again, Shane looked surprised. He had obviously forgotten how people love to talk. 'I was in the shop,' he said, 'and she came over and introduced herself. She knew it was me. Margaret, I mean. I can't look at her now after all this time and think that's my mum, you know? I hardly remembered her from when I was a lad.'

'You never went looking for her in all the time since you'd known that your grandmother was not your mother?'

'I thought she didn't want me. It turns out she did. It was the seventies. They took me from her and she was sent to a laundry. Sure, there are movies made about that kind of caper now. It was pure awful how they treated them girls.'

'Yes, it was, but let's get back to River,' said Linskey.

Shane's eyes fell again. 'I don't know what to say about River. I can't believe no one has found him yet. What have you all been doing?'

'And you had him for the weekend?'

'I did.'

'Where did you go with the boy?'

'Friday evening, we stayed in, ate a pizza, watched a flick. We slept. Saturday … we went for a drive. I wanted to take him bowling, but last time he kept being reckless – wouldn't use the safety ramp. I didn't want to send him back to Zara with a broken toe.'

'What did you do?'

'We played in the yard – a bit of footie.'

'How come his coat was found in the playground at Shaw's Bridge?'

Shane didn't seem alarmed at this, unlike Zara when we had told her. 'River had his coat on when I sent him home,' he said. His voice was ragged.

'Sent him home?' I asked.

'Brought him home.'

'And did you go inside when you brought him home, Shane?'

'No, I sat in the car, watched him go in. Raymond waved out the front window to let me know he ... to acknowledge me.'

'You never went to the door?'

'No, I've never been inside that house till there now.'

'What about River's medication?' Linskey asked.

'What about it?'

'Did you trust River to bring it back into the house with him?'

'Zara only sent me enough to last him the weekend. It wasn't as if he was going to down it on the way in the door. I told you, Raymond was always watching once River got in.'

'Were you on good terms with Raymond?'

'Not bad terms anyway. He was a bit of ... I don't mean to speak ill of the dead but he was a woeful fucker – excuse my French. I thought Zara was being desperate taking up with him. It wasn't a real relationship. She told me they sleep in separate beds. Slept. You know what I mean.'

'But you're on good terms with Zara?'

'Wasn't always. Not great terms now.'

'Yet she tells you intimate details of her life with her new partner?' said Linskey.

I thought the words *new partner* seemed unfitting about a man who was now safely dead.

'Zara might have said something when I was keeping her going about him,' Shane said, 'when she kept bringing up Bronagh. I got caught up in Bronagh, thought it was easier to give up on River, let him have a different family, but

Raymond – he was a waster. I know he was handicapped, but still, he could have done something. He was an accountant before, I think. What does having one leg have to do with number crunching? He was an educated boyo. I'd have been happy for him to play dad if he'd have got his finger out and given the boy a life.'

'You've a strong dislike for Raymond, don't you, Shane?'

'No, not at all. He was just a … disappointment,' he said softly.

'But you were happy to abandon the boy?' I said. I was thinking of how Raymond only had Shane's number because of the barrage of abusive texts Shane had sent him. I had caught a glimpse of them on his phone. All one way, although I guess the other side of the conversation could have been deleted.

'Fair dos,' Shane said. He rubbed the left side of his head; it was significantly puffed up compared to the right. That thick red-brown bruise was sore to look at. He started to tell us about how he co-parented with Zara, how, when he saw how useless Raymond was, Shane returned to Belfast.

'Nothing to do with Bronagh leaving you?' Linskey asked.

He was about to protest, then shut his mouth. He was probably remembering that Cahal was a bit of a talker when he took the notion.

'I was alone for months before I came back,' he told us. 'So if it was a rebound thing, after Bronagh, then no, you're grabbing the wrong end.'

'But you were back in Belfast for four months before you let Zara know you were back,' I said. 'So did you really come back for River? Or was there something in Monaghan you were trying to get away from?'

'I wasn't trying to get away from anything. You could even ask Bronagh.'

'Would Bronagh tell us the same story, Shane? What story would she tell us?'

'Brone wanted a baby and I had one I already didn't see,' he said. 'Her being from England, I knew that if we fought she'd up and leave and take that child away. You have to learn from your mess.' He smiled weakly.

'Shane,' Linskey said, leaning forward – she looked sickened with him – 'Did you or did you not go to Shaw's Bridge with River?'

'I did not,' he said, blinking slowly, that faint smile fizzling away to invisibility.

*

Linskey asked me to let Dunne know Shane's story. 'You do it, poster girl. You carry more bones,' she said.

'I don't at all,' I said.

Linskey was my superior – through time served only – and Dunne was a family friend, but I hadn't the energy to be annoyed with her sniping remarks right then, so I went and rapped my knuckles on his door. He waved me in and set down the pages he was looking at.

His face was bleak. He put his hand out for my notes, scanning them as I told him what they said.

'Chief,' I said, 'Shane Reede's version of events are these: he claims to have left his phone at home and that he was carjacked somewhere near Armagh at five p.m. yesterday. He has given a description of the carjackers.'

'Reede is saying that Ronnie Dorrian came to collect him, is that right, Sloane?'

Now I was under interrogation. It was the equilibrium of the job. It swung in and out of place.

'We'll check his story with his boss,' I said, 'but to be honest, Chief, I don't think Dorrian's the sort to help us. I reckon he puts his name to nothing either.'

'Why didn't Reede get in touch with us?' he asked.

'He said he wanted to get straight back. He was just thinking about River the whole time.'

Dunne read aloud: 'Reede is saying he woke up in some hedges near Armagh, sore and fragile, after this *carjacking*.'

'If fragile is a word that can be used in reference to Shane Reede,' I said.

Dunne squinted at the page: 'Reede was well aware we wanted to speak to him.'

I explained that Shane had said that when he stumbled to a service station at six o'clock that morning, he had every intention of phoning the PSNI but instead he had phoned Dorrian. Dorrian had driven down to collect him and brought him not to the station or to his own home but straight to Zara's. Then Dorrian had driven on to the garage, and the time we saw Shane was the first opportunity we had to.

'Do we have a description on the carjackers?'

'Two of them. Reede said they were both in their early twenties. One had blond hair and a goatee beard, and the second was small and dark, with a line shaved into his right eyebrow.'

'A goatee beard,' Dunne said with a bemused look on his face. 'Do people still wear those?'

'I don't know.'

'I suppose he had to say something. And what about the carjackers, what were they wearing?'

'Shane can't remember. Jeans, he thinks. But it was the blond one who, when Shane sat alone at the lights, pulled the door open and tried to grab Shane. He was wearing a black North Face coat. Shane put up a struggle, hence the bruises, and then the second one was in the passenger seat, pulling on the handbrake and shoving Shane towards the blond man. Shane told them he had no money, and tried to get his hand into his back pocket to give them the money that he did have, which was about ten quid sterling and forty euros. Then they beat him up. Left him unconscious.'

'A strong-looking fella like that, unconscious? Okay, Sloane,' he said. 'We'll play along, if that's what Reede wants.'

Chapter 23

We were tucked into a corner of St George's Market that buzzing late afternoon, at a little makeshift pack-up-by-dinnertime tea room, similar to the one that Father liked on the Lisburn Road, but closer to me and safer; it meant I didn't have to go near that part of town where Jason might be fetching coffee before going back to his home office.

Father looked out of place here; everything was too busy and fussy for him.

'What are you having?' he asked me.

'Focaccia,' I said. All I had the stomach for was bread.

'Focaccia's the kind of thing your mother liked,' he said, sag-lipped. He had a habit of speaking of Mother as if she were dead and not just half a mile away, also near the Lisburn Road, being cared for by private nursing staff.

There was nothing as plain as an Ulster fry on the menu but somehow Father had managed to wrangle one out of the young waitress who sent a finger-drumming rolled-sleeved waiter to the Centra for the specific ingredients.

'Gus is on a one-way path to nowhere,' Father started while we waited.

Coral's fourteen-year-old son had been acting out.

'Gus is alright,' I said.

Father looked at me in astonishment. 'Why would you of all people say that?'

'Why *of all people*?'

'He's breaking the law.'

'Och, Daddy, he was caught smoking. We all did it.'

'I didn't, not once, and everybody else puffing their heads off.'

'I know.' I tore a bit of the bread off with my teeth and began to chew.

'I never even tried it,' Father said.

'But you're stronger than most,' I said, tucking the food inside one cheek.

He skimmed me with a cold eye. 'Smartness doesn't suit you, Harriet.'

Father held his cup up, embarrassed that it was so dainty he had to hold his pinkie out. 'We paid a lot for your educations,' he said.

'Do you regret it?'

'Not. A. Penny.'

'Good,' I murmured.

'There are people who had an opinion about your mother and I giving five children a private school education. They were the ones who smoked – you could be certain of it every time. People are happy to spend money poisoning themselves but they look down their noses at you for investing in your children's future. They're always the very same people who are running around, shouting for the whole world to hear, if and when their own children get accepted into university. They don't mind paying out then because then they can gloat … complain and gloat at the same time.'

He drank the balance of his tea, squeezed the porcelain handle. He was a different man, from all those self-assured years in the RUC; this other version wondering when his retirement was going to come into play.

'People should speak up more for what they believe in,' Father said. 'People should do what they want, and make sure that when they are saying yes they are not saying no to themselves.'

'I know that. You and Mummy always taught me that.'

I thought about Sorcha Seton and how she had been unable to speak up. I remembered her saying she suspected there was something up with Donald Guy, but a mix of worrying about offending him and the kind of things he would say back to her, and her underlying pity for him stopped her from speaking out. Her discomfort about saying something like *I'm going to use another babysitter* ended with her boy Rhys being molested time after time.

'What's Coral going to do about Gus?' Father asked. 'If she'd listen to me she'd take him to the police station and get him talked to. You and I he wouldn't listen to. He needs a scare from a stranger.'

'Bit extreme,' I said. 'Look, I hardly see Coral these days. It'd seem rude … coming from me.'

It was Gus turning out like Brooks was what he was really afraid of. Were cigarettes a gateway to heroin?

'Charlotte couldn't come with us today because Timothy has an appointment about his hips,' Father said as he mopped egg yolk up with a soldier of soda farl and pasted the leftovers into the cup of a mushroom.

'I'll have to call her.'

I took advantage of the lull in the conversation to finish my lunch.

Father left a twenty beside our plates. We walked alongside knick-knack stands and baby-grows emblazoned with corny and often sectarian logos.

'Ridiculous,' Father muttered, 'putting your family values on your child's clothing.'

I rolled my eyes. 'Next time, *you* choose the place, Daddy,' I said.

We walked to my apartment, where I buzzed him into the visitors' car park to fetch his car. He climbed in.

'I still think Monaghan was your best bet. I think that's where the boy is. I think it's obvious now, the outcome,' he said.

But I didn't want to hear it. I closed his door and walked off.

Chapter 24

I limbered up that evening, ran over Queen's Bridge against the traffic and back towards my apartment. Working off my anger. Thinking, running, processing.

At the station the plates were being checked on Shane's jeep. No doubt it had been re-sprayed and was over the water already, or burnt out. Sometimes vehicles showed up in Housing Executive grounds that had unused storage. Owners in the Armagh area were asked to check their garages. I had asked Shane if he'd reported the jeep stolen. He told me he hadn't. What was the point? It had no tax, no insurance.

As I ran, I thought of Shane's brittle scalloped fingernails and his hands, one on top of the other, quivering slightly on the edge of the table. His leg had jiggled, knocking against the table. His nerves must be shot.

When we took Shane back to his house in Brandon Terrace, he had lifted his mobile phone from the kitchen counter and looked at Linskey and I as if to say, *Here it is. I told you.* He pressed the screen.

'Battery's dead,' he'd said and rummaged for a charger. 'River,' he added.

'What's that, Shane?' I asked.

'River … he always moves my charger – transports everything.'

Did he transport his coat too? I wanted to ask. We had questioned Shane about the coat again in the interview room. Unsurprisingly he knew nothing.

Shane's kitchen had smelled clean, clean but metallic. The windows had been on the latch for days. It was cold as a tomb.

'Are you renting here?' Linskey asked.

'Yep,' Shane said, still palming his mobile. He gave up looking for the charger, perhaps thinking it was for the best that he couldn't turn his phone on.

Thinking about Shane and his mobile made me wonder about his mother. How had Margaret McGuire let him know she was unwell?

We went into his living room while he went upstairs to get changed for the station. An overhead light doubled as a fan and had a chain hanging from it. The room was scattered with toys – Ben 10, Power Rangers, mainly little figures. Having nephews who were about ten years old I knew they were toys for older boys, not the kind of things River might have been into. Shane had probably got them cheap from a charity shop for his weekend home. There was the comic his neighbour saw him buy in the shop: *The Simpsons*, a new issue. Six DVDs were stacked by the TV.

'Shane, don't do anything with those clothes,' Linskey shouted. 'Remember, there may be DNA of the carjackers on them. If they're in the database—'

'I don't care about the car,' he shouted down the stairs, cutting Linskey off.

It's easy not to care about something when it isn't yours, I thought. Linskey raised her eyebrows, then cocked her head to listen out for anything more he might want to say.

'Still, we need to take them,' she said.

'Finding River is the main thing now,' Shane said, walking into the room. 'That, and being there for Zee.' The same pet name Raymond had for Zara.

For three days River had been the main thing, the only thing we cared about, even though he wasn't ours. Shane and Zara seemed too calm, but grief – and it was grief, in a way, because they were both anticipating the possibility of it – it worked on people differently. For Zara, I could tell that it had outdistanced her.

Then Shane escorted us to the front door to say goodbye. His black bin was the only one in the street. He gave us a nod, opened the bin lid a crack and peered in, shut it and bounced it up the kerb to pull it through the house.

*

I ran home, got into the shower and thought about River. The poor little soul, stunted, and slipping, out there alone in the cold.

Linskey phoned me. It wasn't often she did that.

'Do you remember Brody Pottinger?' she asked. 'Remember Sandy Hammitt was talking about him and his mother Verda?'

'Yes …?'

'I was just about to go off shift when Brody walked in. I lingered at the desk because I thought I recognised him. I know it was ten years ago, but this fella had these big sad looking eyes that you just don't forget.'

'Okay,' I said as I squeezed the ends of my hair inside a towel.

'He said he wanted to report a case of long-term abuse. They got him a room, and I hung around to find out.'

'Was he there about Verda?'

'He was. So I said that I used to work on his case, that I have a vested interest.'

'You aren't leaving me, are you?'

'No,' Linskey said.

'What age is he now?'

'Seventeen. He's saying his mother hid him in the roofspace, that she abused him for years.'

'Did he say why she did it?'

'Liked the attention.'

'Christ!' I said. 'We do everything in our power to get a child back with their parents but we can't help what happens afterwards.'

'Don't say that,' replied Linskey.

I thought about Brody Pottinger, Sandy Hammitt and his interest in true crime. I thought about the fact that his information was on the money. That night, it felt to me that Sandy Hammitt must have known the case was about to be reopened. I intended to ask if I could work on Brody's case, once we got River back. And we would get River back – I was adamant we would.

What I wanted to do was to look into Verda Dolan to see if I could see anything of her in Zara. I wanted to see if she had cried like Zara, if Brody's mother had a history of tying the boy up in his room too.

Chapter 25

The next morning Markus Gourley, the video analyst, looked at multiple screens in front of him, his glasses on top of his head. He pointed at one screen, like a black-and-white blinking eyeball.

'This is us here,' he said. He took off his glasses and swung them by the leg, put the end in his mouth. 'And there's Donald, standing there.' He zoomed in so we could see better.

The picture was blurred and grainy, but I saw the innards of the warehouse, the outline of a man in a dark fleece counting items on a shelf, writing something down on a piece of what looked like cardboard.

'He's there one minute,' said Markus, 'then the whole rest of the shift – from twelve o'clock till four – he's gone.'

My skin crept. The thought of River abducted by a paedophile. I hadn't truly believed it until now.

'So he did leave work?' I asked.

''Fraid so,' said Markus. He put his glasses down on the end of his nose and removed the video tape from the player. 'Now you can get the bastard lifted,' he said, hiking his thumb at the door.

*

I was prepping paperwork, sorting through notes, when the woman who lived next door to Zara phoned the station, asking for me directly. Vanessa Bermingham – Ness, as Raymond had called her – wanted to come in to talk. I tried to find out from Ness what she wanted without the need for a meet. We had this information on Donald Guy and we needed to speak to him as a priority, find out where he had been.

Ness was coming in at nine in the morning. She couldn't talk at the house, which made me think maybe she had something important for us, something that Zara hadn't been told about. Could it have been about Raymond's death? It seemed straight forward, but perhaps his wheezing like a bicycle pump, his general ill health, was throwing Linskey and I off the scent of a crime. Since I had turned thirty-seven, forty-five seemed youthful, relatively speaking, but technically Raymond was middle-aged.

I got the impression that even as a boy he would have been a placatory character, the polar opposite of River's personality, by all accounts. How would a man like Raymond have kept up with the boy? And Zara, too, afraid to take River out in case she ended up getting into an argument with someone over his behaviour. You couldn't be a hermit and be a good parent, surely. But Zara was tough, although she gave off a vibe that a softer centre was in there, underneath it all.

Ness entered the room, a short woman with soft jowls and a too-small mouth, incessantly tucking her titanium locks behind one ear. She wore a camel-coloured twinset teamed with black trousers; on her feet were unbranded white trainers.

First off, she told us about a car she had seen driving around.

'I've already given a witness statement to Sergeant Simon and Constable Higgins,' she said, 'and I didn't remember anything significant in the first lot of hours after River's disappearance, but now things are coming back to me. They said, if you remember anything …'

'What kind of things, Ness?'

'This car, it would drive around after midnight. I'd thought nothing of it until yesterday.'

'What type of car was it?'

'I have no idea. A small car.'

'What colour?'

'I couldn't tell you. Dark-coloured.'

'Did you take down the number plate?'

'No.'

'Has it driven about since River went missing?' I asked.

'No. Isn't that strange?' She drew in a sharp breath. It turned out that she did this after every statement made that she agreed with, even when she had made the statement herself. It was highly irritating and enough to put us off talking to her for long.

'Is it possible that it was someone visiting or someone who lives further down the road?' I asked her.

Ness drew her lips tight then she slowly relaxed them, exposing tea-stained teeth. I knew that she sat watching out of her window every night. She probably knew everyone's business.

'There's nowhere to go,' she told us. 'Anywhere else you can get to directly some other way. This car, it usually slows down outside Zara and Raymond's, then does a turn and heads back out.'

'When was the last time you saw the car?'

'The start of last week – Monday, a week ago.'

Linskey took notes. 'That's helpful. Many thanks for coming in,' she said.

Ness drew another breath. She wasn't ready to leave just yet. She stayed where she was, adding that a parcel came for her address and that she opened it before realising her mistake.

'It was something perverted,' she said, her eyes all big. 'It was a video, for sex. It was for Raymond.' Ness creased her face at us, wanting reassurance that we knew what she was talking about without her having to describe it. 'A porn film.' *Sharp breath.*

'Did you give him the parcel?' I asked.

'No, it would have been obvious that I'd seen it. It was opened – DVDs of girls – and you know what, they were wee-weeing on each other.' She picked at her eyelashes.

I thought about Ness watching it out of curiosity.

'Then there's this man,' she said, when she saw we weren't interested in this information about Raymond. 'He wears a hoodie, walks his dog by the house at five in the morning, goes to the bottom of the street and turns.' Another sharp little breath.

'Can you tell us any more about him? What height is he?'

'Average height for a man.'

'His build.'

'He's a chunky bug. Stocky.'

'The dog?'

'Sorry, you must think I'm of no use,' Ness said.

Linskey was quick to reassure her that she was far from useless.

'The dog left a big pockle of dirt in my front garden once. That's why I started watching out, in case the man lets his dog do its business there to annoy me 'cus I was banging the bedroom window at him. And then you wonder if you should have made such a fuss. I was a bit scared then, the way he looked up at me.'

'Did you see his face?'

'A bit. His hood was up, sure. Always is.'

I got the feeling we weren't giving Ness what she needed, which was attention. But who would know how to expose a family better than the person who lives next door?

'Ness, is it true that River is a bit of a climber? Has he ever climbed into your trees, for instance?' I knew I was being as subtle as a blade. Linskey threw me a look as if to say it was a waste of time asking.

'He is.' Ness nodded. 'Zara and I had words often enough about it. He snapped a bough, you see. What happened was, River was messing all the neighbours about – not intentionally but just boisterous. If you told him off he'd give you the doe eyes. It takes a community to raise a child, I told Zara when she came to my door, nearly having a nervous breakdown. She's overprotective. All I said to him was "Ach, come on River, you're going to fall and hurt yourself or break something." Zara was screaming, roaring she was, that if my cat so much as looked at her wrong she'd complain to the council about him.' Ness sighed.

'What does that matter now?' she asked. 'Zara just couldn't grasp that I was trying to look after my property, same as anyone would. But she must think I'm soft that she comes to my door and shouts at me. Everyone in the street has had issue with River and she never went near any of them. Zara knows they wouldn't stand for it, whereas I, for a good year, was at her beck and call. I'd get her groceries, get Raymond his lotto done, even though she's not working. All she does is a breastfeeding class in the community centre and that's the height of it. But him and her not working, missy got too comfortable.

'Then my son came around one day and saw everything I was doing for them, and me not well myself. He told me they were a bunch of entitled moochers and made me promise to stop. So if she asked me to get Raymond his lotto I was to say no. After that, after I stopped being their skivvy, Zara turned on me, dirty looks and all, and then the time River was in the tree, when I told him to get down, she went biccies. So we never spoke again ... until Monday. Once River went missing it was a different story. I went to get them some shopping. I just hope she doesn't expect it from me all the time. I wouldn't really mind but – don't think poorly of me – it's just that she wouldn't give you the steam off her piss in return. I'd do anything for anybody who'd show the same compassion back. Zara'd give you nothing – not a hello, not an ounce of patience. She's what you'd call a user. Anyone with a bit of humanity goes into their house and anyone with a scrap of sense doesn't make a habit of it.'

'What about the other neighbours?' I asked. 'We heard there was an incident involving a neighbour putting their hands on the boy.'

'That's right,' said Ness. 'River ruined the ornaments in Ian's front yard. He had the poor child by the scruff. Zara went mad at that, right enough, but I couldn't blame her – he's a horrible, horrible, little man. Small man syndrome, that's what he has. All the kids hate him. But River kept running away. Zara told me once, when I was delivering their lotto tickets, that she'd get these calls to the door and it would be someone or other returning the child to her and she didn't even know he'd gone. River would wait until Zara was loading laundry or washing the dishes and then he'd let himself out. And I remember, when I used to be in there after getting them shopping, when someone kept phoning and hanging up and they both seemed very fidgety. Raymond and Zara.'

Chapter 26

Donald Guy twirled a ring on his little finger; it was silver, broad and flat. Then he rested his hands on the table. He stared through them, almost looking like he was praying.

'Donald,' said Linskey, 'where were you on Monday between the hours of midday and four p.m.?'

He smiled out of the corner of his mouth. 'At work,' he said, sitting up and wiping his palms along his trousers.

'We need your cooperation, Mr Guy,' I said. 'Why did you leave work in the middle of your shift?'

'I didn't,' he said, 'not at all.'

'Not even to get lunch?'

'Not even to get lunch.'

His eyes flitted from Linskey to me and back again. Donald was different from the last time he had been in this room with DI Amy Campbell and me. He didn't seem to give a damn any more. His mother was dead; she had died at the end of his court case. Way back then he was ashamed for her sake, but now she was gone he didn't care what people thought of him. He wasn't asking me for my opinion any more. There was no shame behind his eyes. Maybe that was a good thing. Maybe it meant he hadn't touched River.

'Where did you get lunch then, Mr Guy?'

'In the staff room.'

Though there wasn't a CCTV camera in the lunchroom, Markus had watched each tape Alice had given us and Donald was notably missing for half of the day. But this wasn't working, so I let Donald know that we didn't believe him.

'You weren't at work. So where were you?' I asked.

He flapped his hands at me. 'I'm the target here?' he said. 'Why aren't you out looking for the boy instead of wasting time here with me. I told you, I don't have those urges any more.'

He was so matter-of-fact. *Urges*, he said, like he was talking about hunger pangs.

Something was irritating his skin. He kept scratching his hands until they were red with raised white bumps, licking his fingers to soothe the skin. I felt sick just looking at him. The truth was that I did judge him. I hated him almost more than I hated anyone. Almost. He was a monster. A vile everyday monster.

I went quiet and looked at Linskey. She could deal with him.

'Your boss Alice seems to like you,' she said to him. 'Are you two friends?'

'She's as much my friend as she's yours.'

'Donald, the facts are that we have spoken to your place of work and they have given us their CCTV footage,' Linskey said. 'And the fact is, you did start work at eight a.m., as you normally do. But then you disappear and are not seen again, even though your shift isn't over until four p.m. Your boss said you work mainly in the warehouse but there's no sign of you on the tapes. So where did you go?'

'Those are not the facts,' he said. 'Those are not facts at all.'

*

There was a baby doll on a corner chair in Zara's house; it was wrapped in swaddling. Its opened eyes were the most peculiar colour in the tangerine glow of the midday sun that spilled in through the window. It wasn't a dressing-up doll, a clicky-eyed toy, but a doughy, chubby wee thing, blotchy, with milk spots and an irregular hairline. It was more lifelike than any doll a parent would buy for a child, especially a four-year-old. I'd heard about strange women like Zara who bought those type of things.

'Please talk some sense into Shane, will you?' Zara said. 'I think he has pneumonia. He won't go to the hospital. I don't want another person dying on me.'

I ignored her. I couldn't care less about Shane's health.

'Does River sleep with this doll?' I asked, running my hand over its head. I swore I could feel a soft spot. It was almost warm; it seemed to reverberate.

'No.' Zara folded her arms.

'The house is very tidy, considering you have a four-year-old,' I said as if it had just occurred to me.

'Thank you,' Zara said, the words scaling upwards in question. 'Well, when River went with Shane I tidied. Believe me, it's the only time it isn't like a bomb site.'

Zara sighed. She seemed to be struggling to adjust to the fact that she was now being asked things instead of being comforted and reassured. There was a tidal change in the atmosphere as if we were no longer a help to each other. When cases get to that stage there is little anyone can do about it.

'By the time he got back on Sunday night,' said Zara, 'it was straight into bed for River, and for Raymond. He hadn't been feeling well either.' She rubbed her forehead with her wrist.

'And neither had you,' I said.

'Maybe it was a bug or something.'

It felt like I had it too, but it was autumn, the season for sickness, for viruses. 'He slept well on Sunday night?' I asked.

'Who?' Zara uprooted herself from the sofa, walked to the mantelpiece and straightened River's photo. 'Who are you on about now?' she muttered.

I couldn't tell if Linskey had caught Zara's last remark. Her face was inscrutable.

'River. Did River sleep okay?'

'Certainly.'

'But he didn't always?'

'When he was a baby he didn't sleep. That's true,' said Zara.

'Was he ever locked in his room?'

Zara pouted. 'Detective Sloane, I take it you don't have any children.'

'That's right,' I said.

Zara looked relaxed. Perhaps it was medication of some sort. Maybe she had been dipping into Raymond's cupboard of potions.

'The dressing-gown belt is an alarm of sorts,' Zara said. 'It's tied loosely around the door handle, and when River comes out of his room in the morning, he pushes it off himself. It makes a bang. Why am I even explaining this? It wasn't used all the time. If I had've used it on Sunday night, I'd have heard River leave his room. We wouldn't be here, doing this. He'd be here. So just stop.'

Linskey stepped in, her eyes on the doll but the words aimed directly at Zara. 'Mrs Reede, did you ... or Raymond ... ever give River anything to help him sleep?'

'What like?' Her voice was pitched high.

'We've been talking to your doctor. We know that you asked for something to help River sleep, but with his epilepsy medication—'

'Those were febrile convulsions. They can *lead* to epilepsy. I'm not convinced,' she said.

'But the doctor must have been or else she wouldn't have prescribed them,' I said as gently as I could.

'And?'

'Mrs Reede, did you ever give River part of one of Raymond's sleeping pills?' Linskey asked, her words threading a step back to Raymond and his anecdote about the neighbour putting her cats on birth control.

'No, I did not indeed!'

'And Raymond didn't either?'

'I don't have to listen to this,' said Zara, her face tightening.

I looked at the doll and thought about how the kitchen and Zara's bedroom were an expression of her parenting ethos – the star charts, the books. There was no expression of the child himself, only his photo. It was like a grandmother's house, not his own home. There were no loose ends, no green coat on the rack, no Lego bricks under the sofa. Shane's home, in truth, was homelier. Here, all evidence of River seemed to have been scrubbed, his climbing, his running, erased.

Zara didn't know that at the station was the man we suspected of abducting her son. We couldn't say that at that point; we only tried to reassure her that a local man was helping them with investigations, and she was easily reassured, which was weird in itself, but maybe she was just naïve. She got angriest when we were taking her PC.

'So I'm a suspect now?' she asked.

Half of her was in shadow, a pyramid of light settling on the empty patch of sofa leather to her right where Raymond would have sat.

Chapter 27

I'd known Amy Campbell for a long time. We went to grammar school together, and at one point, before Jason came along, I was dating her eldest brother. She came from Short Strand originally. She had cinnamon-coloured hair that she wore in a huge bun structured around a hair doughnut, and she always wore fancy impractical shoes, no matter the workload. That day, she teetered about in heels that looked like something from Ali Baba: all golds, blues and glitter.

Campbell shuffled her papers. 'You can't keep Donald Guy,' she said.

'What can we do, then?' I asked her. 'He left work for four hours.'

'I know. You said on the phone. Look, Harry, I'm worried that there'll be a vigilante attack on him if this gets out, if there's an arrest. We have someone checking in on him regularly at home.'

'How often is *regular*?'

'The required amount, the convenient amount.'

They weren't the same thing.

'Okay,' I said, 'we need Donald to stay away from work. I don't think they'd have him back now anyway. We need to find out where he really was on Monday afternoon.'

Campbell shook her head; the bun didn't move. 'Alright, we'll get some officers out to Donald's place of work to ask when they last saw him.'

'We have the footage. He wasn't there.'

'I get your point, but I have to make sure it's safe for him.'

'What about safe for kids like River Reede?' I ripped the boy's photo off the board and waved it in front of her.

'My job is to look after people like Donald. I have a duty of care to him as an individual.'

'Well then I pity you.'

'Harry, I'm only doing my job. Like you are.'

'No, not like me. You're not his solicitor. You don't need to stick up for him.'

'I just know him now, and I don't think Donald would do it again. He's been proactive in changing.'

'You *think* he wouldn't do it again, but you don't know for sure.'

I pinned River back on the board. He smiled at me.

I felt as if I'd let the child down.

Chapter 28

'Donald's prints don't match either of the adult fingermarks on River's coat,' Higgins said as he sat at his desk eating takeaway for a late lunch.

'That doesn't rule him out,' I said. 'You never told us what the woman living behind Zara and Raymond said. Did River climb into her garden?'

'Ah, no. About that... we concentrated on Witham Street instead.'

Linskey slammed her coke bottle down on the table. 'I specifically told you, days ago, to go to the house that backs on to the Reedes'.'

'You told me, did you?' Higgins snarled.

'It helps to give us the bigger picture,' I said.

Higgins sat back in his seat and ran his fingers through his hair. 'We went round the nearby streets asking people if they'd seen anything,' he said.

'But we needed you to speak to that specific woman,' Linskey said loudly, not caring who heard.

'Raymond was nailing up the fence between them the morning the investigation started,' I explained.

Simon was nodding. He glanced at Higgins. Their partnership was so one-sided it was going to topple at any minute. I felt sorry for Fergus Simon, paired with this waster.

'We needed her spoken to, Simon,' I said. 'The woman at the back of River's house.'

'I know that,' he said. He looked exasperated.

'Maybe you should have done it then,' said Higgins.

'Obviously I should have,' said Simon.

'Not you,' said Higgins. 'The Nolan Sisters here. Youse should have done it if you're that concerned.'

'The Nolan Sisters?' I repeated.

Higgins laughed.

'He means us,' said Linskey. 'Cheeky sod.'

'They were a girl band in the seventies,' explained Simon.

'Christ, Carl,' I said to Higgins, 'even your insults are retro.' He clapped his hands in delight that he had got a begrudging laugh. 'And anyway, we've been busy, flitting about the country. Can't you be trusted to do anything?'

'Obviously not, so just do it yourself,' Higgins said. He got up and left just as Chief Dunne came in.

Linskey stood up. 'Chief, I want little drummer boy pulled off this case.'

*

In the end we did call ourselves to see the woman in Ribble Street.

'We're here to ask you a few questions about the young boy at the back of you who went missing on Monday,' I said as I stood on her doorstep.

'Oh, c'mon on in.' She was staring at our feet, ushering us in quickly with a wave of her hand.

The hall was long and ran the length of the house; it was an old house and deceptively big from the outside.

'Watch there, loves,' she said, closing the door behind us as two dogs rushed out of the living room.

'Hello,' said Linskey, crouching to pet them.

So she had two *small* dogs. It wasn't what I was expecting from Raymond's mention that River had no fear of the dogs. These weren't the type that would invoke fear in anyone, except spaniels.

'You have a dog?' the woman asked Linskey. She spoke from the side of her mouth; it was hard to make her out.

'No,' said Linskey, 'I work too long hours. Someday, maybe. When I'm retired.'

'Do you have kids?' the woman asked.

'Two,' Linskey said.

'People don't have dogs cos they're too much work,' she said looking into my eyes. 'But yet they have kids and they're more work.' She laughed heartily to herself, so convinced she was funny that it would have been impolite not to at least smile; so I did. 'But these two are like babies, I s'pose. One gets jealous of the other. What is it you want to see, the garden?'

'Yes, please,' I said.

The woman's name was Lila Smith. She was in her fifties, short – little more than five feet tall – and had her hair cropped in a blonde bob. She had lived in the same house for fourteen years, she told us.

She led us into the garden. It was divided in two; the back half was grass and slightly elevated, a raised flowerbed, the other part nearest the house was dull, grey concrete. From where we were standing we could see Zara in her kitchen at the sink. If she looked around she would see us. But she didn't. And there was the hole in the fence, the part that Raymond repaired.

'The man who lives there was fixing the fence when we called on Monday,' I commented.

'Yes, drubbing away rightly,' she said. I saw that one side of her face was paralysed.

'Did the boy ever climb through into your garden?' I asked her.

'No,' she said, shaking her head. 'Just woulda put his hand through to pet the dogs. His dad woulda told me to chase him and not let him, in case he got bit. But they'd never do anything to anybody. More chance he'd hurt them.' I noticed Lila had no trees, nor a shed or a garage.

'And he'd never have hidden in your garden or anywhere?' I asked.

Lila shook her head.

Back at her front door I noticed the car outside her house was a Volvo. 'Has anyone spoken to you about the case already?' I asked.

Lila put the dogs in the living room and stood in the doorway. 'Yes,' she said, 'I went into the station to tell the officer, a good-looking young man, Higgins, to tell him I had been in the park at Shaw's Bridge and hadn't seen anything. I can't remember seeing anybody there. It was freezing. No one was about.'

'You're the woman in the park!' Linskey said as it dawned on her.

'Yes, is that not what this is about?'

'We called with you as a neighbour.'

'Didn't you tell Constable Higgins that you're a neighbour?' I asked.

'No, I didn't think to. I've never even walked down Witham Street since those new houses were built. Sorry, I'm not a good person to ask. I didn't see a coat. I was only asked about that.'

'The park is quite a distance from your home. Why did you go there, instead of walking around here?'

'The kids round here are too cheeky. When you're trying to walk here they say stuff to you and video you on their phones. They ask me why I talk funny. They aren't like that at

Shaw's Bridge. Up there it's a good long walk, and people ring their bells on their bikes when they go past so you can step out of the way. No one annoys you, and sometimes there are people out on the water. Not now, of course – it's too cold. Other times there are families. The kids don't go to the playground unless they have a parent with them, and they're playing like good children do. There's nowhere for kids to play here, so they congregate outside of here cos I'm on the corner. Cos I'm a woman living alone, they mess me around.'

'But there's a park through there,' I said, pointing towards the end of the street.

'Aye, and the big kids race through there on scramblers and terrify the wee ones. Or they put the wee ones on their knees and race, no helmets on their heads and they go down the greenway. That lovely park they built, that community centre and that's what they do! If you say anything they tell you to eff off.'

'Do you know River?' asked Linskey. 'Would you know him if you saw him?'

'I would,' Lila said, turning when her dogs started scratching the living room door.

Chapter 29

Zara's PC was bulky and aged and she had not deleted the internet searches that would incriminate her.

How to love your child more.

She would have loved to think of herself as a perfect woman, I thought, a mum who breastfed a preschool child and had a disabled older partner, a wonderful stay-at-home mother who denied her child's ADHD and epilepsy. Yet here she was searching for natural cures for both on the internet, scouring the World Wide Web for salves to cure the mess of her life.

Linskey winced at the screen. 'Poor girl,' she said, scrolling down.

'Poor River,' I said. Now it was there for us to see that Zara was having difficulty loving him. 'So that's what the books are for.'

'Books can't help you in that respect,' said Linskey.

'But a website can?'

'Maybe she had postnatal depression.'

'I don't know ... this search was last year. He would have been three.'

There was all the perfect mum stuff too: star charts, how-tos, researching the ideal nursery, going on Netmums to ask advice and complain about Olivia Sands, the leader at Strandtown Preschool, when River fell from the climbing frame there.

I had the perfect mother: glamorous – she knew colour like no one else – successful, allowed us kids their freedom. That's how I knew Zara wasn't it. And another thing, I found it repulsive when people cared too much what other people thought.

I fetched a glass of water and looked out at the station car park. The Chief was coming in from a meeting. He locked his car, the headlights of oncoming cars sidling under the car parked beside his, light sliding out from the shadows. It was almost as if he could feel my eyes on him. He looked at the window and quickly walked inside. Higgins wasn't far behind him.

'I think you owe me an apology,' Higgins said so Chief Dunne could hear.

'What in the world for?' I asked.

The Chief went into his office, disinterested.

'For claiming that I didn't speak to that woman when I did,' said Higgins.

'Unwittingly,' I said. 'You spoke to Lila Smith *unwittingly*.'

'I spoke to her. You can't claim I didn't.'

'Okay, Higgins.'

'I'm waiting for it. Where's that apology you have for me?'

'You'll have to wait a bit longer.'

'No, Sloane, I want you to acknowledge that you and Linskey were harassing me for not talking to her, when I did.'

'That was a coincidence, Liam,' said Linskey, her eyes still on the screen.

'Liam?' asked Higgins.

'Liam Gallagher.'

'No, Alan White, you mean. White was the drummer,' I said.

'I'm impressed,' he said.

'Don't be.'

'Too late now,' he said. 'Anyway, some cases hinge on coincidence. It's the universe solving the puzzle.'

'Well, we'll tell that to Zara and Shane shall we, that we'll just let the universe find their boy?'

'This is different,' he said. 'Obviously it is, but most things sort themselves out, I find, if you don't get yourself het up. Worrying is a waste of energy.'

'You're paid to waste energy,' I snapped.

'Nothing is ever a waste,' said Linskey. She hated to think of anything as a time wasted, even her twenty-year marriage. At least she got two kids from it. 'Look out the window and tell me what you see, Higgins,' she said.

'Fujitsu?'

'Beside it.'

'What?'

'The JobCentre.' She winked at him.

'Okay, do you see what's beside *it*?'

'What?' asked Linskey. She leaned on her desk and looked out. 'Nice!'

'What is it?' I asked.

'Funeral directors,' she said. 'What the fuck, Higgins!'

'Don't put words in my mouth,' he said.

'Stop it, children, please,' I said.

Linskey called me over. 'Harry, this should interest you. Someone's been doing their own investigation.'

There it was on the screen: *detective Sloane, detective inspector Harriet Sloane belfast.*

'She's onto you,' Linskey said and laughed.

Dunne walked in. 'Sloane, Linskey – so we have it back from the coroner's that Raymond's death was not a heart attack as suspected. We need to wait for toxicology now.' He turned his attention to Higgins. 'Aren't you supposed to be assisting Simon?'

Higgins gave me a salute as he left the room.

'He loves himself,' said Linskey. 'Thank God you didn't tell him what Lila Smith said about him being good-looking.'

'What's this?' Dunne asked.

'Oh, nothing,' I said.

'Chief, take a look at this,' said Linskey.

I felt myself redden when my face appeared on the screen. It was an article about a crackdown on drugs that I'd headed earlier in the year. There I was with my greens on, just for photo purposes, being quoted that I had no children of my own but I was adamant that other people's children would not be dragged into drugs, that dealers were a blight on our society.

I cringed when I read it. It had been written by some peckish journalist that the press office had sent my way. He'd casually asked me if I had kids, like that had anything to do with anything, then kept in my reply when I'd asked him not to. I also thought about my addict brother Brooks reading it. Was he the blight on our society? Was it any surprise he stayed in England, away from his ex-RUC Chief dad and DI sister, with a judge for a mother, a social worker sister, a minister brother, and Charlotte, our earth-mother sister who was probably the angriest of us all with our eldest brother.

'That's how Zara knew you have no kids,' Linskey said. Dunne was reading it over her shoulder. 'And get this – she looked this one up four times.' Linskey clicked a link.

There was my family, minus Brooks and Father, doing a charity relay marathon for the Huntington's Disease Association. It was before Timothy was born; after his birth, our family charity changed to the Buddy Bear Trust.

'You've got yourself quite the little superfan here,' the Chief said, breaking into a rare smile. 'Give me a shout if there's any more news. Right, enough surfing the web. Get back to work.'

'Yes, Chief,' I said. I sat at my computer and did my own search: *zara reede Belfast*.

And there she was: 'Mother Leaves Boy on Train'.

Chapter 30

When Jason and I got married, we lived in an apartment and we saved. What we were saving for I was never quite sure.

Jason's father was an architect too, and together with Alex, Jason's brother, the Lucie men had designed and built a place on the corner of Bawnmore Road and Osborne Gardens off the Lisburn Road. Alex and his wife Verity lived there. It was cream and red brick, and the windows were mere slits. Next door, an old house hidden by trees, like most in the avenue, had an apple tree that would drop its fruit onto their patio. We used to go round there for barbecues.

One time we gathered in the kitchen because it was getting chilly outside. We were in front of the TV that was anchored to the wall. Alex stood behind Verity, I remember, his hands on the puddle of her belly. Their new baby was in a Moses basket on the dining table, somewhere under all that netting.

Jason was watching him. He was mesmerised by him, even by the crying, those soft squawks that surely weren't stressful to its own doting parents. I know that was what he was thinking. But that cry stung my ears. Their toddler had run around excitedly outside, the yammer of him, like a tractor starting up. When he wasn't ticking over, he was stringing words into sentences that were truly Shakespearean. Jason, like all men, pretended he'd have all the time in the world for children. But with men, work always overrides childcare. As far as I was concerned, women are the same. I certainly wasn't prepared to shut work down for the formative years, like my mother had to.

I examined the TV screen, not sure what I was supposed to be looking at.

'Is it an iceberg?' I asked.

Verity smiled at me. 'Old Arctic ice,' she said.

Jason walked over and draped his arm over my shoulder so the four of us were standing in two teams, watching the ice go. 'Twenty-seven years of ice,' he said, 'melting in seconds.'

'What a waste,' I said.

'It's the wonder of nature,' Verity said, lifting the letter that had been resting on the counter, then stepping back into Alex's arms.

She gave the letter to me, keeping her eyes fixed on the screen. I held it up to the light. Alex had ended up frying everything in the kitchen when the gas ran out on the barbecue, and grease from the counter made transparent clouds and comets on the words on the paper.

'Oh, you've got the planning permission,' I said, running my eyes over the letter. 'What are you going to do with this house? Sell it?'

Lucie and Sons Architects were going to design a new home for them, a home for a growing family. Now they wanted more room – playrooms, a games room, a boys' room for a snooker table. Jason had showed me the designs when it was only a pipe dream.

'Um, I have some news too,' said Jason.

I turned to look at him, those pale lips, that white, white skin. The moon comes up the same colour as his skin. Verity turned too. I saw excitement doctor her face. The thing about being in your late twenties and married was that whenever either of you said you had news, you had to quickly follow up by stating *we're not pregnant*.

'Harry, Alex has offered us first dibs if we want to buy this house,' Jason said. He linked his index fingers under his chin, expecting me to be thrilled.

'Oh, we'll need to talk about it,' I said, my heart beating faster. The skin on my face chilled, my frozen smile too heavy to hold up.

Everyone was looking at me. I felt the weight of their frowns. I just knew Jason would start a whole thing on the short drive home. He would just expect me to bend and fit into his plans.

What happened to the house we were designing, I asked later? The only thing I could say to appease him was that we might outgrow Alex's house too, if we had kids. That would make him happy. But work was slack; he would start on plans. The thing was, I had a vision of an atrium, a big kitchen, a high-ceilinged drawing room like the house I had grown up in at Malone. That was the kind of space I wanted – height, space, room to grow, not big rooms meted out. I didn't want to be meted out.

When we married, I told Jason I didn't want kids. He kept trying to change my mind, making sure I heard him read his nephew a story, hogging the newborn as if that would persuade me, reminding me that the prep schools were right on our doorstep at Osborne. I felt like I was already forgotten, melting away from Jason.

Already gone.

Chapter 31

A year or so before River's disappearance – two months after he turned three – he was left on the train coming back from Bangor. A woman, the only other passenger in the carriage, arrived at a deserted Bridge End with River's hand in hers. Zara was not there waiting for him, so instead, the woman stayed on board and took him to Central Station where staff phoned the PSNI.

It was Inspector Seymour who brought River to Strandtown Police Station until eventually Zara came and retrieved him.

There were two news stories: the national story about the mother who got off the train and left the child there, eventually coming for him, tangled and threadbare; and the one in the local press, Zara's version, which was very different.

She said she got off the train at Sydenham and that River slipped her hand when the doors shut too fast. It had all happened before she could press the button to alert the driver. River was stuck on the train and Zara, on foot, ran to Bridge End. But, naturally, by the time she got there the train was long gone. She had no phone and there was nobody around. She was crying and walking along the carriageway when a man stopped his car; she explained what had happened. He gave her a lift to Central Station and said he would wait for her in the car park and bring her on to Great Victoria Street if needed.

There was an accompanying photo of Zara with her arms wrapped around River, her big eyes like a child's and River's thumb nuzzled into the palm of a hand she had resting across his chest. He had on that coat, the green puffa. It was September.

Linskey was still scouring Zara's internet history.

'Check her history from Monday, Diane,' I said. 'Did Zara look up if the coat had a hood like she said she did?'

'No,' said Linskey. 'There's been nothing searched regarding the coat.'

*

Shane had not been lying; someone had phoned him on the Sunday night. It was a number with a Monaghan area code. I dialled the number expecting a woman to answer, expecting Shane's mother, Margaret McGuire. But there was no answer at all – no dialling tone, just a dead line.

I asked a colleague to find out who the number was registered to and Linskey asked me to call out the number of the last person to have phoned Shane. She dialled it, spoke furtively, then with familiarity. When she hung up she turned to me: 'That was Cahal Cleary.'

Late afternoon, Detective Amy Campbell called me to her office. She had four screens running on her desk.

'Before you say a word,' she said. She held a chair out and I sat in it. She joined me, leaned forward and pressed pause. 'A few things to tell you. We went to Donald's place of work.'

'Okay,' I said, my stomach rumbling; I was holding out for dinner.

'The manager was there.'

'Alice?'

'The proper manager – Crispin Arthur. He was back.'

'That's right. Alice was the area manager.'

'Crispin was able to give us a roster, and there were four other members of staff working on Monday.'

'What did they say?'

'They all claim they had nothing to do with Donald all day, so they couldn't be sure.'

I smiled at this.

'Hold on, I'm not finished yet,' said Campbell. 'So we pushed them – they hadn't seen him at all? They all said they saw him clock on, then around ten a.m., then they saw him at the door with his coat on at lunchtime.'

'And there's no staffroom footage?'

'That's right. But for four members of staff, who all work in different departments, to have all seen Donald at the three exact same times seemed very suspicious.'

'Not really,' I said. 'Clock in, eight a.m. – tea break, ten a.m. – then lunch. Those are times their paths would cross, surely?'

'Or, like you, they're trying to bend the narrative to suit the end result.'

'In what way?'

'Would *you* like to find out that you work with someone with a conviction for sexual crimes against children?'

'Of course not.'

'Well, there you have it. Neither did they.'

'You seem to be assuming that they're ganging up on him, maybe to get him sacked.'

'It wouldn't be the first time.'

'He's still our lead suspect at this point,' I said.

'I beg to differ.' She pressed play; the time on all four screens said 19:00. 'These have all been synchronised,' she said. 'There's Donald, clearly visible in the warehouse.'

'He worked a split shift?'

'No, he didn't work a split shift, remember?'

At six p.m. on Monday, Linskey and I were at Donald's house. I watched the scene again, him lifting a box onto a trolley. This wasn't right. We were his alibi.

'Harry, look at screen one,' said Campbell. 'You can see this lady on the till serving a customer. Now look. She's in the warehouse, making her way to the staff room with her dinner in her hand. She says something to him and he laughs. Yet this woman claims she didn't see him, didn't speak to him, that he was gone by the time she came on for the one to nine shift.'

'So you need to speak to her.'

'Someone with a bit of video editing knowledge has framed Donald to get rid of him,' she said. 'One thing is very clear, there's real hatred for the man and I wouldn't want him going back there now after things have been said about him, especially by this Gary.'

'Gary was hanging about when we were there too. Alice said he was the one who told her about the conviction. He's the assistant manager. He was making out that Donald had abducted a child before.'

'Yes, his name has already cropped up,' said Campbell. 'We need to speak to Gary Pinnock. Seems like he might know who doctored these images.'

'You'd think Markus would have spotted this,' I said.

'That's why I went over it. Markus has a habit of just looking at the relevant timescale and not looking before or after it.'

'But what about during the night, before Donald started work?'

Campbell gave me a smile. 'How can he prove he was at home in bed and not abducting a child? It's not up to him to prove that he didn't,' she said. 'It's up to you to prove that he did.'

Chapter 32

I called Father on the way to Charlotte's. 'How's Mummy?' I asked.

'I didn't go today,' he said like he was proud of himself, as if Mother was something to be weaned off of.

I knew he shouldn't go every day, just as long as he did something better and didn't mope about. The only thing that alleviated my guilt was knowing that he was visiting her.

'I think you should go back to Monaghan,' Father said. 'Speak to Cleary again.'

'We're going to call him.'

'Harry, listen to me, he'll talk more freely in person.'

Father couldn't retire from the force completely and I suppose that was partly my fault – I told him too much; I called him every day. It gave him something to think about, but at times he tried to take over.

'Cahal isn't the problem,' I said, but I didn't want to get into the Donald situation, the possibility that there might be a network of perverts involved.

'I don't know,' he said, 'I think you're missing a valuable person there.'

'So when *are* you going to see Mummy?' I asked to get him off the subject of work.

'I'll go soon,' he said. 'What about you?'

'I won't get there this week what with this case,' I said, sounding like he used to.

'Don't forget what matters, Harry,' he said.

'Finding River Reede matters, Daddy.'

*

It was nine p.m. when I pulled into Mount Eden Road off Malone and pulled up at the double-faced white home of my sister. I liked going to her place at that time, when there were no L-plate drivers slicing up the road. It was a street for learners. If you weren't careful you'd get sandwiched between two of them, slowly perfecting their three-point turns and usually making many more points before they actually turned.

Charlotte was in the shower when I let myself in. David was unscrewing a bottle of wine in the kitchen while keeping an eye on the gravy. I was interrupting their monthly date night, every fourth Friday. Timothy went down to sleep at 7.30 p.m. in his own bed. Charlotte was yet to let him sleep over anywhere else; anyway, it was highly unlikely that David's mum would have him. The arrangement was mutually pleasing yet restrictive at the same time.

David gave me a glass of wine. He threw a tea towel over his shoulder, stepped backwards to tilt the pan so the oil formed a web. He fried some fish while a cheese-sprinkled baguette breathed under the grill. He may not have been a great father, at least not a bathing, nappy-changing, hands-on kind of one, but he was a good husband to Charlotte. He was a good, old-fashioned father, the kind there didn't seem to be any more.

Charlotte was bent this way and that. It was a relief at least to see that she had David, who although he wouldn't cook for the family and expected her to be a good housewife most of the time, was quite handy when it was date night or her birthday; he even baked cakes. This makes it sound as though she was lucky to have David, maker of meals, hunter-gatherer, but really, she had kept up her end of the bargain. Five babies later and she didn't look any different from when we were teenagers.

Charly and I may have been twins but we made sure there were differences. I had my hair long while hers was shoulder length; mine was chestnut brown while she had copper streaks in hers. She had facials, botoxed away the wrinkles; I barely wore make-up. She was proud to be the only mum at school who didn't wear shapeless grey clobber; I didn't give a toss what I wore so long as it was comfortable.

She came down the stairs perfumed and primped, the ends of her hair still damp. A pale blue shirt gaped at her chest and she wore a pair of washed out jeans and peep-toe stilettos; her toenails were painted pillar box red.

'Harry, come here a minute,' she said. She held out a silver necklace for me to do the clasp. 'We had a viewer.'

'Probably a time-waster,' David chirped.

Their home was on the market. Charlotte couldn't carry Timothy up to bed any more. They had talked about building an extension to give him a ground-floor bedroom, but they decided to explore the idea of moving house.

'When should you expect to hear if they like the house?' I asked.

Charlotte put on the monitor in Timothy's room; it could tell if he stopped breathing and would sound an alarm.

'The viewers were making all the right noises,' Charlotte said.

The doorbell chimed.

She took my wrists. 'Listen, we're having a friend coming round, a fella who David knows from five-a-side.'

David skipped past us for the door.

'No, Charly, I'm not staying,' I said.

'Oh come on,' she said. 'Don't be awkward.'

'I'm seeing someone,' I insisted. My boyfriend – known to her too as Paul, not Greg – must have seemed like an apparition.

'When you can't go to your sister's house with your boyfriend, you know he isn't worth it,' Charlotte said. 'Or he isn't real – one or the other.'

Standing behind David was a very real man. He was about three inches taller than David, so about six feet tall.

'This is Paul,' Charlotte said with a laugh. 'An actual Paul,' she whispered in my ear.

I felt myself blush as he reached out to shake my hand, the wiry cuff of his winter coat scuffing my wrist. Stupid me, thinking I could be included in date night without an ulterior motive. The only ulterior motive I'd considered was that Charlotte wanted to stick her nose in the River Reede case.

Paul stood there, smiling, scratching the light stubble on his jaw, looking as uncomfortable as I felt, only he obviously hadn't had this blind date sprung on him. He had had a chance to spruce himself up. I hadn't bothered with anything.

'Just in time, mate,' David said to Paul, hand on his arm. 'I'm just gonna plate up.' David walked through to the kitchen and gathered the cutlery. 'Charly, sweetheart, will you help set the table?'

They put on a show of married life, when I knew that too many times my sister battled the chores alone, or that David was on at her for buying a new outfit and trying to pass it off as old. He noticed; he noticed everything about his wife. I was only half jealous of this. At least they were still fighting the little things. That was married life, the fight.

We all sat down, David chattering away, trying to alleviate the awkwardness. We ate the fish he'd prepared; as good as it looked, it tasted metallic. David was talking about this woman who, at the last minute of having her windows fitted, said she had ordered brown UPVC and not white, because she thought the white was cheap-looking.

'I mean, she waited till the last one went in and then she spoke up,' he said.

'Didn't you have her order?' asked Charlotte.

'Yes, and she was absolutely right,' David said. 'We put the order through right, but there was a mix-up at the delivery end. When I arrived on-site to help the lads, I thought they'd already checked.'

'Did she kick up?' asked Paul.

I imagined he thought the story petty, being an anaesthetist, as Charlotte made sure to tell me straight away as if she was trying to sell me this stranger the way she was trying to sell her home. I certainly found David's work problems trivial in comparison with my week, but Paul looked interested enough. He was certainly polite.

'The woman was out looking at the windows loads, according to the lads who started the fitting,' David continued. 'But then she took me aside, said that it was wrong. They were all sealed in by that time.'

'Stupid woman,' said Charlotte. 'What did you tell her?'

'The woman said she had noticed but was embarrassed to say. In case she got anybody in trouble.'

Charlotte rolled her eyes. 'So then you're home late.'

David lifted the gravy boat. 'You want a double helping?' he asked, smiling.

'Stop it,' said Charlotte, but I could tell she was glad, now that their guest was looking at her inquisitively. 'I think David's trying to see if you recognise us,' she said to Paul. He sat slightly open mouthed. 'Gilberts' Gravy Granules? You want a second helping?' Charlotte asked, all animated. I noticed how Paul's face lit up when my sister spoke.

We had appeared in just the one advert when we were ten. Mother thought it would be cute, and the novelty of twins was a winner. Then there was an article in the paper about us being the kids of the Chief of police. That was the end of our acting careers.

'Yes, I know now,' Paul said. 'That advert was out again quite recently, wasn't it?'

I nodded. 'It was Gilberts' twenty-fifth anniversary,' I said.

That had been a nightmare, a couple of years earlier, being at Strandtown station and noticing the billboards on Pomona Street with my own face smiling back at me in innocent amusement.

Paul smiled at me. Charlotte was murmuring something to David to give Paul and I a chance to talk and pretended she wasn't paying attention to us.

'You work for the PSNI?' Paul asked.

He'd obviously had the low-down already. I could have killed Charlotte. I could be at home waiting for Greg to phone. Maybe he'd even call round if he could get away from work. We'd started to watch a boxset together and that was enough for me.

'Yes, I'm a Detective Inspector,' I told Paul.

'She's going to be promoted again soon,' Charlotte said, looking self-satisfied.

'Don't … It's not confirmed,' I said.

'You must feel great, getting promoted,' said Paul.

'You'd think,' I replied, 'but really you just get a whole new set of insecurities.'

David poured more wine; I asked him for soda water for mine. Paul was offering to drop me home if I wanted to drink. The subtext was obviously that I'd maybe invite him in. That was one of the things I hated about men my own age; if they had got to their mid-thirties and were still single, the desperation just reeked off them. They were always trying to close the deal. They'd often try to impress me with their jobs and their cars: 'I'm a partner, so I'm kind of tied into my career, and I'm driving a Boxster these days.'

But men talking to other men was what really took the biscuit, how they competed over jobs and family, who worked the hardest. Keepie-uppies. Greg was unaware of competition in that regard; it was part of my attraction to him. There wasn't a self-conscious bone in his body. He drove an average, typical car, worth far less than he could afford and he never boasted about his position.

Paul, on the other hand, was young, broad-shouldered, with beautiful blue eyes and blond hair. He caught me with a smile when I looked at him. But he'd managed to fit in that he drove a BMW and owned a kit car he'd put together himself.

'Harriet, Paul has just completed a triathlon,' David said.

'Really?' I asked. 'What made you do that?'

'I like to set myself physical targets. Plus it's something to talk about at dinner parties.'

I laughed, unimpressed. 'Well worth the effort then.'

After dinner, the men went out for a drive in the kit car.

'What's your deal with Paul?' Charlotte asked me. 'He's a honey and he likes *you*.'

'You better stop before you gush yourself into the ground, Charly,' I replied.

'Why didn't you tell them off for driving? They've both had a drink,' she said.

'I'm off-duty, thanks. And I'm not saying I don't like him. I'm just not interested.'

'You're never going to have a kid at this rate.'

What good was it doing Mother in Bethany Nursing Home that she had five kids? And there was Timothy upstairs, his whole family having to uproot to accommodate him.

'When are you next going to visit Mummy?' I asked Charlotte.

'I'm busy this week. Timothy's got the doctor's. Go by yourself,' she said. 'Mum'd love to see you. Doesn't always have to be us together.'

'Charly, have you ever not loved Timmy … because of his handicap?' I asked.

'Handicap? He's not Rory McIlroy!'

'I mean disability.'

She laughed. 'Fucken hell!'

'Sorry.'

She squinted at me. 'Sometimes. I suppose. In answer to your question. But most of the time I love him more because of it. Why do you ask anyway? Is it Mum? Is it the Huntington's? Coral's talking again about the rest of us getting tested.'

There was a fifty-fifty chance that we would inherit the disease. It was in a box I'd locked up and disowned. Charlotte hated to face it too.

'River Reede.'

'That little boy gone missing?' said Charlotte. 'You working on that?'

I nodded.

'His poor mum. I know her, you know. She runs a breastfeeding group at the community centre.'

'That's right.'

'Yeah, and she's a right bitch.'

'Seriously?'

'Oh yeah! When I couldn't feed Timothy, before we knew ... she was on at me to keep trying. At the time it made sense with the low muscle tone. Plus I don't sweat.'

'What's that got to do with it?'

'Sweat glands is all they are. Have you ever seen me sweat?'

Thinking back to when we were at school, Charly would get slightly pink around the cheeks after playing in netball tournaments. The other girls would grudgingly get into the shower afterwards but Charly would refuse. 'See, fresh as a daisy,' she'd say, lifting an arm. 'Don't sweat.'

'But you didn't breastfeed the others, did you?'

'Obviously not.'

'Was it obvious?'

'Believe me, H, you'd know,' she said. 'Breastfeeding mums make sure they tell you. No, that's a lie – they ask first if you breastfeed. If you don't, they look at you like you're a monster. If you say you did, they ask how long you did it for. Fuck, I even told someone I had when I hadn't. They asked how long and I said three months. She said, get this, *sometimes I wonder why I bothered doing it for a year when no one else bothers*.'

'Surely it's personal choice.'

'You'd think so, wouldn't you? Tell the midwives that. Even I caved with number five. Last chance to do things *right*. And it was fucken horrendous. Timothy had to go back into the hospital – UV lights, lost too much weight.'

'I remember. Where did you meet River's mum? Was it at the community centre?'

'She'd just had a baby too and was feeding him. Everyone else had a shawl over them or tried to be discrete, but she just sat there, titties out. And her husband! Now, he was a creep. The beast from the east I called him. Not to his face.'

'Certainly not.'

'He was taking photos, making them black and white, and she was posting them on Facebook. A few mums complained.'

'Which community centre?'

'In East Belfast, Connswater. Zara was really Breastapo. Smoked like a chimney, too.'

'You sound like Daddy.'

'Breastfeeding nicotine should be a crime,' Charlotte said. 'I get that breastfeeding is great if you eat and drink well. Some of the diets they were on would have made you sick. I remember, there was this girl, about nineteen, and she was admitted back to hospital. She had awful problems and was pumped full of meds. Nearly died. I bumped into her at Forestside a few months later. It turned out that this Reede woman made her feel awful about not breastfeeding her child, turned up at the hospital and told her that she had to keep breastfeeding. I mean, give the girl a break! The baby couldn't come into hospital with her mum, so the granny had the child. Well, didn't Zara go round claiming that Kassie told *her* to breastfeed the child, like a wet nurse. Zara sat in the child's bedroom, whapped her tit out and fed the child. They have this sense of superiority because they can breastfeed. It'd be like me boasting that I never had postnatal depression, you know?'

'So you never had postnatal depression?'

She laughed. 'Was that not obvious either? No, I had depression alright when Timothy was diagnosed, but that was circumstantial, grief-dependent.'

'Do you think Zara Reede suffered from postnatal depression?'

'Who knows. They were saying on the radio the other day that it can sometimes take four years to come out of PND. In some ways I was really lucky – five kids and no sign of depression. Mostly lucky.'

I thought about the last time I had been talking to Zara. She said she didn't want to leave the house, so a neighbour brought her breastmilk to the hospital for her. This was what she had been doing since River refused the breast a couple of years earlier – donating milk. The night before Raymond died the hospital had sent someone to collect it. They used it for preemies. Even with all her own problems going on, Zara still sat morning and night with that pump on her nipple like a martyr.

When David and Paul came back from their drive, we all had coffee. Paul was still looking at Charlotte as if he was infatuated with her. He seemed to have a Pavlovian response to her, watching any parts of her where her skin was exposed. I was sure David must have noticed; maybe he was proud. Paul was one of those men who saw himself as a family man, who wanted to have it all. Just like someone else I used to know.

Paul's reaction to Charly was more sexual than the way Jason used to look at his brother Alex and his sister-in-law when we were in their company, like there was the picture he wanted to be part of. It rendered him speechless and jealous as hell. Aren't we all jealous of something?

But I missed Alex and Verity. It had been a relief to get shot of the people who made my life worse, but what I hadn't realised was that I'd also have to get rid of some good people too. It was tough, but you had to cut them out too, you had to remove some of the good tissue to make sure you obliterated the cancer.

*

At three o'clock that morning I was a little girl again, dreaming about dropping down by Jamesy's side, angling my ankles away from his giant swollen hands. I wrenched Father's Barbour off his head; those eyes, which I expected to be milky, were technicolor blue, and fixed in a somehow familiar hooded gaze.

That night, Jamesy wasn't another variation of the same theme; he wasn't River, nor Timothy, nor Brooks. He was Mother, looking unfocused at a spot in the cooling dirty white sky behind me, her flesh goose-pimpled from all her years floating.

When I jolted awake, I turned the volume up on the telly and sat with my arms circled around my knees on the sofa. I allowed myself to think about Mother for once.

Despite Diane Linskey saying that no change was good, there was nothing good about it. Mother was seventy and had been in a nursing home for ten years already. Huntington's was taking its time with her, longer than anyone had thought, or wanted. And what was so bad about that? How awful did it sound that I wanted it to be over? If I sniffed the sadness hard enough it could go all the way into my lungs.

Mother had become forgetful. She scalded her legs with hot spud water one family Sunday dinner, Sunday dinners which incidentally stopped at the same time as her diagnosis. She was the thread that held the family together.

Father had gathered us in the drawing room of the old house: marble, fires and bread. We were seated loosely around the room. I remember noticing how the sofa seemed to be holding her up. Father was on the opposite end, already distancing himself from her. Then he told us about her Huntington's, his language laced with self-pity, though never again after. We're all allowed an off-day, I suppose.

And Mother, she looked utterly lost. Traceless.

Addam was telling us that God never did anything without a reason. I wondered what these mysterious reasons might be. How Addam could continue to defend them? He hated homosexuality; he was opposed to abortion; he was supposed to be about love; yet he was the sibling I felt least loved by. Too many stipulations came with his love.

I always believed he latched on to Christianity to differentiate himself from the rest of us, and from Brooks, the way brothers who are close in age try to show that they are different.

Addam saw Mother every other day. I couldn't remember the last time I'd seen either of them. I had suspicion that neither of them missed me.

Brooks's disappearance helped me with Mother's illness. It was my first experience of someone going missing. I wanted to thank him for that. Then Mother dripped away.

Chapter 33

The next morning, I phoned Olivia Sands on her home number, it being the weekend, to ask if she remembered what the car was like that Zara arrived in at the nursery.

'It had a cover on the spare wheel that said *I like it dirty*,' she told me.

'So you could see the spare tyre? Was it a jeep, then, rather than a car?'

'Yes, it was a black jeep.'

'Did it have anything hanging under it?' I asked.

'It may have. Something odd …'

'A pair of tights that looked like testicles?'

'Sorry, I never noticed.' She gasped. 'God, that's revolting!'

I relayed this to Linskey who was exfoliating her notes.

'So Shane drove past the house,' she said. 'He was obviously more involved than Zara lets on. Not quite the spurned dad.'

I was exhausted by information and couldn't find a clear space in my head. I would have loved to have gone for a run, but I was empty.

'I'm nipping out for some air,' I said.

'Just keep bringing the coffees,' Linskey joked.

Outside I rested my back against the wall. It was muggy, with dark clouds brooding over everything. I thought about Olivia's remark, about the jeep being the vehicle that collected River, about Zara and Shane together then, and together now. Olivia never knew Raymond.

Constable Higgins was walking about.

'Have you spoken to everyone? Bet you haven't,' he said, and he was right.

I walked away. In the communal kitchen I grabbed two cups and poured some thin coffee into them.

'Have we let Hammitt off the hook too easily?' I asked Linskey as I handed her a cup.

Just because it wasn't Sandy on the ferry didn't mean he was in the clear. I looked again; there was his business card, pinned to the board in front of us. There was his daughter's number.

'What about Hammitt's daughter?' I asked.

Linskey looked up at the ceiling, casting her mind, like a net, back to the start of the week. 'She stayed at theirs,' Linskey said. 'Wasn't the daughter house-sitting?'

I took Meggi's number from the board, the name and number that Jan Hammitt had written down for us. 'We should give her a call,' I said.

'Couldn't do any harm.'

I keyed in the phone number. It was a solicitor's office. I excused myself to the receptionist who answered and hung up.

'Wrong number?' asked Linskey.

'I don't know.'

I opened a webpage on my browser and typed in the name of the solicitor's office: *Selby and Selby*. There they were, based in Carrickfergus.

'I think Sandy Hammitt's daughter is a solicitor,' I said. 'Meggi Selby and Nigel Selby.'

Suddenly Linskey was interested. 'Hold on,' she said, going into the database and looking up an old case. 'I *knew* I knew that name. I've had a couple of dealings with Meggi before. Husband and wife team.'

'Not any more. Didn't Jan Hammitt say they were getting divorced?'

'That's a mess,' said Linskey, 'working with your other half in the same profession.' She clapped her hands. 'There! Got it!'

I stood behind her and looked at the screen. Meggi was Verda Dolan's solicitor; Verda – the mother of Brody Pottinger, the boy in the attic. Beside the case was the word 'Reopened'.

'Do you think this is all coincidence?' I asked.

'No, not coincidence,' said Linskey. 'I know what this is. This is a daughter who clearly breaches confidentiality by telling her crime-buff dad too much about her cases.'

'And now the minute Hammitt mentions it, this Pottinger boy crawls out of yesteryear's newspapers to tell the PSNI that Verda was abusing him for years,' I said.

'Well, that might be coincidence,' said Linskey, 'but don't tell Higgins.'

Chapter 34

We didn't talk about the science of trying any more. Jason knew my monthly cycle better than any blueprint – better than I did. It was like clockwork, regular.

Four nights a month, no matter what had been said between us, no matter what had happened at work that day, he rolled over and worked his hands over me. I couldn't say a thing. They rest of the month we didn't touch; we barely spoke.

We'd moved into Alex's old house as planned. Our eldest nephew's old room became Jason's home office for Sunday night sketching, and masturbating over Pornhub the rest of the time. I had the younger nephew's room as a dressing room, with a safe for my gun knocked into the back of the wardrobe.

I had come home from work, changed and sat down to dinner with Jason. Then, almost on autopilot, we fucked, my face pressed against the wall so we didn't have to look into each other's eyes. Then we went to bed to read and sleep.

The next morning, we woke to face the same day all over again. We fucked, a cold, empty transactional fuck. Then I pulled on Jason's hoodie, but when I went to the dressing room to get ready for work, I found the safe open and empty.

'Jason,' I shouted, 'I have to phone the station. Fuck, fuck, fuck!'

He was standing in the en suite, his back to me. He wasn't pissing. There was a soft rain of pills falling into the toilet water. I grabbed his arm and pulled him back. He turned, the empty blister packs of my medication in his hands. My gun was on the toilet cistern.

'You're still on the pill, you lying bitch,' he said. 'How long have you been back on the pill?'

He walked me into the bedroom and whipped me with the pistol, catching me in the hairline.

'You're not going anywhere. You're not going to make a fool out of me any more.'

With nothing to say, I got into bed and lay there, fear swimming in my gut, blood pouring into my eye. Jason sat on the end of the bed, pointing the gun at me with one hand and tapping something into his phone with the other. He read something on screen.

'We're not moving for three days,' he said then, pressing his face against mine. 'Three days of fucking. One will take, you devious cunt.'

He phoned Alex to say he wouldn't be in to work. He called Strandtown and told whoever answered that I was in the early stages of pregnancy and was very sick, that I might not be back at all. Ever. Then he paced the room. It was the only time he took his eyes off me. He only let me leave the bed to use the loo.

Over the next few days I slept twice, in short bursts. I woke both times without forgetting for a moment that he was there; Jason didn't sleep at all. His skin was almost purple with exhaustion. I opened my eyes to see him on the floor, pulling his hair and crying, his nose streaming blood. I knew I could overpower him, but he was in the wrong mental state for me to do anything.

The only time I tried to fight him he straddled me, put the gun in my mouth and told me that if I tried to do anything he would blow my brains out. Then he pulled at my pyjama bottoms and his own and forced himself on me for an endless assault he couldn't finish to his own satisfaction.

I believed him when he said he would kill me if I told anyone what happened. I knew he had to leave the house some time – leave me – but it was how I might be left that sent a jolt of fear through me. I just wanted to live. I could fix my shattered body afterwards. My bruised palate and chipped tooth could be repaired; the scar on my forehead could be hidden by my hair.

Chapter 35

'Hello, Detective,' Cahal said down the line.

'I'm investigating the calls on Shane Reede's phone,' I said.

'What is it you want with me?'

'Your number is on Shane's phone. You phoned him on Sunday evening.'

'I didn't call Shane Reede,' he said, quite adamant and abrupt.

'You called Shane at eight fourteen in the evening.'

In the background, I could hear Bernadene Cleary reminding him – or giving him a story.

'That's right,' he said sheepishly. 'I called him to say that an official-looking letter had arrived for him.'

'Did you ever find out what it was?'

'No. I gave it to him when he came here. I wasn't sure if Shane was using the address for dodgy dealings.'

'Has he before?'

'What it is is that we once got a phone call – hold on, it's the missus. I'll put her on.'

'Hello? It's Bernadene Cleary here.'

Mrs Cleary told me that she once got a hill of letters from various companies, then a phone call about a loan application. 'There seemed to be a mix-up,' she said. 'Shane had given the wrong address. Sometimes that happens easily enough the way these houses are set out, but for him to have given our phone number was something else. It was hard to know if it was an innocent mistake or not.'

'So this official-looking letter – it was in Shane's name, was it?'

'No, it was in the name of Marsh.'

'Raymond Marsh?'

'It was Mr Marsh. I don't recall the details.'

'What made you think it had something to do with Shane Reede?'

'Because he had been getting the same letters to his own cottage when he was gone. Same envelope. I ended up looking up the address on the back, and then with these calls for Mr Marsh and the letters, I phoned the company and told them to stop sending the letters.'

'Bernadene, did you hear that young River's stepfather has died?'

'I didn't know he had one.'

'His name was Raymond Marsh.'

'Oh no!' she said.

'So you'll understand that I need to know about this letter, this official letter that arrived for Mr Marsh.'

'I'll get Cahal for you, love,' she said.

Cahal explained that the envelope had red print on it, a final reminder, and that there had been a summons for Shane. He had told the garda his suspicions about the fraud and they were trying to talk to Shane, but Cahal couldn't give them an address for him up North.

'Why didn't you tell me this when we were down speaking with you?' I asked.

'The two things aren't related – the child and the loans. Sometimes these minor things overshadow the bigger things.'

'I promise you they wouldn't have, Mr Cleary.'

'Then why do you need to know?'

'Why would you tell the guards and not us?'

'I told them because I thought Reede was going to ruin the credit for our son at that address. I just wanted to let

Reede know that they were on to him, that the guards were looking him.'

'Did you tell Shane this?'

'I most certainly did,' he said.

'And did you tell him about the boy, like you told DI Linskey and I you did?'

'I did,' he said, softer. 'I told him about the boy too. Without question I did. He was away like the wind was under him.'

'Cahal's not so big and clever now,' I said to Linskey later back at the station.

'Mistakes are always nice when they're made by someone else,' she said.

'Hmm, like toast.'

She let a laugh slip and nudged me. 'Make us a wee slice of toast, would you? I'm famished.'

'I'm not hungry,' I told her.

'For God's sake, do something for someone else for once,' she said, and glanced at me. 'Fine. I'll get something in a minute. What about the neighbour who throttled River – Ian somebody or other. He hasn't been spoken to in any depth.'

'We'll speak to him,' I replied.

'Raymond sits uneasily with me,' Linskey admitted.

'What would have been Raymond's motive though?'

'He didn't seem to think a lot of River. There was no affection for the boy. You saw how he was.'

'Wouldn't he cover that up with fake affection?'

'Hold up – the sleep medication. Maybe there was an accidental overdose and he couldn't live with himself after.'

'That's all I have too,' I said. 'But his body language … I don't know.'

'Can't always go on that, Harry. People lie to your face day in, day out.' She looked down at her notebook. 'What about Zara?'

'She loves her therapies,' I said. 'Charlotte had this magazine about disabilities in her house and I flicked through it one night. It was talking about kids with autism being accidently killed during therapies. There was this one for deep pressure. Some kids died from suffocation.'

'Okay, so we have that line of questioning, plus we have to think about the epilepsy.'

'What are the therapies for it? I'll look into it.'

'What about if River had a bad seizure and Zara's trying to cover it up? Seeing as she doesn't want people to know about the epilepsy.'

'I don't know. Didn't she just cover it up to get him into nursery? I wouldn't say that she ignores his epilepsy altogether. She did go to the doctors. Put River through that intensive sleep trial – brain scan too.'

'I honestly don't think it's anything to do with Zara,' Linskey said.

'What about our man Shane?'

Linskey looked more serious now. 'He's our best bet, isn't he?'

'And what does *he* have in the way of a motive?'

'I really don't know, not now I've seen him and Zara together. There seems to be something between them.'

'Grief and pity?' I suggested.

'I don't know about that. Something more. Shane said he's staying with Zara because she's used to a full house.'

'He's seizing his opportunity to get close to her again. Some men love nothing better than a vulnerable woman.'

'There doesn't appear to be bad blood,' said Linskey.

'It seems wrong, the pair of them.'

'Zara and Raymond seemed more wrong.'

'Let's get back to River. Why would Shane take his own son? Why would he hurt him?' I asked.

'I've left a message for Bronagh Shaw. Maybe she can shed some light.'

'She's in England, then?' I said.

'She is.' Linskey frowned down at her notebook again. 'Shane went to Monaghan on Wednesday afternoon for an alibi.'

'We need to find out more about this mother of his – Margaret, isn't that her name? – if he was with her or not,' I said, imagining what my father would advise. 'Could River be in the South with this grandma? Has Shane decided to give the boy to someone else? Is he downplaying his relationship with his mum? Was he really carjacked and left lying in the bushes unconscious?'

But I had a feeling, the way I sometimes did, that Margaret was a dead end, and that what we really needed to zoom in on was right under our noses.

Chapter 36

The desk sergeant came to get me from the office at midday. 'Alexander Hammitt's here to see you.'

'What does he want?' I asked.

'Well, it was Linskey he was wanting, but she's left now.'

'What do you think he wants?'

'He says he wants a word,' said the sarge.

I went out to reception and found Sandy, his index finger hooked over his shirt collar.

'Mr Hammitt, you wanted to see me?' I said.

'Can we talk?' Sandy asked.

'We can. Go ahead.'

'No, not here.' Sandy eyed the sergeant, who was looking back at him.

'Okay, come through,' I said, bringing him into an interview room for privacy. 'Why don't you take a seat, Mr Hammitt?'

Sandy sat down and locked his hands in front of him. 'I've done something a bit stupid,' he said. 'I'm cross with myself.'

'What have you done?'

'My DNA might be on the coat.'

'Why would that be?'

'Because I touched it. I lifted it down and looked at it, saw that it said River on the nametag and put it back. I made sure to put it back the way it was, though.'

'But when you called the station, weren't you told not to touch it?' I asked. 'Didn't you tell us you knew not to, when we arrived at Shaw's Bridge?'

'Yes, but it was too late then. I told my daughter, who's a solicitor. She told me I better say.'

'And that's the *only* reason why your DNA might be on the coat?'

'God, yes! Don't say that. I'm not … I just saw the coat.'

'Okay. We're going to need your prints. And forensics will need to go over your car.'

'I just want you to know that I did touch the coat …'

'You may have contaminated evidence, Mr Hammitt.'

'I know. I should know better. I feel bloody stupid. I just thought, what's the likelihood that this coat is … you know what I'm saying?'

Sandy went back to get his prints taken. I watched him, wondering what he would say if we could link him to the other fingermarks. When he was done, I asked him if he needed a lift home, since he couldn't use his own car, but he said that Jan was coming to get him.

Chapter 37

It was four o'clock on Saturday afternoon and the wind was up. An empty drink can made music on the pavement. From the outside, Zara's house looked as if it was in darkness. Inside, it wasn't much better. It was dull and empty, like my apartment when I came home to it alone, when no one had breathed life into it all day. Death filled the place, and it was hard to imagine light, or sound, or laughter ever being there again.

Raymond was gone and Shane had now taken his place on the sofa. Man of the house. He was wearing a grey hoodie and jeans. The swelling on his face had not gone down; it had just got darker. He was holding her hand.

'There probably won't be any news now,' said Zara. 'I feel like one of those mums who has to live in limbo for years – for the rest of her life – not knowing. That's it. It's all done now. It's been five days.'

Shane tightened his hand around hers. There were no tears any longer. There was a sad acceptance that was strange to me. I thought it might be because Zara was including her son while she grieved for Raymond. Two birds one stone. She was mentally preparing herself for the darkest part.

The weird doll that had been on the seat was away. In its place was that sad little cross-stitch cushion, the one about the messy house and children, only there was no mess and no child. The wind whistled down the chimney above the remains of long-dead fire.

'We're looking into a few lines of enquiry, Zara,' Linskey told her. 'We'll solve this.' She was saying this for Shane's benefit and we kept our eyes on him, but he continued to look at Zara's hand, at her chipped nails and frayed cuticles. I never saw her biting her nails, like I never saw her smoke, but I knew she did both. She was the kind of woman you could never imagine doing the things she did. I thought about her in Kassie's house, having the cheek to play wet nurse to someone else's baby. She didn't look as if she'd have it in her to be so audacious.

We wanted to ask Zara about the neighbour who throttled River but didn't want Shane to hear. We didn't want him to think he was off the hook. Shane was a compulsive liar, a fraudster, a tax evader. I wanted to let him know that these were offences that would, in time, be dealt with.

'Shane, Mr Cleary said that he gave you a letter on Wednesday, is that right?' I asked.

He looked baffled. 'I can't remember.'

'What was the letter about?'

'Is this necessary?' said Zara.

Linskey was looking at me as though she was thinking the same thing.

'That's right – it was my phone contract,' he said.

'Shane, were you getting credit at another address?'

'Yes,' he said and looked me dead in the eye, daring me to do something about it.

'The guards have been looking for you over loan applications made in other people's names.'

Linskey frowned as if to say *not now*.

'I'm not perfect,' Shane said. 'I've made mistakes.'

These things were small fry to him. I just needed to let him know that there was the stain of suspicion on him that wasn't going to go away anytime soon. But he was confessing too easily. He was using it as a deterrent.

'Okay, we'll get to that soon,' said Linskey. 'You're obviously aware that you've been operating on the wrong side of the law, Shane.'

I could tell by his face that he wasn't aware. He had no record, a couple of cautions. But hurting people, violence, was not part of his history. It was greed that had got him every time.

'Zara,' said Linskey, crouching down to her level like she was a child, 'tell me, is there anyone else you think we should talk to? Is there anyone with a grievance against you or your family?'

Shane was staring at Zara, waiting for her response.

'Being a parent means you're ten per cent uncomfortable all the time,' Zara said. 'You're expected to bond with strangers because they are parents too. Because they had sex around the same time you did.' She scoffed. 'When you have a kid like River it becomes more like fifty per cent. People have grievances with me every day because he can't behave. It's invisible disabilities, isn't it? Because he just stares at them. I overheard his nursery teacher say that he gave her the creeps. A four-year-old giving her the *creeps*? Talking about River as if he's an adult who's responsible for his behaviour.'

There was a tear in Shane's eye. His nose twitched. He looked up and down, avoided looking at anyone in particular, his hand was still around Zara's.

'I know it's hard,' said Linskey. 'We expect kids to all get along when we adults can't manage it, and we're better equipped apparently.'

Zara smiled thankfully. 'River doesn't try to annoy people,' she said. 'He's just brimming over with energy. All day long. He can't sit still. He has this little thing in his brain that makes him get up to mischief, but he'd never hurt anybody. That's what annoyed me about these other mums. You'd think he was trying to harm their kids or that he was something *less* than their kids. How would they like it if it had been their son born like that? He's a pure-hearted boy. Their kids are the ones who fight … and lie.'

We watched a marked police car slowly drive past outside. Zara ran to the window. But it went to one of the semis at the end of the street. I called through to see why it was there. It was for Ian, the little blond man who almost throttled River. There was a warrant for his arrest. Apparently, he pulled a kitchen knife on a twelve-year-old for riding a scrambler past his window and taunting him by calling him Ian Anus.

'I know him,' Zara said. 'River went into his yard once and he got River by the neck. *You need a licence to own a dog!* he said to me. He's an ignorant old pig.'

'What's he done?' Shane asked, but I stayed silent.

This Ian man was brought out of the house and put into the police car. The neighbours were flocking outside. 'Good riddance!' one shouted.

'The neighbours will tell me if you won't,' said Zara, looking out of the window. 'They like me again now … now they think I'm someone to pity.'

'Why didn't you tell me he had River by the scruff?' Shane asked her.

Zara sneered. 'The epilepsy diagnosis is just the start,' she said, ignoring his question. 'The label doesn't change anything. It just means I can say, my boy has a condition. It's not his fault.' Zara started to sob. 'I'm never going to get over this.'

Shane got up and walked to her, held her in his arms. He put his chin on her head and rubbed her back; the cuff of his jumper went up.

There was a scorch mark on his wrist.

Chapter 38

'Three days,' Jason threatened me. But it had been four days in January 2015, in the bedroom I once loved, with the man I once loved, him breaking down before my eyes and breaking me and everything else in our lives simultaneously. By the fourth day I didn't dare dream that I was going to make it out alive. I kept thinking, this is something I feared happening while I was on the job; never for one minute did I think it might happen inside my home, within my marriage, our bed. I just lay there; I was crushed. Jason had collapsed on the floor, blood crusted around his nostrils and upper lip from a screaming-induced nosebleed.

My gun was clenched in his hand. His hoodie, which I had been wearing over my pyjamas, lay crumpled on the floor, spattered with blood that was probably mine.

It's now or never, I thought. I pulled myself up weakly, feeling like my wrists could snap under me. I took care not to make the bed creak, or any floorboards or stairs. I didn't breathe as I stepped down them; it was as if I was being pulled down by the front door. I quietly lifted my long, padded winter coat from the coat rack and grabbed my trainers by their heels. I took my purse and the car keys from the hall table, squeezing the keys tight so they made no noise at all.

I didn't close the front door behind me. I ran to the gate, my heart pounding inside my head, and threw it open. Then I went back to the car and got in, throwing my shoes, coat and purse on the passenger seat. I swung the car out of the drive and into the street, and didn't look back.

How many times had I told other women, victims of domestic abuse, to go to the PSNI, or the hospital, or Women's Aid? The answer was far too many. Yet there I was, driving around Belfast on a cold January morning, pulling my duvet-like coat over my lap and down my shins, over my nightwear, so thankful I wasn't naked. Would that have mattered? I was out, with no idea where to go next.

I tried to work out what day it was, but I'd lost all sense of time. I thought it was a Saturday; it looked like one on the Lisburn Road. I could drive to the hospital, but the part of the hospital that rape victims needed wasn't open on Saturdays, so I drove to Charly's, where I sat for a moment, hunched over the steering wheel, waiting for Jason to appear in my rear-view mirror. Then I saw my nieces through the window and thought, what am I doing, leading him here in his state, and with my gun on his person?

I reversed out again and headed for the motorway. I had had no food or sleep for days, but I was hypervigilant. I can't remember how I got to Fermanagh or how I found our old chalet. It was years since I'd been there. Father hadn't used it at all since Mother got ill, and not often before then, not once the Sloane kids had all grown up.

I took the key from the coal bunker where Mother always left a spare and let myself in. It was a cave of darkness full of this powdery dampness that made me sneeze and hurt all over. I had a cold shower and found some old clothes of my mother's that smelled like an old dead fire. Then I rang the Chief.

'Are congratulations in order?' he asked. It was the first time he ever spoke to me like a human. I clung to it.

'They are,' I said. 'But only congratulate me because I got out of that house alive.'

'Well, that's the best any of us can hope for, until we don't,' he said.

A wild, tired laugh escaped me.

'What is it, Sloane? Do you need to speak to HR? Or to Linskey?'

'No,' I said. 'Everyone else is too sappy. I can't take that right now.' I felt completely hollow as I looked out at the lough.

'You don't sound like yourself. Maybe you need some personal leave,' he said. 'Awful American invention, but you know what I mean. Sometimes it's necessary, I hear.'

'Thanks, Chief, but no,' I said. 'I've loads of overtime accrued from Christmas. Use it for the days I've been off, and just know that I'll be back … give me four days. Just four. That's all I need.'

I wanted to buy back a day for each one that had been stolen from me. It would be that easy. I was not the typical victim. I was a detective and I was strong.

'If you're sure,' Dunne said.

'Positive.'

I texted both my sisters to see if Jason had been around, or if he had killed someone, even himself. It was what I pictured – him hanging from the apple tree at home. Then I felt like a coward for running away, for tiptoeing off and saving my own skin. Another picture filled my mind – of *me* overpowering *him*, me grabbing the gun and shooting him right between the eyes. And wouldn't he have deserved it. He'd raped me. Repeatedly. My own husband. In our own bed.

I looked at Mother's old clothes on my body, a nautical-style Jaeger jumper and tight creased trousers that I left unbuttoned. They were pulling me tightly at every seam. I thought about the men she'd let walk free from her court and the women and children who had been stalked and abused and beaten. Now I knew how they felt, and now I knew how I felt when I promised them protection and meant it. Mother had often blamed the law for her having to let those men walk free, but once I knew the law, I knew it was her fault.

Since she had been diagnosed I had allowed her to become this paragon. But really, she never looked after women who had to stand in her court and tell the details of their rapes, be raped again where they stood, in essence. Mother stayed poker-faced and let the bastards walk. And it still played out like that, mostly. The law hadn't changed much since her day. There were still judges who automatically took the side of the accused.

I pulled at the neck of her jumper until it tore at the seam and the fabric sat out from my skin in two fist-sized bunches. I wanted to hate her. I wanted to blame this ordeal on someone I had not chosen to have in my life. Until that day, I had always portioned half the blame of each and every crime to the victim because somewhere along the line, that was what I had been taught. I caught a punch in my cupped hand and screamed. Then I took a breath and looked at my phone.

There were still no replies to the texts I'd sent to my sisters. In the end, they each took hours to get back to me, which told me that Jason wasn't looking for me, and although I knew he wouldn't remember that our family had the chalet, I still imagined I heard his car or heard his winter boots outside. Even the sounds of the lough seemed just like him calling my name.

And indubitably there were the dreams. Bad, bad dreams about cells forming and eating me up from the inside. Which they were.

Chapter 39

Chief Dunne sent Higgins and Simon to check out the scene of Shane's carjacking in Armagh, then on to speak to Cahal Cleary in Monaghan to find out more about these letters that had arrived for Shane and about Margaret McGuire. 'A weekend away,' Higgins joked.

'To get you out of the way, more like,' Linskey joked in return.

The Chief had ordered them to go to the hospital if they needed to, to check out the story about Margaret having a stroke. He clearly thought Linskey and I had missed something, just like Father had. I asked why I couldn't go. The Chief was eating pizza from a box at his desk.

'I think you should stay here,' he replied.

'But Cahal knows us now,' I said.

'You need to stay here. I want you to bring in Zara and Shane again and quiz them.'

'I agree, but we don't have grounds to arrest.'

'Find grounds. Every contact leaves a mark. There has to be some physical evidence.' He was probably thinking about the public, that it was days now and there hadn't been an arrest. 'There's a tip-off from a neighbour. Vanessa Bermingham phoned to say she saw a man go into Zara's house and she recognises him. I need you to look into it. Higgins and Simon can do their thing in Monaghan and you can pull the strings up here. Okay?'

'Okay,' I said, turning to walk out of the office; then I turned back. 'When will I see you, Greg?' I asked him.

'I'll be tied up until we have a conviction, darlin',' Dunne said.

Linskey was walking into the office, her hand poised to knock. She turned on her heel.

'Diane,' I said, rushing after her, 'we have a tip-off from Ness Bermingham.'

Linskey glared back. 'Find another mug,' she said.

'What's wrong?'

'I know when people are lying to me. It's a skill I have. Believe me, you aren't the first.'

'What are you talking about?'

'You and your Chief. I suspected it this last while but you've just confirmed it. What on earth are you playing at?'

'I don't know what you're talking about.'

'Does this kind of thing excite you, talking about *Paul*, this man you're involved with, and it's Greg all along.'

'I didn't want to lie to you. My father and my family know Greg.'

'Yeah, you're right to hide it from them. Charles wouldn't like this at all. He had standards.'

I was surprised. I'd always thought it was well known that Father cheated on Mother. With all the praise he had had for Linskey as her mentor, Mother even believed at one point that there was something going on between them, and I hadn't cared.

'Greg and I know how to be professional,' I said.

'Yes, there's a level of proficiency in the way he does this to Jocelyn, but I thought you had more sense.'

Linskey went and made herself a coffee. I waited until she was done; eventually she sat down.

'Jocelyn is crying on my shoulder, telling me she knows he's seeing someone again. It's what he does, don't you know that?'

'Then why doesn't she leave him … if she knows?'

'Why do you think he keeps his distance from me, Harry? I've told her repeatedly to leave him. This is the position you've put me in. I could lose Jocelyn as a friend. She might think I've told her to leave him to leave the way clear for you.'

'I don't want him full-time.'

Linskey laughed. I remembered her telling me that as soon as Geordie had cheated on her, the trust was gone, and so was she.

'You had a good one in Jason,' she said. 'You didn't give yourself time. Greg has taken advantage of you.'

'I'm not some stupid kid, Diane,' I said. 'What do you know about Jason really? That he didn't cheat? There are worse things you can do than that … and anyway, the first thing we're taught here is to believe no one.' My phone was going in my pocket. 'We'll pick this up again in a minute.' I told Linskey.

I had been avoiding Charly, but now it seemed preferable to the tirade of aggro Linskey was heaping on me.

'I didn't want to phone you, Harry,' Charlotte said hysterically. 'I know how busy you are, but I just want you to know that Timothy's in hospital. He's stopped breathing.'

I instantly forgot the texts she'd sent about the dinner party with Paul, her insistence that I give the man a chance, my last text telling her to butt out and get herself a hobby.

'Coral has the boys,' she said. 'David's parents have the girls.'

I felt jealous of Coral for being asked to do something I knew I was in no position to do. But Coral had always been a caretaker. Certainly, she had helped me in 2015. And I allowed her, telling myself I could be weak for four days, but that was all. I was no victim.

'Will you let Daddy know?' said Charly. 'I can't call him. He'll start going on. You know what he's like.'

'I'll let him know. I'll get there as soon as I'm done in work,' I said.

I could tell she was pissed off I had to put work first, but at least she knew where her boy was. Zara Reede, I now fully believed, did not.

Before Charly hung up I said, 'Timmy will be fine – my little man will be okay.'

It reminded me of the neighbours outside Zara's at the start of the week, how empty words were, how they didn't make a damn bit of difference.

*

At the Royal Victoria Hospital was Addam and his wife Sylvia. They always dressed like grown-ups: he was in his suit and she in her silver and blue layers that hid the great little figure she had, like it was something to be ashamed of. Her long grey hair was tied in a low ponytail at the nape of her neck. We were waiting out in the corridor.

'Timothy has to have an operation,' Addam said. 'Charlotte's with him now.'

What capacity was Addam there in – uncle, brother or minister?

'God will look after him,' Sylvia said.

'Cool,' I said, 'we'll tell the doctors they can have a day off, shall we?'

'Don't speak to her like that,' said Addam. He was clutching his Bible in one hand and Sylvia's hand in the other.

'Sorry, Sylvia.'

'It's fine,' Sylvia said through clenched teeth.

Charlotte and David came out of the room and saw us. David was quiet, his mouth twitching as he bit the insides of his cheek. Charlotte's eyes were dark, her body shaking slightly, hand held aloft as though she was carrying a torch and had been using it to help her see a way through.

I hugged her. Charlotte didn't react.

'How long will they be, do you reckon?' I asked David when I let go.

'An hour – maybe more. I have no idea.'

'I'd like us all to pray together,' said Addam.

He held the Bible in both hands and closed his eyes. Charlotte reached out for me with one hand, David with the other and made this half-circle while Addam prayed for Timothy. As much as I wanted to resist, I didn't. I wouldn't, not if it helped someone. Silently I added River to the prayer.

Chapter 40

The wind had nearly blown the day from the bone when my mobile went. I was sitting in the car at the hospital. Timothy had been brought to intensive care and I had just spent the last two hours waiting in the corridor hoping for news.

It was Paul on the phone. He wanted to meet up – he had a spare ticket to a show in the Grand Opera House. The old spare ticket excuse; I found it weak and presumptuous.

'We can dovetail in together,' Paul said.

'Do you really like opera?' I asked.

'I like it if you like it.'

'Look, I'm already seeing someone, Paul. Charlotte knows that, so I don't know what she was doing trying to matchmake us.'

He went quiet for a while. 'Come to the show, just as friends,' he said. 'You can never have enough friends.'

'Thanks for the offer—'

'I promise, as friends,' he said, interrupting me. 'I don't see what the problem is.' But I detected a sharpness in his tone.

'I don't need this, Paul – not right now.'

'You know, you could be a bit friendlier to the people who're nice to you. I know you're seeing someone. It's obvious. So who is he ... married?'

'That's none of your business.'

'That's right. You keep on doing what you're doing – see where it gets you.'

I hung up on him, missing the effect of slamming down the receiver on an old phone. I tapped Greg's number.

'Can you speak right now?' I asked when he picked up.

'Go ahead.'

'Are you coming around later? It feels like I haven't seen you in ages. Not properly.'

'There's no chance. I'm not going to get away from here tonight. How's your nephew?'

'Seriously ill.'

'Do you think you'll get back to the station soon?'

'I will and I need to tell you something.' Really, I needed to tell him two things: that Linskey knew about us; and the bad news, that I was late, really bloody late. My breasts were heavy, and I hadn't had a bleed in such a long time. I hadn't been keeping record, but I knew it was a long, long time. After the science project Jason had made of it in the past, I refused to monitor it.

'I've just been asked out,' I told him instead. 'Charly tried to set me up.'

'Are you going to go?' he asked.

'Of course not. Why? Do you think I should?'

'I'm really busy here, Sloane. As you well know.'

'What have Higgins and Simon found out?'

'Nothing. There were no tyre marks where Reede's car was supposedly stopped. Anyway, you'll be updated when you're back on shift.'

'Perhaps Shane was at the lights and already stopped,' I suggested.

'Try to rest in your downtime. Do something to take your mind off your nephew.'

'Downtime? Ha! Or maybe I'll go on this date to the opera, since you don't seem to mind.'

'Opera? … If you want to.'

'Do *you* want me to?'

'It doesn't matter what I want.'

'Really?'

'Okay then, I don't want you to.' Greg coughed.

'Then tell me that.'

'I don't have time for these games. I'll see you tomorrow, Sloane. Not tomorrow night. In the morning.'

'I know what you mean. Greg?'

'Yes?'

'My period's late,' I said, before I could back out of it again. I held my breath. 'Really late.'

'Can you find out a conclusive result and then let me know?'

'A conclusive result?'

'We'll need to run a risk assessment on your position.'

'Is that all you have to say?'

'Harry, I can't talk about this now. Do you know the stress I am under? You're being ruled by your emotions right now. This isn't the kind of person I thought you were.'

'It is actually. And I'm glad I'm not a fucken robot like you.'

'Come in, Sergeant,' Greg shouted. 'Look, I have to go now.'

I could hear Higgins in the background. 'Is this the search warrant for Brandon Terrace?' he was asking.

Chapter 41

Mostly Belfast is grey and brown, and the sky reflects this in its ceiling-mirror up above. But the city has a different character at night; it might even be called beautiful. And with a bit of green and the introduction of some colour in the summer, the place can be positively festive.

I blamed the Mela for that, for bringing the colour two months before. Charlotte's kids loved throwing coloured powder at each other. It hit them – hair, skin, clothes – and exploded, bright and vivid. The girls shrieked and laughed and chased the boys who kept their mouths shut tight; Timothy, in his wheelchair, had his mouth wide open like he wanted to eat the colours.

I watched as the sky above puffed into clouds of magical hues: pink, yellow, green and purple. Everyone was happy and dancing; drums were pumping on the stage. Charlotte sprinkled yellow powder onto my head. I turned to grab her, my hand full of coloured dust, ready to retaliate. Then I saw him.

Jason.

He was covered in yellow and green, a smear of blue under one of his eyes.

It could have been any man his height, his build, but there was a feeling I got when I sensed he was nearby. My stomach would flip and I'd plummet into a visceral spell of seasickness. No one else has ever made me feel like that, and I have dealt with some out and out scumbags over the years.

To think that this was the man I once signed up to be with for the rest of my life. Now, the mere thought of him appearing, the anticipation of it, made me ill. In actual fact, I didn't know if he was still stalking me, or if it was just the imprint of it that had not yet dried.

At the end of Mela, feeling far from protected and repaired, as I should have after the festival, I got Charlotte to drop me home rather than stay on with the family for dinner. I needed my own apartment, sofa and wine. I drank a full bottle of Merlot before Greg arrived, straight from work, with the added protection of a baseball cap.

He poured himself a finger of scotch. It was all he drank, and he only drank with me because I did.

'You're looking very vibrant,' he said, setting his cap on the table and sitting down on the sofa beside me.

Something was unearthed in me with these colours. I had only wiped my face; the powder still sat in my hair, on my clothes. I felt languid and submissive. I took off my shirt. Greg looked greedily at my body. I walked to the window in my bra and looked down, angry now. If Jason was there, I couldn't tell. There had to be a point when I stopped looking for him, stopped allowing him space in my life.

'I love you, Greg,' I said.

We fucked then.

'I'm going to have to head,' Greg said after, putting his trousers back on.

I watched him out of the window, baseball cap on, returning to his car and going home to his family.

Chapter 42

I headed out through the grey Saturday afternoon streets of East Belfast to Shane's house in Brandon Terrace. I had to see for myself. Simon and Higgins were there with the search team and had been for hours.

'Have you nowhere better to be?' Simon asked me.

'Doesn't look like it,' I said. 'How did it go in Monaghan? How are you back so soon?'

'We didn't go in the end. We were about to, then Higgins thought we should call Cleary first. In fact, the guards phoned us.'

'Well?'

'Cleary had told them everything he'd told you. The guards searched the barn and Shane's old house again.'

'No joy?'

'No.'

'And the carjacking?'

'We did get as far as Armagh. There were no tyre marks where the carjacking was alleged to have taken place. CCTV in the area isn't up to it, I'm afraid.'

'Dunne said that. And what about Margaret?'

'Cleary did have one piece of new information – there is no Margaret McGuire. Shane's mother's name was Janice Bell and she's been dead years.'

'Really?'

'According to Cleary, Janice Bell moved to New Zealand when Shane was a kid. Married a man out there, had a family. She died in ninety-eight.'

I gloved up and followed Simon into the kitchen where Higgins was emptying drawers. More officers were taking the house apart. Simon and I stepped over the piles of papers, receipts, old keys.

'Oh, look at you, Higgins,' I said, 'actually doing some work for once.'

'Ha! Fergus tell you the news?' Higgins asked.

'Yes, about Janice Bell you mean?'

'Oh that? Yes. But the second set of prints – they aren't a match for Sandy Hammitt's.'

'Really,' I said.

'You didn't think he did it, did you?'

'Most of the time, no.'

'Yes, I hadn't got to that,' said Simon. 'We can rule Hammitt out. So now we're looking for someone else, someone who hasn't been into the station at all yet.'

'How's it going?' I asked Inspector Seymour who was walking down the stairs with a computer.

'There's nothing that stands out. Not yet,' Seymour replied. 'We've received orders from the powers that be to seize this.'

I walked into the living room. There were toys strewn across the floor, some with the price sticker still on them, and a stack of DVDs beside the TV. I rifled through them. Six for a pound, read the Oxfam sticker. The top one was *The Magdalene Sisters*.

'I'm just going to turn on the TV,' I said to no one in particular.

Behind me, Higgins laughed. 'Do you want me to get you some popcorn?'

The DVD player was on pause; the solid blue light at the front stared back at me. I pressed 'Play'. It was the final scene of the movie, followed by the end credits. Margaret McGuire, played by Anne-Marie Duff. I paused it again.

'Good film?' asked Higgins.

'Very inspiring, thanks.'

I went looking for Simon who was looking at the kitchen wall.

'Is that blood, do you think?' he asked.

I squinted at the marks. 'Could be,' I said.

Then I saw something else on the wall. It was so tiny it could easily be missed. In fact, last time we had missed it. It winked at me as the light caught it.

Chapter 43

I jumped back into the Skoda and hightailed it to the station. Linskey was there and talking to Greg when I arrived.

'Can I see you in my office?' he said to me.

He led the way. I stood in front of his desk.

'Harriet,' he said once we were alone – no 'Sloane', no 'Harry', definitely no 'darlin'. 'I'm taking you off the case.'

'What? You can't do that! I'm the crime scene manager.'

'Why didn't you tell me that Linskey knows about us?'

'What does it matter?'

'It's not professional for you and her to work together in the present circumstances.'

I looked him in the eye. 'Greg, please don't do this. I'll talk her round.'

'We need to get someone else briefed,' said Dunne. 'They found something in the roofspace at Brandon Terrace – the spare tyre from the jeep with *I like it dirty* on it. But it's not enough to hold Reede. Anyway, there's another case I want you on. Brody Pottinger – it's a reopened—'

'Please don't. I have the Reede case. I can do it.'

'So where is River Reede? Can you tell me that, Sloane?'

'No, but I know I can get Shane to admit to taking the boy. Give me the chance.'

'Linskey refuses to work with you.'

'She wanted Higgins pulled off the case and you ignored that.'

'This is different.'

'Why? Because your name's in the mix?'

'We're in work now, Harriet. Be professional.'

'Yes, Chief,' I said. 'Linskey's okay talking to *you*, but you're the one who's married.'

'Linskey's barely speaking to me,' Chief Dunne said. 'This might ruin the case if it were to come out.'

'I'm sure you've taken these risks before.'

He looked numbly at me. 'If you can't talk her round, you'll have to get taken off this case.'

'I'll smooth things out.'

'If you're staying on, a black Suzuki Vitara has been found burnt out in a field three miles from the scene of the alleged carjacking in Armagh. It's in the CSU garage being analysed by forensics.'

'Okay, Chief. Thanks,' I said, and went looking for Linskey.

I'd been expecting him to ask if I'd done a pregnancy test yet. He really didn't care one way or the other. He'd been kinder when I thought I was pregnant by my ex-husband than he was now, when the mess was his. I knew Greg would throw money at the problem, if it came to it.

Linskey was in the briefing room with Shane Reede's solicitor.

I stuck my head round the door. 'DI Linskey, can I have a word?'

She probably wanted to tell me to fuck away off, but the solicitor was Lance Worth. He represented a lot of legal aid folk and was a total piss-take: an ex-copper who used that knowledge to help people who he knew full well shouldn't be helped. As much as Linskey felt angry at me, she hated Worth more so she came out.

We went into a side room where she stood examining her fingernails, her mouth drawn tight, hard as a nut.

She sighed. 'I don't really blame you for all this,' she said, still refusing to look at me. 'I don't blame you for getting with him, but there's something far worse going on. It's what you've done to Jocelyn. You don't care about other women, Harry, that's what I'm learning about you.'

'Bull!'

'You're sneaky. You've been trying to get me to tell you things about Greg and Jocelyn's marriage, but that's playing dirty. You think Charlotte is stupid to have kids. You think Zara murdered her son, or is at least covering it up, because she creeps you out. Why? Because she's too motherly. For days Zara has been sentenced to this worry, but you don't get it because you aren't a mother.'

'That's low.'

'It's coming down to your level.'

'Sometimes you're wrong about other women, Diane. You like to believe that we're all on the same team. Brody Pottinger's mother was far from perfect, but you skimmed over her old convictions.'

Linskey shook her head. 'Ninety-nine per cent of parents would never do anything to harm their own child. What about Sorcha Seton? We were right to listen to her when she came to us about Donald Guy.'

'You weren't there for most of that.'

'No,' she replied, 'I was putting my own family back together.'

I felt another sting in her words. ' So I didn't choose to have one,' I said.

'But you still have a family, whether you're a mother or not. You still have family responsibilities.'

'Is it my mother you're talking about?'

'Not necessarily—'

'Are you saying I don't have any sense of responsibility for my nieces and nephews? For Timmy?'

'I didn't say that.'

'He's still in intensive care. I've gone there, spent time with my sister and her family. I don't need to feel guilty about anything.'

'But do you not feel guilty about Jocelyn?' Linskey asked.

'Greg has affairs – always has done, and everyone knows it. Why should I feel guilty about her when he obviously doesn't – never has. If you were a true friend to Jocelyn you wouldn't stand by and listen to her complain about him. You'd tell her to get out, get a job and a life.'

'Everyone has their own battles,' Linskey said, looking as if I had smacked her. 'You don't know what else Jocelyn is going through.'

'We've kept it between us all this time, Greg and I,' I said. 'There's no reason why we can't continue to do that. No one needs to get hurt.'

'With affairs, sooner or later someone always gets hurt. You need people to lie for you.'

'I'm not asking you to do that. In fact, go and tell her. I don't care any more.' There were footsteps outside the door. 'Di, what's the craic here with me and you?' I asked her softly.

'We're done,' she said. 'I need to be able to trust my partner. It's important to me. I can't do this any more. Not with you.'

'Okay, Jocelyn can find out about me and Greg or she can go on living a lie. She doesn't need you to fight her battles when she doesn't care enough to fight them for herself.' My voice was thick with tears. 'But everyone's life is fucked up in some way, yours included, and right now Zara Reede's life is fucked up more than most. Can't we set aside our differences for now and close this case – for Zara. For River?'

Linskey glared back at me. She seemed willing to lose our partnership for a superficial friendship with a woman she had nothing in common with apart from failed marriages. It was why she liked Zara, why she had once liked me.

I waited for some kind of response. Then she nodded just the once.

'But we're done once this case is over,' she said, as she swept past me out through the door.

Chapter 44

In February of 2015, a month after Jason and I 'split' – as Coral believed it to be – she came into the toilets on the ferry to check on me.

'I'm fine,' I told her, despite the fact that I was cramping up a storm and dropping more blood into the bowl than I'd imagined possible when there had been so little of anything to lose.

The place was disgusting. The sanitary bin was already overflowing and I had to find somewhere else to tuck the two sodden maxi pads I'd been wearing for the last half hour.

'You obviously aren't fine,' Coral replied, the toes of her brown leather boots pointing my way underneath the toilet door. 'We should have stayed another night in the hotel.'

'I can't do that,' I said, standing up and losing more blood with the effort. 'I've missed enough work of late.'

I washed my hands in the corner sink while the ferry pitched in a way I had become familiar with. It was how I'd been feeling for weeks – almost ghostly, like I too had left this body.

'I'd have been happy ordering pills online,' I said into the mirror.

'Even though it's illegal?' said Coral, fetching me a bundle of paper towels to dry my hands.

'It's a stupid law.'

'Be that as it may …' She stopped herself. She looked as though she dearly wanted to give me a lecture, her silly little sister, silliest when with her twin and just about tolerable on her own. 'You need to keep yourself right, Harry,' she said.

'I need to keep *myself* right?'

'I know you're going through The Split, but I'm here now. I'm here to help you.'

'Sorry that's fallen to you,' I said.

'What do you think Jason would think about this jaunt to England?' she asked, rubbing my arm. I pulled away. 'Forget I said that,' she said softly. 'It's your body and it's done now.'

'It certainly is done,' I said.

'Are you okay if I go and get us a drink?'

I nodded. 'I think I could manage a glass of Merlot,' I added.

'I'll get us both tea.' She pulled the door open and left me there.

I waited for a few moments, then went onto the deck and watched as the loaded grey sea pulled and pushed against itself, as if possessed by demons rising up from under the water. It was raining, just a mizzle you could barely see against the mist. It sat on my face like sweat.

I pulled my long winter coat around me and felt the potential of a baby I couldn't take a chance on leave my body in hot, fresh drips.

*

Two days after I returned from my 'jaunt' to England and vacated the spare room in Coral's house for the peace of my new apartment in St George's Harbour, I spoke to Chief Dunne on the phone.

'I've no right to ask if you are … pregnant,' the Chief said, 'only from a safety point of view we will need to run a risk assessment, understand?'

'No baby on board here, Chief,' I promised my boss. 'No husband either, any more. But I do have a new home. Actually, I need to speak to someone about changing my address, for the record …' I wanted to leave hints of the wars I had just survived and be asked if I was okay by someone I truly respected.

'HR,' the Chief simply said, but I knew that if I got back to the station and stuck by his side, he'd give me something more eventually.

And two months later, he did. We were delivering training at the Police College at Garnerville that April when he said over a canteen lunch, 'You should be higher up the ranks, you know. You, Sloane, deserve to be Superintendent more than anybody on our team.' Then he told me how much he respected the fact that I'd left a 'personal situation' because it wasn't right for me; it must have taken 'real guts', he said.

It doesn't sound like the start of a great romance, but it was.

A year and a half later, I was still sitting at the same rank and pregnant for the second time in my life. It was downright dysfunctional, but somehow it felt like the right time – for me, at least. I couldn't care less what was best for Greg Dunne. He already had his family, and who knew if I'd ever have the chance to be pregnant again. Or if I'd ever want to be.

When I returned from England I spent a week in bed, fearing that at any second I could die. There followed a year and a half of being stalked by my husband until I had shrunk to a tiny, barely visible creature, unless they needed me to be their voice or their hero. Then, when he seemed to have finally let up, came the solicitor's letters.

I could depend on no one. I'd have this child and I'd heal, at last. It would be no part of Jason. Or Greg. It would spell out a future. That plan, it seemed to me, was the one that took the most guts.

Chapter 45

Lance Worth had the bearing of a lawyer in a US court drama. I didn't bother sitting because he never did until he had to. It was his way of exerting leverage. He patrolled the floor, leaned over, put his hands on the table like he was born to be in the courtroom and his reputation preceded him

I leaned against the wall and folded my arms across my chest. My trousers were tighter across my swollen ovaries.

'Your ex plans to take you to the cleaners, I do believe,' Lance said.

Jason, knowing how much I hated Worth, was using a colleague of Worth's for the divorce. I ignored Worth's attempts to throw me off. People are like rules: the better you know them the easier they are to break.

'Do you have anything on my client?' Lance asked.

'You already have our disclosure,' I replied.

'Fine, you have twenty-four hours with Mr Reede. After that you have to charge him or let him go.'

'Well, since you took your sweet time in getting here, we have even less.'

Lance's smile lit up his entire face. 'Before we start,' he said, 'I need to take a shit. I'll try not to take too long, but I can't promise. I think it's a bug.' He winked.

*

At five p.m., or thereabouts, Donald Guy was at the desk, the custody sarge taking his details, and Higgins standing guard. Simon was putting Donald's ring and watch into a bag.

'What's going on here?' I asked.

Donald ignored me.

'We had an incident,' said Simon.

'What kind?'

'Guess.'

'Hello, Detective Sloane,' Donald said. He looked defiant.

'To what do we owe the pleasure?'

'More of the same,' Simon said.

'Images?'

Simon nodded.

'Donald, you know you aren't allowed to have a smartphone or a computer,' I said.

'I don't.'

'We got a call to the library by the Holywood Arches,' Higgins explained. 'Guess who was up to no good in the computer suite? He was trying to access banned sites. Do you want to hear what his searches were?' Higgins went on.

I stared at him. 'What are you doing, Donald?'

'I'm sorry. That wee boy wasn't the only one. It's a good thing I'm caught now. I can come clean.'

'Exactly what do you need to come clean about?'

'Over the years I've been bad to a lot of kids. I've been bad to lots of kids, caused them pain.'

'River?'

'No, not him. The kids I'm talking about, it was nothing other than touching.'

'Christ!' said Higgins.

'Constable!' I reprimanded him.

'Finish processing Mr Guy and I'll talk to him later,' I told the desk sarge.

I walked off, dying to tell Amy Campbell that my theory about men like Donald had been right all along, that they couldn't change their spots. Not much felt better than that.

Chapter 46

A sweat broke on Shane the moment we got in the room. It was like watching a fish move; they have to swim their entire lives. His leg jiggling under the desk. His eyes told their own story.

Linskey read him his rights. He listened, his ruddy face cocked sideways, his fingers spiralling the sagging elastic of his cuffs so we wouldn't notice the burns up his arms.

'Mr Reede, where were you on Sunday night?' I asked.

Linskey sighed. Everything I did or said seemed to be annoying her.

'No comment,' Shane replied. This was Worth's favourite tactic but not everyone heeded his advice.

'Come on, you know the drill, Mr Reede,' I said. 'We need your cooperation. Did you have River to stay on Saturday night?'

'No comment.'

'Does River like the park, Shane?' Linskey interjected.

'No comment.' He sipped the sweat from his top lip.

Worth was smiling to himself as he watched his client play his game. He didn't care that we were searching for a four-year-old boy.

'Do you know that River has epilepsy, Shane?' Linskey asked. 'Do you know how serious a condition that is? Without his medication he could be seriously ill.'

'No comment.'

Linskey looked at me.

'You said you went to stay with your mother in Monaghan,' I said.

'Is there an address for her?' Linskey asked.

'No comment.'

'It strikes me as odd that you wouldn't have got in touch with her when it was made public that your son was missing.'

He said nothing.

'Shane?'

He sat up abruptly. 'No comment.'

'Where were you going without a spare wheel?'

He was silent.

'Why would someone take that off their car?'

Nothing.

'Is it because a distinctive wheel cover like that would make you stand out?'

Shane's knee was jiggling away. He was a tic-ridden mess.

'Our colleagues have spoken to Mr Cleary, Shane,' I said. 'Do you know Cahal Cleary?'

He glanced at Lance. Lance shook his head.

'No comment.' He looked down at the table.

'Mr Cleary seems to think that your mother moved to New Zealand when you were very young and died in the late nineties. That that was why you were living with your grandmother. Does he have that right?'

Shane lifted his head and looked into my eyes. The skin around the perimeter of the bruise on his face was going green.

'No comment.'

He looked down again.

'Do you know that Bronagh Shaw is not Shaw any more,' I said. 'She got married and she's two months pregnant. Isn't that lovely news?'

He looked as though he knew this. He licked his bottom lip and didn't speak.

Bronagh had been quick to get back to us. She said she was always telling Shane to get in touch with River, but he didn't want to.

Shane stared at the wall now. Lance sat back, hands behind his head and smiled. I had to block him from my vision in case I punched him in the face.

'It took you a while to come through as a dad, Shane,' Linskey said, 'but I know that to all intents and purposes you have River's well-being at heart, don't you?' She spoke softly. 'Don't you just *adore* that boy?'

Shane went to answer, then he shut his mouth.

'And Zara is very good with River too,' added Linskey. 'She's very close to him. Any little problem and she finds a way to help your son. I know you do the best for River when he's in your care.'

I placed a hand on the desk. 'What Detective Linskey is saying, Shane, is that we know you want River home safe and sound, every bit as much as his mother does. Wouldn't you agree?'

Shane coughed, his eyes pricked with tears. He started to blink furiously.

'I think we'll have a half-time interval,' said Lance.

'No, not yet,' I said. 'Shane, Zara was a bit over the top, don't you think? All these rules about your son. It must have been hard to stick.'

Linskey scowled at me.

'She's overprotective, wouldn't you agree?'

He sighed.

'Shane, speak to me. We're all on the same side. We're all on River's side. Help us.'

Shane closed his eyes.

'What do you think about all this healthy eating, this breastfeeding palaver … all the things Zara did for River that other mums didn't do? Was she overcompensating, do you think?'

He looked like he could be asleep.

'Shane!' I yelled.

He opened his eyes and yawned, rubbed his head.

'What about the star chart?' I said. 'There's one in your house too, so maybe it didn't annoy you. Do you try to keep things consistent for River?'

'No comment.'

'I need to go to the toilet,' Lance said. 'Apologies, folks, I've had a dicky stomach all day.'

'Did you make the chart or did Zara give it to you?'

'No comment.'

'It's just that there's this one thing, Shane,' I said.

He suddenly looked up and I could see the penny drop.

'The chart is on your kitchen wall at Brandon Terrace. And you did fill it in, Shane. In fact, tucked up the side of your microwave is four months' worth of charts, so you were filling it in like Zara wanted you to. Most dads wouldn't, not if they were separated and they thought the child didn't need them.' I paused to give him time to absorb what I was saying. 'Some people have hinted that Zara was pedantic, but you mustn't have thought she was. You must have seen that the chart helped, because River has more and more stickers on each one as time goes on. You even started adding ones that Zara didn't do at her house. I see that you have ones for River tidying his room, and one for feeding the dog, isn't that right?'

I looked him over. He was a sorry sight – unshaven, smelly, dressed in the same scruffy grey hoodie he'd been brought in in two days earlier.

'Do you have a dog, Shane? Because we've had a call about a man who used to walk his dog in the early hours of the morning past Zara's house. We were told that this man wore a hoodie, a grey hoodie. Might that have been you, Shane?'

'I really must insist we break here,' Worth piped up. 'Mr Reede clearly has nothing to say. You clearly have nothing to charge him with. And I have clearly said that I need to use the bathroom – quite urgently.'

I disregarded Lance and looked Shane in the eye. 'Why was there was a star in the chart on Monday morning?'

'A mistake,' he said.

'May I remind you, Mr Reede, that you don't have to answer,' Worth instructed his client.

Linskey looked up at Shane, then at me. She seemed to think I was making this up.

'What did River do to warrant a star on Monday?' I said.

'*Was* he with you on Monday morning, Shane?' asked Linskey.

'No comment.' He pulled his cuffs down over his hands.

'You took him back to the house on Sunday night, didn't you.'

Shane coughed. 'No comment.'

'You missed River. A weekend wasn't long enough for you,' I said, 'so you got the boy to come down, open the door and you brought him back to yours again. You were in a habit with the chart so you carried it on.'

Shane covered his mouth like he might be sick. He shook his head.

'We also noticed how spotless your kitchen is. That's quite surprising for a man like you. But forensics did some testing for blood and they found traces on the floor, on the mop, and spattered up on to the oven door. You need more practice at cleaning, Shane.'

'No,' he said.

'What's that, Shane? Where were you really between leaving Belfast on the Sunday and seeing Cahal on Wednesday?'

He closed his eyes so he couldn't see the words come out. 'I was in a guest house.'

'Where?'

'Donegal.'

'Donegal? We have reason to place you there on another occasion. Your prints were on our database from a burglary there on 6 January this year.'

He blinked.

'And the jeep?'

'I changed the plates,' Shane admitted.

'Where did you do that?'

'In work.'

'But your boss said he didn't see you. Or was Ronnie lying for you, Shane?'

'No comment.'

'Now seems like a good time to take a break. I'm going to cease recording here,' said Linskey.

I directed Shane to his cell where he now wanted to talk.

'I would never hurt my son,' he said. 'Never.'

*

'Worth's a joke with his dicky stomachs,' I said.

'That's always his game,' said Linskey. 'And the no comment interviews – no surprise there. The worthless shit!' She gave me a wry smile.

My mobile bleeped. 'It's Charly,' I said. 'I have to take this.'

It turned out to be David. 'Timothy is really sick,' he said. 'Charly is beside herself with worry. She's going mad. Will you talk to her?'

'Put her on,' I said.

'What will we do if we lose him, H?' Charly asked me.

'We won't.'

She groaned. It sounded like it came from an animal.

'I'm coming straight there as soon as I can. Hold tight. I promise you, he'll be fine.'

'Okay,' she said, her voice cracking.

David came back on the line. 'I'm going to call around everyone,' he said. 'Timothy'll be okay.'

'Without a doubt,' I said.

After I hung up I stared at my phone; I couldn't breathe. Linskey was standing by my side asking why I never told her about the star chart. I managed to get out that it was because she wouldn't talk to me.

'Look, we need to working together again properly, for River's sake,' Linskey said. She should have been annoyed, only it was hard to be angry when we finally had our man.

Dunne called Higgins, Simon, Linskey and I into a meeting room where photos of River were up on the board.

'We've found our young man. We've located River Reede,' he said.

*

Shane sat facing us again, Lance to the right of him. He wasn't smiling now. Everything was different.

Linskey pressed record and spoke into the machine. 'Shane Reede, Saturday 22 October 2016. The time is 8:37

p.m. Shane,' she began, 'your solicitor is here for advice. You don't have to listen to him. You are over eighteen.' She paused. There was no rush now for anything.

'You were helpful enough before, Shane,' I jumped in. 'Please help us take this in the right direction.'

Lance nodded at Shane.

'No comment,' he said.

'River has been found,' Linskey said.

Lance and Shane darted their eyes at each other, at Linskey, at me.

'We know now, Shane,' I said. 'We know. So think carefully, and I would strongly advise you to say something at this point.'

He shook his head.

'For the tape, Mr Reede is shaking his head. Can you speak instead? Is there anything you want to say?'

He blinked back tears.

'Can you tell us where your son might have been found?'

'Just tell my client where his boy has been found and if he's safe,' said Lance.

'I'm quite sure Mr Reede knows where River has been found, and the ... condition of the child.'

'Why did you put River into a suitcase?' Linskey asked. 'Why did you throw his body into the ocean?'

Shane started breathing rapidly, shallow noisy breaths. I kicked the table leg.

'What happened to River?' I shouted.

'I really have to ob—' began Lance.

'Talk to us, Shane,' Linskey said.

Shane let his head fall into his hands. His leg was jiggling so furiously now everyone could hear his heel knocking up and down off the ground. Then he straightened up, pulled at the neckline of his hoodie, as if he was fighting for air, and his eyes went out of focus.

Chapter 47

When I heard the news, I recalled Jamesy Lunney and his missing fingernails. I thought of Hanna-Caitlin Clarke, the restaurateur's daughter, and how she had felt her father's warm hands on her throat, how the last thing she had seen were the black seeds of Hans' eyes.

And I thought about the twelve-year-old girl who, on a nature trail with friends from school, knelt in the sand at Buncrana Bay that Saturday evening and prised open a brown leather suitcase that earlier that day was tossed to the shore by the boiling surf.

Inside the case had been the body of a young boy, coiled like a fossil. His skin was pocked and frayed and washed clean of blood.

River's small body was covered in holes. A preliminary investigation found that he had been savaged. His sodden blue and green pyjamas were shredded and clung to him; his nappy had disintegrated although the stickers at his hips were still fused. There was a semi-circular scar on his thigh from the old burn.

River Reede, our young man, lay in the morgue at Letterkenny Coroner's Court as we sat in the interview room with his father, with his murderer, while our odontologist checked River's small fund of dental records.

Chapter 48

Linskey relayed the details of the find to Shane Reede. How bluntly the words fell from his tongue.

'I only went upstairs for a shower before I was going to bring Riv home on Monday,' he said. He choked on his son's name. 'I just wanted one more night with him, you see. It's hard in a house by yourself.'

'Did you go into Zara's house and lift him?'

'No. I threw a handful of stones at his window. He looked out his curtains and came downstairs – let himself out.'

'You don't have to say anything,' Worth told him, defeated, setting his pen on the desk and folding his hands in his lap. But Shane was in full flow, haemorrhaging facts; he needed to unburden.

'When I came downstairs, the dog had him gripped in his jaws. I couldn't stop him. I kicked the dog – punched him. He was tossing River about like a rag doll.'

'But there's no evidence you have a dog,' I said.

'It was a security dog for work. Ronnie had him for the garage, but there were complaints about him. He'd whimper all night, so I brought him home in the evenings; during the day he sat in RAD.'

'Didn't you have a bowl for the dog?'

'Yes. But I threw all the dog's belongings – food, bowl, collar and lead, bedding – in the wheelie bin and put it out for collection.'

'This is the dog that was found drowned at Shaw's Bridge?'

Shane nodded.

'Can you speak for the tape, please?' said Linskey.

Worth sat back, hands behind his head again, only this time he was a spectator. His game was over and no one had won.

'Who threw the dog in the water? And tied up River's little green coat? Who did it with you?'

'Nobody.'

'Was it Ronnie Dorrian?'

'No comment.'

'Is that a yes? Did Ronnie help you clean up?'

'No. He only came to get the dog.'

'And the coat?'

'And the coat.'

'What did he do with the coat?'

'Left it in the park.'

'Did you arrange this?'

'No. He just said he'd sort it – make it look like River had wandered off. He only told me what he did with it when I called him from Armagh.' Shane scratched the side of his face.

'And the suitcase?'

'I threw it from the cliffs. My son … my son. I tossed him away the same way Ronnie did with the animal that savaged him. I took that animal in because I pitied it, and that animal destroyed my boy. I may as well have done it myself.'

'Where's the jeep, Shane?'

'Burnt it.' He pulled his sleeves up to show the burns. He was weeping. 'I would never have hurt River. Never.'

*

I was on the phone to the press office, telling them that I needed to inform Zara before news of the boy's body could be released, that she mustn't find out from the television.

'The other fingermark must be Ronnie's,' I said.

'I bet that little immigrant car washing squad Ronnie has aren't legal either,' said Higgins. 'Some trafficking caper going on.'

'Maybe, but prioritise,' Linskey told him.

Simon came bounding in. 'Linskey and Sloane, you're both needed in the medical room. Reede has tried to slash his wrists with his zip.'

When we arrived, the medic was attempting to treat the wounds, while Shane tried to fight him off. After everything I'd heard that day and I was still alarmed by the violence in him.

'I can't live with this,' he shouted. 'Please, just let me get on with it. Please.'

'Shane, you need to calm down,' I said, trying to establish eye contact.

'Zee can't know how Riv died,' he said.

'She has to know, Shane,' said Linskey solemnly. 'It's her right.'

After an hour Shane had quietened enough to talk to us in an interview room.

'The dog wasn't a bad dog,' said Shane. 'River must have had one of his seizures ... maybe he fell to the floor. I thought I heard a scream, like they do before they drop. It's the only way this could have happened. When I collected him on the Friday, there was no epilepsy medication in the bag. Zara was at the hospital doing her milk run. Raymond must have forgot. I should've just gone back at bedtime when I realised I didn't have it. I didn't though – didn't want to go out again once we were settled. I thought, he's only on a small dosage now, maybe he's not on it at all any more. That weekend River was really settled, more than usual. I thought the medication must have been messing him up. I should have called Zara. I didn't.'

'Maybe River screamed because the dog was attacking him?'

'No, no, Razor wouldn't have attacked him for no good reason. Once when I was really drunk – stocious – and fell asleep on the sofa, he bit me.' Shane pointed at the scars at either side of his eyes. 'But he was only trying to wake me up. Razor wasn't a bad dog.'

'Okay, Shane,' I said.

'I wanted Zee to be able to live with hope,' he said. 'Hope keeps you going.'

Chapter 49

By one o'clock on Sunday morning, it wasn't as cold as it had been. The rain stopped as we pulled into Witham Street. I sat on in the car, trying to psyche myself up to break the news, but then Zara looked out, wide awake and waiting for us. When she got to the door and saw us bow our heads as we entered the hall, she opened her mouth in a wide silent scream, hit out at the air and crumpled to the floor.

It was me who picked her up, but it was Linskey, naturally, who told her what had happened. We made her tea she didn't drink. Linskey put her arm around her and let her cry. We stayed with her until the sun came up.

She said she knew about the dog – River had told her. Zara said that she had raised it once with Shane but he had dismissed her fears.

'I'd nagged him enough – to do the charts, to give the medication. I didn't like the thought of River being in the room with a security dog, but I didn't speak up enough.' She dabbed her eyes with a tissue. 'I didn't want to give Shane an excuse to abandon River again, not since Riv had started to look forward to seeing him. I should have been a nag. I shouldn't have trusted him. I was just sick of having to fight for everything.'

At 6 a.m., Ness came in to sit with her. Zara put on a home recording of her, Shane and River. He must have been eighteen months old in it. He was climbing a tree and smiling, and suddenly real in a way he had not been to me before.

There was a boy who now was dead. He had light brown hair and blue eyes, and even in the video he was being kept on the straight and narrow. There was a boy who didn't quite fit, who should have had the time to learn how, like we all have to. That time had been taken from him. River lived only for a short time, but he had lived before he died. I saw that now.

Ness watched, struggling to keep her own emotions in check, as we all had to. We had to be strong for Zara.

Back at the station was when it escaped me. I dabbed at the tears dripping from my chin. Linskey pretended she didn't see them. She told me she'd asked for a transfer to another district and that Dunne had said he'd see to it with immediate effect.

'We can work around it,' I said, taking my running clothes out of my locker.

Linskey didn't reply. I knew she thought I was incapable of friendship, but what she didn't see was that I thought of her more like a sister, and that this job was my family. That if I had to choose one, I would always choose this.

Epilogue

Linskey brought the parakeet back to the station just before Christmas, saying she had no time to look after it. But what I heard was, Why should I care about anything, Harry, when you clearly don't?

'That's fine. I'll give it to my father,' I said, trying not to react to her sting.

I had called into Witham Street later that day, just to see how Zara was holding up. I suppose I'd become attached to her. After we talked, she followed me out to the car and she saw the parakeet.

'Is that the bird that flew into Strandtown the day Riv went missing?' she asked, her eyes lighting up.

'Yes, it's the same bird,' I said.

'It's been living in a police station since then?'

'No, it had a home, but—'

'Does it need a home now?' she asked.

'It does.'

She put out her hands. I lifted the cage from the Skoda and gave it to her. She peered in at the bird.

'Okay,' she said, 'I'll take it.'

I tried to tell her that she didn't have to, but she had already walked back inside the house, turning only briefly to nod at me and say thanks, then closing the door gently with her foot.

At the coroner's court today, I asked Zara how the bird was.

'The bird's fine,' she said thoughtfully. 'He's company, like how some people leave the TV on. He's noisy ... so that's good. Sometimes I let him fly about the room. He can be quite affectionate, believe it or not.'

Zara was holding River's stuffed Thomas the Tank Engine. When I asked her how she was holding up she told me she still did her milk runs. Now it's what she lives for, until they tell her to stop, which soon they will.

I was trying to hide my bump behind piles of paperwork, but she saw it and clammed up. I thought for a moment it embarrassed her. I waited, but no colour rose up her blue-white throat. Still, Zara couldn't wait to get away. Ness was waiting on the steps for her, speaking with Linskey, who was keeping her distance from me. I could hear that they were talking about Shane, who was on charges for manslaughter, for knowingly being in possession of a breed of dog that is banned, for breaking and entering in Donegal the previous year, for two counts of automobile theft and destruction, and for perverting the course of justice. He is facing years.

I wish I could say how that will go. Truth is, you never know.

I said a brief goodbye to everyone after the inquest, then rushed to the hospital, where the great grey concrete planters had broken out in crocuses and a cool breath of January air wrapped itself around me. I walked to the maternity unit, my yellow folder clutched against my swollen belly.

The nurse nodded at me. 'Your first?' she asked, as she did the initial checks.

They all ask that, no matter what you say to them. There is more than an air of condescension in it. I always hesitate, but I suppose this one is my first.

She sent me to the waiting room and I sat with two other women, who were also at the half-way mark, and their partners. The two couples were chatting amongst themselves;

it was baby number two for them both. They smiled knowingly at each other when I said number one. One couple were going to find out the sex and the other wanted a surprise.

I was called in first. My bladder was bursting; I felt poisoned by the tank of urine inside me. During the scan, the midwife left to fetch the doctor and I found myself thinking again about seeing Zara on the day she got the news.

I saw the paused image of River on the screen and couldn't stop worrying. I was thinking about Timothy too. What if my baby was disabled in a physical way they could see in the scan, or what if they couldn't, and then it'd be too late to do anything except love him – or her – once they were born.

There was this awful crying coming from the room next to mine; one of the couples I'd been chatting to in the waiting room. I think the woman must have lost her baby. I felt like I was outside my own body. Then the doctor came in, a Filipino lady. She scanned my tummy.

'Don't look so worried, Harriet,' she said over the top of the crying, as if it wasn't happening. 'Your babies are fine, strong and healthy.'

'Babies?' I was dazed.

I couldn't stop wondering which couple I had heard grieving. And when I was leaving I couldn't see either of them, so maybe I'll never know. But I remembered the doctor's last words to me: 'Next time, don't come alone, alright?'

I went straight from the hospital to see Mother. I hung my coat and scarf on the back of her door. Her blue eyes barely took me in. I sat in front of her, held her papery hand in mine. It felt weightless, nothing but skin and marrow.

'Charly told me that she and Timmy were here to see you earlier,' I said, looking at the outdated Christmas cards still on the wall. One was a Christmas tree made from Timothy's handprints in green poster paint. His trademark handprint art. A website I'd found the night before said that at this stage of my baby's development it would have friction ridges on its fingers by now.

'Mummy, wait till you see this,' I said.

I opened my handbag and took out two images of my new humans that looked like sand blown into a shape with a straw. Mother blinked at them. I examined them myself.

'The boys are outnumbering the girls this time round,' I said. I'd asked the nurse about the gender, wanting nothing else in my life to take me by surprise.

I sat with Mother for an hour. I brushed her hair, talked until my voice was raw, and left ten minutes after Coral arrived. I told her the news about the babies. As I left, I had to drive past my old house near Osborne Gardens, the house where Jason had held me captive at gunpoint. The place sat in darkness. I couldn't tell if he was there or not.

*

I've admitted to Brooks that I never wanted to be a mother, that I don't think I'll make a good job of it. Brooks says I'll be fine. Much as I love him, I take everything he says with a pinch of salt.

I'm still getting used to the fact that sometimes the lost can be found. But in a way, he's still lost, that's the strange thing. He can be sitting there watching TV with me, we can be laughing at the same jokes, eating the same meal at the same table, and I know he has left parts of himself everywhere.

He is lying on the sofa watching some Sky Arts documentary when I get back to the apartment.

'You're late,' he says, pretending to tell me off like a huffy child.

'What for?'

'Not a thing.'

I look at my brother, so paper-thin you could fold him and post him. He still hasn't put his things into the spare room, kidding himself, but not me, that he isn't going to stay long enough to make himself comfortable.

'I went to see Mummy,' I tell him, resisting the urge to lower the volume on the TV. I'm allowing my life to make sounds again, getting ready.

'I'll go see her tomorrow,' he says. 'What time will *he* have left?' He means Father.

'After two,' I say.

They have yet to set eyes on each other since Brooks showed up at mine last month.

Brooks has exhausted the friends he can call on, and he needs to avoid them if he wants to keep his sobriety. I'm his last port of call. Addam is cold and uppity with him when their visits overlap. I'm not the only one who is lucky to have sisters.

'Wasn't it the inquest today?' Brooks asks. 'So, what did the coroner say about the boy's stepdad?'

'Accidental overdose,' I tell him. 'Raymond was taking chloral hydrate to get to sleep, amphetamines in the morning to wake him up, antidepressants to quell the storm, and Librium for his anxiety. But it was the Nembutal that finished him off. It was all too much.'

'Did he buy it on the internet?'

'Yes,' I say.

'It's so easy to get stuff online. It's the new street corner.'

'The coroner said that chloral hydrate affects short-term memory, so Raymond may have forgotten that he'd taken the barbiturates and took a double dose, judging by the high levels in his bloodstream.'

'It happens,' says Brooks. 'Did he rule the death accidental?'

'Yeah.'

Brooks holds my scans in his hand. 'I got your voicemail. Twins, huh?'

'Yep.'

'You're sorted, then – one for you, one for this ex of yours.'

'Now there's an idea!' I say. 'Are you coming to the next scan?'

'Wouldn't miss it.'

'Ha!'

I go to my bedroom where I hide my gun and purse in the safe. It's also where I keep my jewellery and everything else that has any monetary value. It's standard practice when living with a junkie; they're the gifts that keep on taking. I had somehow forgotten that part.

The neighbours above are getting ready for a night out. I hear their music, the beat of their feet on my ceiling. In the kitchen I see that Brooks has made me a plate of food. I lift it, sit down at the table and take in the view out over the Lagan.

It doesn't occur to me to look down at the bridge.

Acknowledgements

There are many people I want to thank for their support and friendship: Claire Savage, Sharon Dempsey, Jane Talbot, Jo Zebedee, Catriona King, Roisin Coleman, Wilma Kenny, Kate Burns, and Paula Matthews.

I owe much gratitude to the Arts Council of Northern Ireland, Irish Writers' Centre, John Hewitt Society, Ards and North Down Borough Council, Belfast Book Festival, Aspects Festival, all the staff at the Tyrone Guthrie Centre, Paul Maddern at the River Mill Writing Retreat, Damian Smyth at ACNI, David Torrens at No Alibis bookshop, and the amazing members of Women Aloud NI.

Thank you to Valerie, Maddie, Jude, Jonah and Martha.

Most of all: Ryan. You never stop encouraging me to write. Thank you for that.

KELLY CREIGHTON
The Bones of It

Thrown out of university, green-tea-drinking, meditation-loving Scott McAuley has no place to go but home: County Down, Northern Ireland. The only problem is, his father is there now too.

Duke wasn't around when Scott was growing up. He was in prison for stabbing two Catholic kids in an alley. But thanks to the Good Friday Agreement, big Duke is out now, reformed, a counsellor.

Squeezed together into a small house, with too little work and too much time to think about what happened to Scott's dead mother, the tension grows between these two men, who seem to have so little in common.

Penning diary entries from prison, Scott recalls what happened that year. He writes about Jasmine, his girlfriend at university. He writes about Klaudia, back home in County Down, who he and Duke both admired. He weaves a tale of lies, rage and paranoia.

Out now in paperback and ebook.

KELLY CREIGHTON
Bank Holiday Hurricane

A woman picks up what is left of her life after her release from prison. A young couple are about to set off for Australia when a leaving party changes everyone's fate. Lifelong friends keep deep secrets that could fracture each other's lives. In Manchester, paths cross for two people who have not seen each other since the genocide in Rwanda.

Bank Holiday Hurricane is a collection about dislocation, disenchantment and second chances, told through linked stories set in and around a Northern Irish town, and further afield.

Out now in paperback at doirepress.com.

Printed in Great Britain
by Amazon